THE RUSSIAN'S WRATH

ALSO BY CAP DANIELS

Stand-Alone Novels

Novellas

THE RUSSIAN'S WRATH

AVENGING ANGEL
SEVEN DEADLY SINS SERIES
BOOK #7

CAP DANIELS

ANCHOR WATCH
PUBLISHING
** USA **

The Russian's Wrath
Avenging Angel
Seven Deadly Sins Book #7
Cap Daniels

This is a work of fiction. Names, characters, places, historical events, and incidents are the product of the author's imagination or have been used fictitiously. Although many locations such as marinas, airports, hotels, restaurants, etc. used in this work actually exist, they are used fictitiously and may have been relocated, exaggerated, or otherwise modified by creative license for the purpose of this work. Although many characters are based on personalities, physical attributes, skills, or intellect of actual individuals, all of the characters in this work are products of the author's imagination.

Published by:

ANCHOR WATCH
———— PUBLISHING ————
** USA **

13 Digit ISBN: 978-1-951021-71-9
Library of Congress Control Number: 2025941998
Copyright © 2025 Cap Daniels – All Rights Reserved

Printed in the United States of America

THE RUSSIAN'S WRATH

Russkaya Gnev

CAP DANIELS

'Tis said that wrath is the last thing
in a man to grow old.

— ALCAEUS

Ona Dolzhna Zaplatit'
(She Must Pay)

Chicago, IL, Late Summer 2015

Cigar smoke rose like a spirited demon escaping the pits of Hell and slithered through the dead-still air of the mahogany-paneled sanctum where four men sat, speaking in Russian and sculpting the demise of Anastasia Anya Burinkova.

"This little traitor has cost us a quarter of a billion American dollars, and it must end now."

The man's glistening dark hair was combed straight back, exposing seven decades of a furrowed brow.

The man to his left, and a quarter century his junior, leaned forward and pointed his Cuban at the older man. "Ilya, you are correct about this vermin who turned her back against her own people, but I believe your estimate of our losses is quite low. If she is allowed to continue, she will more than double your number in another year."

The older man groaned. "Perhaps you are right, Yakov, but if you are telling the truth about this mysterious source of yours, we will rake the flesh from her body and send her bones to the bottom of Lake Baikal."

Yakov said, "Question my source again, old man, and it will be the greatest and final error of your life."

A ruddy-faced bald man, sitting mostly in the shadows of the darkened lair, examined the golden-brown wrapper of his two-hundred-dollar cigar. "Gentlemen, I understand that tensions are high, but I must be the voice of reason here. We cannot turn against each other. This is precisely the sin of comrade Dmitri Barkov's seed. We must remain unified against our common enemy."

Yakov glared back at him. "This is but one more of the lies you've been led to believe, Oleg. Anastasia Burinkova is not the daughter of comrade Barkov. Half of her blood is American, and I'm quite certain you know her father well."

Nikita, a dark-eyed elf of a man, and the fourth and final Russian in the room, snapped his fingers—a habit for which he had become known but could not break, regardless of endless attempts. "Who this wretched woman's father is has no bearing on the necessity of killing her. She must die, and it must be done in the unholiest of ways, by the least human creature we can unleash upon her."

"Agreed," Ilya said. "But before that can be done, we must know every detail of her alliance with the Americans. If Yakov is correct—"

The younger man said, "Do not question whether I am correct. You will soon fully understand just how valuable my informant is."

Oleg said, "Tell us, Yakov. How did you come to recruit this American spy?"

"You forget that I was trained first by the KGB, and then SVR, and after that, FSB. I am a graduate of one of the most prestigious universities in the United States, and I have run more American spies than all of you combined."

Oleg shrugged. "Perhaps, but none of this makes you immune to falling victim to a trap by the Americans. Did this man come to you, or did you seek him out?"

"How I nurtured and developed my spy is none of your business. All that is important to you is that he is trustworthy and extremely well placed inside the American government."

Oleg waved a hand. "You are beginning to sound like an arrogant politician, Yakov. You spoke only of your grand accomplishments, but you failed to answer my question. Did the source approach you, or did you pluck him from the bushes?"

"He came to me," Yakov said, "but only after weeks of small, delicate grooming by me and my operatives. The man is scorned and shunned by his own government."

Oleg took a long draw and let the white aromatic smoke escape his lips. "I thought you said he was well placed inside the American government. Now you are trying to make us believe he is an outcast in his own country. Which is true, young Yakov?"

As his ire rose, Yakov said, "Listen to me, you bunch of dinosaurs. I am risking my life being here in this godforsaken country, and I'm doing it in the name of restoring the motherland to her former glory and might on the world stage."

"Bullshit," Nikita barked. "You are doing this for the enormous fee you are being paid and nothing more. Do not wave the flag of a patriot in our faces. You were for sale, and we bought you. That makes you our property, and by extension, it makes any source beneath your wing ours as well. Do not forget this."

Yakov leapt to his feet. "Let me make one thing clear, comrades. I could walk into Anastasia Burinkova's bedroom tonight, press a pistol to her head, and dispatch her from this world."

Oleg and Nikita laughed, and the dwarf said, "You could walk into her bedroom, but someone could walk out of that same bedroom with every piece of you in envelopes. This woman isn't the kind of person who is easily dispatched. She is a Kremlin-trained red sparrow and assassin."

It was Yakov's turn to laugh. "Yes, she may have been trained in State School Four, as well as the Red Banner Academy, but she is merely mortal, just like all of you. And she has become softened by her station in the West. Her razor grows rusty, and her vigilance now slumbers, when in the past, it would never rest its head."

Ilya crushed his cigar into a heavy crystal tray. "This woman you call 'soft' and 'lacking vigilance' faced off against six of our most established brothers, and now, each of those men is either in an American prison or the grave because they underestimated a beautiful woman who spoke their native tongue while driving daggers through their hearts."

"I know what I'm doing, Ilya. I am what the Americans call a spymaster." He paused and tore open his shirt, exposing the flesh of his chest and neck. "I have played this game—the world's deadliest game—for thirty years, and look at me. I bear no scars, no marks of bullet or blade. I do not fail. I do not get caught. And most of all, I never underestimate my foe nor overestimate my source."

Ilya said, "Okay, Yakov. You have convinced us. Now, tell us what you know about the daughter of Katerina Burinkova and the American, Robert Richter."

Yakov poured himself four fingers of vodka without offering to refill the glasses of his countrymen. "This is what I know about Anastasia Burinkova. She defected to the United States after failing the mission assigned by Colonel Victor Tornovich of the SVR. She was to seduce and recruit an American by the name of Chase Daniel Fulton, a bumbling idiot trained by the CIA. Instead of successfully recruiting him or killing him, she believes she fell in love with him."

Oleg cocked his head. "Victor Tornovich was killed, and his body was burned in Virginia. Was this the work of Burinkova?"

Yakov looked away. "I do not know, but that is irrelevant. What is important to understand is that the American Department of Justice apprehended our target in the city of St. Augustine, Florida."

Oleg continued staring at Yakov. "Pardon the interruption, but am I mistaken that Ms. Burinkova killed four federal agents that night?"

"You are not mistaken."

Oleg nodded. "That is what I thought. Killing four American agents doesn't sound like the work of a woman who is complicit in her cooperation with the so-called Department of Justice."

Yakov said, "At first, she was not cooperative, but the supervisory special agent who was running the operation, known as Avenging Angel, was highly skilled in manipulation. His name is Raymond White, and he is now retired from federal civil service, as they call it."

Ilya said, "So, we are expected to believe that this Raymond White person manipulated a Russian assassin and sparrow into working alongside the American Department of Justice. Is this what you are asking of us?"

Yakov smiled and relaxed in his seat. "No, comrades, it is not me who is asking you to believe this. I am merely asking you to listen to the information provided by my source."

Oleg raised a finger. "No, no, no, Yakov. Remember, you are bought and paid for. Your former source is now *our* source."

Yakov raised his finger in response. "You forget, Oleg, that I am perhaps bought, but not yet paid for."

Nikita said, "Bring in this so-called source, and if we believe you have delivered something of value, you will be paid."

Yakov slowly shook his head. "Do I look to you as if I am a fool? Once you have my source in your hands, you and I both know I will never be paid, and I will likely never be seen again. This is not how I do business. When I see proof of the wire transfer, you will have your source, but not a moment sooner."

The cigar clenched in the dwarf's teeth looked enormous in contrast to his impish head, but the look in his eyes was nothing short of ice. He pressed his cell phone to his ear and said, "Send the money."

Yakov typed a password into his iPad and watched the number appear on the screen. "You transferred only four million dollars. I can only assume you wish to have only half of my source. Do you prefer the upper half or the lower?"

Nikita said, "You'll get the rest when we are satisfied that you have delivered what you promised."

Yakov said, "If I fail to deliver what I promised, I know full well that I will be dead before the moon rises over the Kremlin, and eight million dollars isn't enough to protect me from your reach. Send the rest or I walk away."

Nikita made the call, and Yakov watched the balance of his Swiss account double in size. "Thank you. It has been a pleasure doing business with you, comrades."

He placed his iPad on the desk facing the three oligarchs, and a man's face appeared on the screen. He was in his thirties, clean-cut, and perhaps slightly afraid of what was to come next.

Yakov said, "Comrades, meet former DOJ Special Agent Johnathon McIntyre. You may call him Johnny Mac."

2

PRINTSESSA VOINOV
(WARRIOR PRINCESS)

Special Agent Guinevere Davis dangled her feet from the smooth, massive boulder on which she was reclining and relished the feel of the icy water of the mountain stream caressing her skin. "This place is amazing, Anya. How did you find it?"

Anya Burinkova sat up and brushed her long blonde hair from her eyes, tucking a strand behind her ear. "I came here once when I was very lonely. Is beautiful place and makes me feel calm and relaxed."

Gwynn smiled up at her friend and former Department of Justice partner. "Loneliness sucks."

"Yes, it does," Anya said with her native Russian still lingering in every word she spoke. "This will sound silly in English, but I feel like this place inside mountains is like arms of beautiful lover."

Gwynn joined her friend in sitting upright on the rock. "What do you mean?"

"I told you this would sound silly."

Gwynn shook her head. "No, it's not silly at all. I wish I spoke Russian well enough to hear you describe that feeling."

"I can maybe do this in English, but it will not be, maybe, uh . . . poetic."

Gwynn laughed. "Come on, Anya. I've watched you gut men like the pigs they were with only a knife. Nobody expects poetry from a warrior princess."

The Russian sighed. "I could have been maybe poet. I could have been many things if my life had not been stolen from me. I would have been wonderful gymnast or maybe dancer inside Bolshoi Theater."

"Yeah, that's true. I'm sure you could've been anything you wanted, but if you'd been anything other than what you are, you and I never would've met."

Anya laid her hand on top of Gwynn's. "Having you for friend is worth everything I had to endure to come to this place."

Gwynn closed her eyes. "That's very sweet of you to say."

"Is only truth," Anya said.

Gwynn raised her arms above her head, stretching her back. "Sometimes the truth isn't so beautiful."

"But is always better than lie, no?"

"I guess," Gwynn said. "But sometimes, telling a little white lie to protect someone from being hurt is okay, right?"

Anya stared through the trees above the mountain stream. "I do not believe lies come with colors. I think all are only black. But sometimes, we tell to ourselves these little lies to protect our hearts from breaking."

Gwynn studied her friend and wondered if there had ever been a more physically beautiful woman. "Do you ever wish you were ugly, for like maybe a month, just to see what life for the rest of us is like?"

Anya chuckled. "This is ridiculous question. What do you mean, rest of us? You are more beautiful woman than I have ever been."

"Stop it, Anya. I'm serious. Don't you wonder how people would react to you and treat you if you didn't look like a goddess?"

The Russian smiled. "I have been that person, friend Gwynn. You must remember when I was beaten and cut so badly on operation with Chase. I was very ugly for more than one year, and I did not like it."

"I guess you're right. Sorry to bring that up."

"Is fine. Is only part of truth and not lie of any color. What lies do you tell to yourself to protect heart?"

Gwynn listened to the water gliding across the stones of the river. "I tell myself that by being a DOJ special agent, I'm doing the most meaningful work I can to make the world better."

Anya frowned. "And you think this is lie?"

"Sometimes."

"Why do you think this?" Anya asked.

Gwynn giggled. "How did we get to this point in the conversation? I want to hear your poetry about this place being your lover."

Anya rolled her eyes. "I did not say this place is my lover. I said is like arms of lover . . . and will not be poem. When I came here for first time, I was sad because I wanted to be someone else."

Gwynn recoiled. "Wait. What? Who else would you want to be?"

"Do not interrupt. This is difficult for me to tell, but I am trying to be better friend to you and have, as you call it, girl talk."

Gwynn made the playful gesture of zipping her lips, and Anya continued.

"First time I came to this place, I was sad because I was not woman who is Chase's wife. I will always love him, even though I know I cannot have him to be my husband." She paused and splashed her feet against the water. "I remember how I felt when he would wrap his arms around me, and it felt like we had only one heart beating. It was like he was part of me and I was part of him. I think I will never have this feeling again. But when I am here, this place holds me and is almost like being in Chase's arms. I feel safe, and my mind is quiet."

Gwynn leaned in. "Wow, Anya. You are a poet. That was beautiful. I've never had that with anybody, and now, all of a sudden, I want the same thing."

Anya scowled. "You cannot have Chase. He is husband for Penny, and even if not Penny, I make first dibs."

Gwynn laughed. "Did you just call dibs on a boy?"

"He is not boy. He is very much man. You have seen him, so you know. And yes, I make dibs."

"Then there's no hope for me," Gwynn said. "I can't compete with you.

And for the record, I wasn't saying I wanted Chase. I meant I'd just love to feel that with someone. It must be amazing."

Anya sighed. "Is best feeling in all of world. Gutting man like pig is close second, but heartbeat thing is first."

"Let's talk about something else. This is getting pretty heavy."

Anya said, "Yes, I agree. We must talk about real reason I brought you here. This is also heavy conversation, but not so much as pitiful try for poetry."

"Oh, the real reason?" Gwynn said. "This should be interesting."

"Is very serious, and you will not like what I have to tell to you."

Gwynn raised an eyebrow. "Stop stalling and spit it out. You're killing me here."

Anya stared into the water as if willing the words to emerge from the gurgling surface. "We have done very good work for six missions together. We took some very bad men from streets and protected thousands of innocent people from becoming their victims."

Gwynn nodded. "We definitely did that. I'll admit that I never knew how prevalent the Russian Mafia was in this country before we started the task force."

"I have also same admission. I did not know how bad problem was inside United States. We did very good work, and as you said, I think we were doing best thing we could do."

Gwynn said, "Yeah, but there's more, right?"

"Yes, there is more. We could continue to tear arms from beast that is Bratva, but these arms will always grow again. I must now slice head of beast from shoulders. In time, a new beast will come, but it will take many years for Bratva to become what it was when we started this."

Gwynn frowned. "You said 'you,' and not 'we.' Does that mean you think you're going after the head of the Russian Mafia by yourself?"

Anya shook her head. "No, I think head of Bratva is maybe Vladimir

Putin inside Kremlin. I cannot get to him, but I can stop the man who is running all of Russian Mafia inside United States."

"You didn't answer my question," Gwynn said. "Are you planning to go after him by yourself, without me?"

"This is very dangerous thing, friend Gwynn. I cannot—"

She cut her off. "Oh, no. You don't get to do that. You don't get to say that it's dangerous and that you're going alone. That's not how partnership works. Remember what you said about having only one heart with Chase? Well, the same thing is true when you and I are on the street. You've taught me to be the most dangerous person, other than you, in any room. You've taught me to find evil where everyone else sees good. You turned me into something I never dreamed I could be. I belong by your side if you're going after this guy. We're better together, and you can't deny that."

Anya didn't change expressions. "Yes, maybe this is true. You are very good fighter. You are sometimes more dangerous than me, but you must understand what it would do inside my heart if you came with me and you did not survive. That would be my fault. I would have to forever carry that inside heart and mind, and I cannot bear to even think about doing this."

"Look at it from my perspective," Gwynn said. "If I don't come with you, and you get killed, then I have to spend the rest of my life knowing you died because I wasn't with you."

"Is not same thing. Is different. You have important job and very good future inside Department of Justice. You will be supervisory special agent soon, and maybe you will one day be attorney general."

Gwynn shook her head. "No, Anya. None of that matters if you get killed, and I'll never be the AG. That's not possible."

Anya furrowed her brow. "You are lawyer with badge and gun. This is perfect combination to be attorney general."

"We're getting way off track here. I can't let you go after the head of the Bratva without me."

"You do not know what you are saying," Anya argued. "This cannot be done inside rules and laws. This is . . . I do not know English word . . . is *mstitel'* in Russian."

"The word is *vigilante*, and I understand exactly what you're saying, but you have to remember that little white lie I tell myself."

"I remember, and is not lie. You are doing best thing by being best agent in all of DOJ. This is what is best for you and for family. You have mother and father who love you. I do not have career, and I do not have family like yours. If I am gone, nothing will change."

Gwynn recoiled. "What? That's ridiculous. You may not have a mother and father, but you've got me, and you've got Chase and his team. We're your family. We're the people who love you, and if we lose you, think about what that would do to us."

"If I am dead, this would be relief for Chase."

Gwynn huffed. "That's stupid, and you know better. Two things . . . Number one, Chase still loves you, no matter how many times he denies it. It would destroy him if anything happened to you. And number two, I'm going with you. We started this together, and we're going to finish it together. We're the Avenging Angels, and that's exactly how it's going to stay."

3

Vremya Chayepitiya
(Teatime)

"Is waste of time to argue with you. I have known this since day we met. But do you really think Chase still loves me?"

The Russian awaited Gwynn's answer as if the world would stop turning if she didn't say it again.

Gwynn lowered her chin and stared at her partner over the top of her glasses. "Yeah, and you know it as well as I do. I've only seen the two of you together a few times, but that man would fistfight a grizzly bear for you. It's written all over him."

Anya smiled as if everything were right with the world. "I would like to see this fight. I would maybe bet money on side of Chase. He is very strong."

Gwynn snapped her fingers. "Come on back, Cinderella. We've got work to do."

Anya recoiled. "Cinderella? This is silly thing to say."

"It got your attention, didn't it? Now, how are we going to find this guy?"

"What guy?"

Gwynn rolled her eyes. "The head of the Russian Mafia in the States. That guy."

"We do not have to find him," Anya said. "He will find us."

"That's a little ominous, don't you think?"

Anya said, "Yes, is extremely ominous, but is also truth. He will first send men for us. These men will believe we are just silly girls and no threat, in spite of being warned. They will have to die."

Gwynn threw up her hands. "Why do you always go straight to killing people? Why can't we just discourage them from wanting to kill us?"

"This is exactly what we will do. There is no better way to discourage them than to kill them. This will send dangerous message to people who sent them."

Gwynn huffed. "Yeah, dangerous for us—they'll send better guys next time."

"You have learned very well, friend Gwynn. When these men come, it will not be so easy for us, but we must—"

"Yeah, yeah, I know. We have to kill them, too."

Anya shook her head. "No. We must only kill some of them."

"How many will there be?"

"Is impossible for me to know, but we must leave one of them alive after he has seen us kill all of others."

"So he can tell us who and where the boss is."

Anya grinned. "Teacher is very proud of her favorite student right now."

Gwynn took an animated bow. "Thank you. But seriously, I've studied the Bratva until I can practically think like them, and there's no definitive head of the organization. How will we ever know when we've won?"

"You can study every word in every file until you are blind and mind is melting, but you will never think like leader of Bratva in America. You do not have same sickness he has inside mind. For this, you should be thankful. Understanding depravity is not easy way to live. I know this because I have also this part of my mind—same as Ilya Gorshkov."

"Who's Ilya Gorshkov?"

Anya stood. "You will have with me some tea, yes?"

"Sure. Tea sounds good. But who's Ilya Gorshkov?"

The pair stepped from boulder to boulder as they made their way back to the cabin tucked beneath a canopy of age-old oaks beside the stream.

Anya filled the kettle and placed it on the flaming eye of the stove. "Ilya Gorshkov is former general in KGB. He is now very wealthy man and also very close friend with Premier Putin."

Gwynn raised an eyebrow. "Premier?"

"Yes, when Putin rebuilds former Soviet Union, he will, naturally, change his title from president to premier."

Gwynn pulled a pair of mugs from the cabinet. "Let's pray that never happens."

"If Putin lives long enough, trust me, this will happen. There is only one way to stop it."

Gwynn said, "Let me guess. Kill him?"

Anya pulled two teabags from the chest. "Very good. Maybe we can do this after we are finished with Ilya."

Gwynn braced herself against the counter. "Do what? Kill the president of Russia?"

Anya shrugged. "Someone has to do it. Why not us? You said we are Avenging Angels, so why would we stop at Ilya Gorshkov?"

"You still haven't told me who he is."

Anya poured the steaming water over the bags dangling inside each of the mugs. "Ilya Gorshkov is probably person at top of Bratva inside America. This is very likely person we will ultimately have to kill."

"Why not arrest him and try him for racketeering?"

The Russian laughed. "Is cute you believe American justice system is capable of stopping this man. Remember, I am Russian inside mind, so I understand how these people think. I know the terrible things they are willing to do. I have been trained to do same things . . . things your American justice system cannot fathom."

Gwynn lifted her mug and blew across the steaming surface. "This is going to be ugly, isn't it?"

Anya laid a hand on Gwynn's arm. "This will be worst thing you will ever do, and I am sick inside stomach that I have brought you to this terrible place."

"You didn't bring me here, Anya. This is what I signed up for when I took my oath and then pinned on my badge and gun."

Anya slowly shook her head. "No, my precious one. Where I am going to take you, badge and gun are toys of children playing inside street. We will look into face of dragon and beg God to protect us."

Gwynn swallowed the lump in her throat and felt it sink into her gut. "Are you sure this is—"

Anya squeezed her arm. "If we do not kill dragon, he will devour us, and everything we have worked for will be for nothing. He is coming for us, so we have only choice to lie down and die for him or stand up and drive spear through his heart."

Tea time was spent in silence as both women imagined what the coming days would deliver to their door and what wrath they could pour out in return.

Gwynn placed her empty mug on the side table. "So, what? Do we just wait around for these guys to show up? That doesn't sound like much of a plan."

Anya finished her tea. "Surely you know by now that I am not player of defense. Of course, we will not just *wait* for them to come. We will first make ourselves easy to find."

"What a relief," Gwynn said. "I'm almost afraid to ask, but how are we going to do that?"

"We simply must do what krot thinks we would do."

Gwynn screwed up her face. "Who is krot?"

"We do not know this yet, but we fill find him in time. Is only necessary that we be patient and not dead."

Gwynn chuckled. "I like the not being dead part, but I still don't know who or what krot is."

Anya furrowed her brow. "*Krot* is Russian word meaning person inside organization who is spy for enemy."

"Like a mole?" Gwynn asked.

"Yes! This is American word, *mole*."

Gwynn sighed. "It's English. American isn't a language."

"This is not truth. If it were, people from England could understand you."

"Okay, I'll give you that one. Maybe American is a language after all. So, tell me about this mole you think exists."

Anya frowned. "I do not think mole exists. There is always mole because there is always someone who is desperate for something. Most of times, money is this thing, but sometimes, it is attention of pretty girl . . . or maybe pretty boy. Krot is easy to find and recruit when we know what he wants."

Gwynn leaned toward her partner. "Are you saying there's a mole in the Justice Department?"

"This is likely," Anya said. "We will do dead bird in coal mine to find out."

"Oh, this ought to be good. What are you talking about now?"

Anya said, "You know this thing. Inside of coal mine, there is bird who needs same air to breathe as miners. If too much carbon monoxide is inside mine, bird will die, and miners will run from inside mine shaft."

Gwynn still wore the look of confusion. "So, we're getting a bird to tell us when the Bratva is coming to kill us?"

"No, silly. This is ridiculous. We will tell to Ray White, and maybe also attorney general, truth about where we are. If mole is inside Justice Department, he will tell to Ilya Gorshkov where we are."

Gwynn said, "That's a canary trap. It's not the same thing as the canary in a coal mine. We're not worried about running out of air. We're worried about who is feeding information to the Russian Mafia."

"Yes, this is what I said. But we must also tell lie in case krot is someplace other than DOJ."

Gwynn asked, "Where else could he be? Nobody else will know where we are."

"There is one person who always knows where I am."

"Not me. I never know where you are between assignments. You always run off and disappear until it's time to strap on our angel wings again."

Anya said, "No, not you. Skipper always knows where I am."

"Skipper? Chase's analyst? You can't be serious. There's no way there's a mole in that organization."

Anya sighed. "I do not believe anyone inside organization beneath Chase could be krot, but there is organization above him I do not always trust."

Gwynn gasped. "Ooh, I hadn't thought of that. Does Skipper report your whereabouts up the chain?"

Anya shrugged. "I do not know. Maybe this is proper protocol."

"Why don't you just ask her?"

"I think maybe I will do this backward."

"Keep talking," Gwynn said.

"I think I will tell lie to Ray White and attorney general. And I think I do not have to tell Skipper anything."

"I'm not following," Gwynn said.

"Is simple. Skipper has way of tracking where I am, even when I do not tell her." Anya paused as if drifting off. "I do not like this. Person needs privacy sometimes, no?"

"Yeah, we all need our privacy. Does it really bug you that Skipper can track you?"

"Yes, it does. I think maybe is telephone, but I sometimes change phones, and she still finds me."

Gwynn said, "Okay, so we don't mention it to Chase or Skipper. We'll just let that network play out and see what happens."

"Yes, and we will tell lie to Department of Justice and watch for killery to come to place of lie."

Gwynn said, "Killery means hit men, right?"

"Yes, very good. Again, teacher is proud of student."

Gwynn contorted her mouth. "Wait a minute. There's a problem with that plan."

"Nonsense. Plan is perfect."

Gwynn protested. "No, it's not perfect. What if the Bratva has a way to track you, just like Skipper does? If they do, that means even if the killery shows up where we are, it doesn't necessarily mean the mole is in Chase's chain of command."

Anya huffed. "You are right. Plan is no good."

"No, don't throw the baby out with the bathwater."

Anya groaned. "Throw out baby? What kind of American saying is this?"

"It means don't throw out the whole plan just because one part of it isn't any good. We keep the baby and throw out the bathwater."

"Is still ridiculous phrase, but I understand now. What are you suggesting we do?"

Gwynn said, "I'm suggesting we call Skipper and find out how she does it. If she's willing to tell us, then we might be able to eliminate that method of tracking, at least temporarily."

"But we do not want to eliminate it. We want them to find us."

Gwynn clicked her tongue against her teeth for a moment before saying, "How about telling no one the truth? That way, the canary trap will work, but it won't be definitive. If the killery show up where we told the DOJ we'd be, we'll know the mole is inside the government. If they show up where we really are, we'll know the mole has to be inside Chase's organization, or the Bratva has a similar—or the same—method to track us. Well, not us, you."

Anya said, "I like this plan. We will keep baby and some of bathwater. Now all we have left to do is decide where we will go and where we will tell DOJ we are going."

"There's a little more to it than that. We have to do all of the above and then find a way to stay alive while trained Russian hit men are crawling all over us."

Anya smiled. "Sometimes trained Russian hit men are very beautiful boys. You may not mind so much to have them crawling all over you."

4

TSENA LOYAL'NOSTI
(THE COST OF LOYALTY)

Chicago, IL

Ilya Gorshkov silently studied the younger man far longer than anyone would find comfortable. Johnny Mac gave an Oscar-worthy performance by staring back at the Russian oligarch without flinching.

Gorshkov said, "So, you are *former* officer of Department of Justice, yes?"

Johnny nodded. "That's right."

"How much is Yakov paying you to commit treason against your country?"

Johnny's performance came to a screeching halt. "This isn't treason. This is me getting what I deserve."

Gorshkov laughed. "What you deserve . . . This is interesting phrase. For you, this means something, and for me, it means something very different. If you were Russian, which you clearly are not, you would deserve terrible death for betraying your country." The Russian shrugged before continuing. "But since you are merely American, you probably believe you deserve very big reward, no?"

Johnny shook his head. "As I said, this isn't about money. Because of this woman who you want so badly, I lost the career I worked for and earned. Because of her, my country had no loyalty to me. Why should I owe them anything?"

"This is fascinating motivation. You wish to punish your country because they allowed this Russian woman to destroy your career."

Johnny said, "No, that's not it. I don't want to get back at the DOJ. I want to watch you kill Anya Burinkova."

"And for this, you are not being paid?"

The former special agent looked away. "Well, of course I'm being paid. Since I lost my career, I'm not exactly flush with cash, so Yakov offered to help me out."

"Help you out? Indeed. How much?"

Johnny drew in a long breath and swallowed hard. "A million."

Gorshkov frowned. "One million American dollars is a lot of money. Yakov, tell me, where did you get this money?"

The younger Russian stammered and answered in his native language. "I haven't paid him. I don't have the money yet, but I'm giving you a gift—"

Gorshkov cut him off. "This is wonderful news, a gift. Gifts do not require payment from recipient, right?" He turned to Johnny and spoke English again. "Go ahead, American *former* special agent. Tell Yakov that gifts are free in your country."

Johnny's eyes darted between Gorshkov and Yakov. "I don't know what he just told you because I don't speak Russian, but I've been completely up front about everything. You know my motive. You know my situation, and you know—"

Gorshkov held up a finger. "You may not speak my native language, but I happen to know everything there is to know about yours. You made grammatical error in any language."

Johnny replayed the previous seconds through his mind. "I'm sorry, but I don't know what you're talking about."

Ilya Gorshkov said, "You told me I know your motive . . . singular. Then you revealed your *motives* . . . plural. You want revenge against this woman, and you want the promised one million American dollars. That is the correct sum, yes? One million dollars?"

Johnny chewed the inside of his jaw. "Uh, yes, sir. I misspoke. I do have two motives. One is a necessity, and the other is my greatest passion."

"And the money? One million dollars is price Yakov promised, yes?"

Johnny nodded. "Yes, that's what he promised."

Gorshkov returned to his native Russian. "Your source tells me you promised him one million dollars. Is he telling the truth?"

Yakov threw up both hands. "Wait a minute. Let me explain."

The elder Russian held up one finger. "Yes, Yakov, please do explain, but do it in English so your source can understand."

"But Comrade Gorshkov . . . You see, I uh—"

"In English, Yakov!"

Yakov lowered his head and spoke barely above a whisper. "Is true. I promised one million dollars."

Gorshkov clapped his hands sharply, sending a crack reverberating through the room. "Speak up, Yakov. Tell me why you promised only one million to this American traitor, but you demanded one-point-five million from me."

Silence prevailed as Yakov's heart pounded like galloping horses inside his chest. "I should have . . ."

Before Yakov could finish his sentence, Ilya Gorshkov drew a 9mm Makarov and sent one round through the man's forehead.

As he watched his countryman wilt to the floor, Gorshkov said, "Yes, Yakov, you should have, indeed."

Johnny sprang from his seat.

Oleg Lepin, the second man in the room who was more than twice Johnny's age, spoke for the first time. His tone was dark and unmistakably ominous. "Do you understand what just happened here, American?"

Johnny stared down at the corpse at his feet. "Yes. Yes, sir. I understand."

"I think maybe you do not," Oleg said. "Yakov was our business partner. He was in what you Americans might call 'circle of trust' for over ten years. What you just witnessed was his first offense against any of us. We loved him, but we are men of loyalty. A good communist always does what is best for the whole, and not what is best for the individual. Yakov tried to —what is it you call it? Ah, yes, extort five hundred thousand dollars from us, and he called this extortion a gift to my friend Ilya. You understand now?"

Johnny continued nodding. "Yes . . . loyalty above all else."

"Precisely."

The dwarf, Nikita Obrosov, let out the chortle of a court jester. "Look at him. The American is terrified. Are you afraid of dying, American?"

Johnny's mouth became the scalding desert, leaving him unable to speak. His eyes panned the room as they filled with disbelief over what he had just witnessed.

The dwarf dragged a duffel bag from behind Oleg's chair and dropped it at Johnny's feet. "There is your money. What you just saw was price that must be paid for disloyalty. Give to us exactly what we want, when we want it, and you can sleep like baby at night. Lie to us just once, and you can spend all of eternity discussing philosophy with our friend, Yakov. Understood?"

Johnny couldn't take his eyes off the duffel bag. Everything inside of him wanted to rip it open and pour the money all over himself, but the desire to remain alive outfought his greed. "Yes, I understand. I don't have any reason to be disloyal to you."

Ilya shrugged. "Maybe, maybe not. That much money can take a man far away and make him difficult to find. When this thought enters your head—and it will enter your head—banish it immediately because I will gladly spend ten million dollars hunting down a man who cost me one million. To your American mind, this sounds foolish, but to my comrades, it is perfectly logical."

Nikita wrestled with Yakov's body until he had rolled the man facedown. "There. Is that better for your American sensibilities?"

"I've seen dead bodies before," Johnny said. "I've even produced a few."

Nikita pointed toward Johnny's pants. "Yes, it is obvious how brave you are. I think you will need to change trousers."

Johnny yanked his chair away from the dead body and replanted himself. "What do you want to know?"

Ilya crossed his legs and lit a cigarette. "First, is Ms. Burinkova working alone, or is she still supported by your so-called Department of Justice?"

Johnny repositioned himself in the seat. "I don't think she's supported by the Department anymore. I think she's rogue."

"You think?" Ilya asked.

"Well, I know the task force has been dissolved, and the supervisory special agent running it is now retired."

"And his name?" Oleg asked.

Johnny's stomach tied itself into a knot. "SSA Raymond White."

"And where can we find him?"

Johnny held up both hands as if surrendering. "He's not part of this deal. I don't have any beef with him. He's just a retired agent who's living out his life in peace."

Ilya leaned forward and tapped the duffel with one foot. "We bought you. That means we own everything you know. Absolutely everything, *former* Special Agent McIntyre. Where can we find retired Special Agent Raymond White?"

Johnny stared at the black bag. "He's got a brownstone in Georgetown."

"See?" Nikita said. "That wasn't so hard, was it?"

Johnny groaned. "It's just that Agent White doesn't know anything about where—"

As had become his custom, Ilya interrupted again. "So, you are asking us to believe task force commander, who created and ran program, knows less than a fired, low-level, former special agent. Is this correct?"

"No, I mean, I didn't want to involve Agent White in any of this."

Ilya said, "It would appear you have some fondness for this man, Raymond White."

Johnny grimaced. "He's been through a lot. He had brain cancer and he survived surgery. He's a good man. Involving him in this would have no beneficial effect. He won't tell you where Anya is. He probably doesn't even know where she is." Johnny paused, caught his breath, and continued. "Besides, if he found out what's going on, he'd report it, and that would bring down an investigation that none of us wants."

Ilya smiled and took a long draw from his cigarette. As the smoke escaped his lips, he said, "We have no interest in questioning your friend, Agent White. We merely needed to confirm your devotion to him."

Johnny frowned and cocked his head, but before he could speak, the dwarf claimed the floor.

"It is like this, American. If you choose to be uncooperative in any way, we can bring you pieces of your beloved retired Supervisory Special Agent Raymond White. My personal favorite is to start with toes and work slowly toward ears."

"Wait a minute," Johnny belted. "This is not—"

"Oh, but it is," Ilya said. "Your rule of law is dead and gone." He paused and glanced at Yakov's body. "Just like your friend, Yakov. You are now living in our world and under our law, where justice is far more swift and perhaps even more brutal."

Johnny's eyes involuntarily swept back toward the bag of cash as Yakov's ever-expanding puddle of blood encroached on it.

Nikita noticed and hopped from his perch. He dragged the duffel away from the body and toward Johnny. "You can go now."

Confusion consumed Johnny's face. "Go? What do you mean?"

The dwarf turned to Ilya, the obvious leader of what had been a four-man team, and said, "Inside bag, you will find a cell phone. No one has number except the four"—another glance toward Yakov changed Nikita's statement—"except the three of us. You may not make any outgoing calls. You may only answer phone when it rings, and absolutely every time it rings, regardless of what else is happening in your pitiful little life. If you are sleeping, turn up ringer. If you plan to travel on airplane, cancel plans. Answer phone when it rings, regardless of everything else. Failure to do so will be considered breach of loyalty, and you have seen how we deal with issues of loyalty."

Johnny nodded. "I've got it. Answer it whenever it rings, no exceptions."

Ilya kicked the bag. "And put money someplace safe. Chicago is crawling with criminals, and one can never be too cautious."

Nikita opened the door and waved Johnny through. "We will be in touch very soon."

Johnny shouldered the bag and squirmed beneath its surprising weight.

Oleg snapped his fingers. "I almost forgot. Make certain you count money. We cannot have any inaccuracies spoiling a perfectly good partnership."

5

PULYA BYLA BY LUCHSHE
(A BULLET WOULD BE BETTER)

Johnny McIntyre sat on the edge of a motel bed, in a part of Chicago with more robberies, rapes, and murders than in some entire states across the country. The black duffel resting beside him was more than enough to add him to the city's already burgeoning list of victims. As the bag lay there, as benign as a stone, Johnny thought that stepping through the door of the room and waving fistfuls of hundred-dollar bills in the air would be safer than the pit of Russian vipers into which he had voluntarily fallen. In spite of his self-loathing for what he had put in motion, the siren call from inside the bag beckoned him ever nearer to the cliffs of despair.

As if unzipping the bag would change anything, he gripped the tab with a trembling hand and slowly pulled. The zipper slid smoothly, with barely any sound, but the fluid feel of its motion did nothing to soothe the burn from the glowing embers inside his chest. When the tab reached its end, Johnny braced himself and parted the opening with only one finger.

What's wrong with me? It's just money and a cell phone. It's not going to bite.

He pressed further into the bag until his fingertips met something firm and blocky. The bedside lamp did little to illuminate the room—and even less the depths of the solid black duffel. The instant he dared take the first block into his hand, a car horn blared from outside, and he leapt from the bed, withdrawing his hand from the bag as if he'd been struck by a demon of Hell.

Johnny gathered his wits and stepped to the door, double-checking the deadbolt and chain. They were both solidly in place, but they weren't enough. He scoured the room with fear-filled eyes until he settled on the solid chair beside what qualified as a desk in the seedy motel. He shoved the chair in place beneath the doorknob and parted the curtain barely more than a sliver as he surveyed the parking lot. A dozen or more shirtless men circled a car and danced as if they were part of some ancient ritual at the farthest reaches of humanity. They yelled, raised bottles of beer, and passed burning joints from hand to hand in a well-practiced routine.

He stepped away from the window and pulled the curtains even tighter than before.

Inside his head, he screamed, *Just do it, Johnny! Do it! What are you afraid of?*

With one explosive motion, he grabbed the end of the duffel and flipped it over. With the other hand, he shook the bag until it weighed almost nothing in his grip. A mound of banded cash spread out on the blanket of the rock-hard bed and flowed like water cascading over itself until coming to rest in a peaceful, tranquil pool.

What am I supposed to do with a million dollars in cash? Where do I keep it? How can I launder it? Is it counterfeit? Am I seconds away from the horde of men from the parking lot forcing their way through the door and leaving me a lifeless, soulless corpse on the carpet?

A glance back at the window did nothing to comfort him, so he took a knee beside the bed and mindlessly recited the Rosary over and over, crossing himself and kissing his fingers after every iteration. The longer he spoke the words, the emptier they became until they were gibberish wedged between sobs and gasps.

I could run. I could change my name and disappear. I'm smart enough. I could find someplace they'd never look for me.

The old Russian's words thundered behind his eyes. "Make certain you count money. We cannot have any inaccuracies spoiling a perfectly good partnership."

Count it. Count every bill. It must be counted. I have to count it.

Johnny grabbed the leg of the piece of furniture that was almost a desk and dragged it beside the bed. He tore the first brick of cash from its paper band and counted one hundred bills.

That's ten thousand dollars. Okay, that's what the band says, and I counted one hundred bills. I know I did.

As paranoia closed in, crushing his faculties between its relentless, vise-like jaws, his breathing came in choppy, convulsive waves until he was uncertain if he'd actually counted one hundred or if he'd only allowed his mind to count what was stamped on the band.

Like a man possessed, he counted the bills again. One hundred and two. Ninety-nine. Ninety-eight. One oh one.

My God! I've got to get myself under control. I have to calm down. The money has to be counted. It has to be counted.

The next instant, he found himself on the ground outside the bathroom window of the motel, lying flat on his back and gazing into the cloudless, obsidian sky. A billion specks of light danced in a chaotic, endless parade, coming in and out of focus. He scrambled to his feet and dusted himself off.

How did I fit through that window? Why am I outside? What am I doing?

Bracing himself against the graffiti-covered wall of the motel, he took several deep breaths until his vision cleared. Staring down at his hand, a pair of bills stared back. They were crisp and new, the kind of bills that only come straight off the presses. The bills weren't street money. They were too clean, too crisp. He wadded the bills into a ball and unrolled them again. They were still too fresh, so he threw them to the ground and planted a foot on top of them, grinding the paper into the filth. Ten more repetitions of abuse left the bills tattered, worn, and street-worthy.

Johnny shoved them into his pocket and rounded the corner of the motel. Before him, in the parking lot, the ritual he'd witnessed earlier continued even louder and more energized. Every step made him feel as if he were walking in quicksand. His feet were concrete slabs, hesitant to move, but he trudged onward toward the crowd that was still dancing, yelling, smoking, and drinking.

As he slowly made his way toward the throng, every minute of his Federal Law Enforcement academy training, coupled with what he'd learned on the streets, screamed inside his head. Approaching the scene without support was tantamount to insanity, but he felt as though he had passed that landmark hours before. He fumbled with the two one-hundred-dollar bills wadded inside his pocket before realizing the gang in front of him might perceive that as aggression, and that was the last thing he wanted. He needed their cooperation, and he had no desire to appear threatening in any way.

"Woah! Hey, man. What you tryna do? Hold up right there. Get that hand out your pocket."

One of the shirtless men waved a pistol haphazardly through the air in front of him, and Johnny stopped in his tracks.

Slowly pulling his hand from his pocket, Johnny said, "I don't want any trouble. I'm just trying to find some weed."

Someone turned down the music, and Johnny had the crowd's full attention.

Their apparent leader laughed. "You a cop, man. You ain't foolin' us. You got cop written all over you. Just get on out of here 'fore this turns into something you ain't ready to deal with."

Johnny held out both hands. "You're right. I used to be a cop, but not anymore. I'm a . . ." He paused and clawed at his brain for any reasonable thing to say next. Finally, he said, "Look, I've got money. I just want to buy a little weed. I've got myself in a bad situation, and I need to . . . well, you know . . . I need to chill out."

The tall, skinny man glanced at his fellow partiers and then back at Johnny. "Come on over here, man. How much money you got?"

"Just a couple hundred. That's all."

The gang laughed in unison, and the man said, "So, you expect us to hook you up so you can lock us up. Is that it?"

Johnny stared at the man's feet. "No, it's nothing like that. I'm telling you, I'm not a cop. You know the law. If you ask, I have to tell you the truth, right?"

The man turned to face a younger man sitting behind the wheel of the car. "What you holdin', Cookie?"

He looked up and said, "I just happen to be running a special today. Two for two for crazy-ass crackers lookin' all five-oh."

The tall man waved Johnny closer. "Come on, man. Don't be scared. We ain't gonna bite you."

As Johnny took his first hesitant step forward, the man jumped toward him and yelled, "Boom! We might bust a cap in your ass, but we ain't gonna bite."

Johnny didn't react. He simply continued walking toward the man who was still waving the pistol.

"Oh, so that's how it be up in here. You ain't easy to spook, is you?"

Johnny sighed. "Not anymore. The stuff I'm messed up in is worse than you putting a bullet in my head."

"You in a bad way, ain't you, Cracker? Lemme see that money."

Johnny extended his hand, and the man snatched the bills from his fingers.

In an instant, the man planted a palm in Johnny's chest, shoving him away. "Get your cracker ass outta here, man. You lucky I ain't shot you already, fool."

Johnny brushed off the shove and stood his ground. "I already told you that getting a bullet in the head is probably better than what I'm doing. Just give me something. I need it bad."

The man turned to his crew. "Can you believe this dude?"

Cookie looked up from the car and held out a pair of tightly rolled joints. "This dude's a trip. Here. Give him these so he'll go on back to wherever he came from."

The tall man took the two joints and stepped toward Johnny. He laid them in his palm. "Two for two, just like the man said."

Johnny closed his hands around the joints and whispered, "Thank you."

He turned to go, but the shirtless man said, "Whoa, wait a minute. I almost forgot. Let me see them."

Johnny turned back to face him and opened his hand.

The man snatched one of the joints. "Consider it a delivery fee or shipping and handling. Now, get outta here 'fore you get your wish and I put a bullet in your messed-up head."

Johnny wanted to throw a punch that would collapse the man's throat, but that was the surest way to make his night worse. Instead of throwing the punch, he glanced down at the two-hundred-dollar joint, closed his hand, and turned away for the second time.

The music returned to full volume, and the revelry continued.

Climbing back into the bathroom window was far more challenging than getting out had been, but he couldn't let the partyers in the parking lot know which room he was in by using the front door. When he finally made his way through the small opening and onto the cool tile floor of the bathroom, he lay on his back, staring at the ceiling and fingering the joint in his hand.

After catching his breath, he slipped it between his lips and lit the tip. With every draw, the chemicals pouring through his lungs softened the sting of the encounter with the Russians. Fifteen minutes later, his heart was beating at thirty beats per minute, his breathing was calm, and the count was one million five hundred thousand dollars.

The hard plastic telephone lay silent in his palm, and Johnny stared down at it, begging it to ring so he could report the overpayment. Anything else would be a death sentence, just like Yakov's.

6

VOSKHOD
(SUNRISE)

Gwynn slipped from her bed inside the secluded cabin half an hour before sunrise and moved quietly to avoid waking Anya. She pulled on the jeans and sweater she'd laid out the night before. The door squeaked, so she lifted the knob, taking a little of the weight from the hinges until she could step from inside without any excess noise. Her boots waited for her on the rustic porch, and she pulled them on as her eyes adjusted to the darkness.

She climbed the trail up the steep incline as the sky took on the first indications of sunrise. The air was crisp and cool, but the climb had Gwynn's heart beating fast enough to keep her body warm. She paused to catch her breath a few hundred feet from the summit ahead, and the sounds of the Great Smoky Mountains National Park awaking for another day engulfed her. Chittering squirrels and the lonesome call of an owl stood out, but even the trees seemed to speak to her. Their leaves rustled as the gentle breeze floated up the mountainside. The sound of something heavy and unafraid broke through the serenity, reminding her that no matter how many tourists a black bear sees in his lifetime, he never becomes harmless.

She held her ground and let the bear pass, but the lingering thought of a second—or even a third—bear roaming at dawn remained fresh in her mind. With the omnivore well south, she continued her climb until the steep trail gave way to the rounded peak of the ridge and half a dozen fallen hardwood trees that had succumbed to the previous summer's tornadoes. Gwynn climbed the trunk of one of the reclining oaks until she was ten feet above the leaf-covered ground, and she stared into the distance as the eastern sky came to life.

First came the deep purples, followed closely by orange strands stretching through eternity. The ghostly silhouettes of the mighty trees morphed into majestic giants standing watch over the Appalachian Mountains as they'd done for eons, but they all seemed to stop their swaying, paying homage to the sun as she made her glorious entrance. Gwynn was just as mesmerized as the forest by the arrival of our nearest star, and in that moment, she felt as if she were little more than a tiny speck on the landscape of limitless beauty. The feeling was warm and rich and reminded her how thankful she truly was for unforgettable moments such as the one in which she floated without a thought of the deadly course that lay ahead for her and Anya. In that moment, nothing beyond the majesty of the mountains existed in her eyes, but that splendor would soon melt away and lie trampled beneath the feet of dangerous men. Those men would stride with singular purpose, but in the end, when the defiant sun rose and set again, the blood of those men would stain the ground, and one more step toward a country unpolluted by the Bratva would be made.

"Good morning, friend Gwynn. Is beautiful, no?"

Gwynn jerked and spun to see her partner nestled in the crook of the tree where a limb jutted skyward. "You scared me to death! Why didn't you tell me you were up here?"

Anya giggled. "You were having little moment, so I was quiet to not disturb you."

"How long have you been up there?"

Anya shrugged. Maybe ten minutes longer than you. Did you see bear? It was mother with two babies. They were so cute."

Gwynn shook her head. "Amazing. I didn't see them, but I heard them on my way up."

"They were probably frightened by you. You make a lot of noise when you walk inside forest."

"I do not. I'm practically silent when I move."

"Inside house or on street, yes, this is true, but with leaves under feet, you are not so good at being quiet."

"I wasn't really trying to be quiet."

"This is good for me to hear," Anya said. "Maybe you could be quieter if you tried. We will work on this on our walk back to cabin."

Gwynn said, "Not everything has to be a teaching moment, you know."

"We should always learn in every moment. This is why I am still alive."

"Good point. And yes, the sunrise was gorgeous. I guess you saw it a few seconds before me since you were higher."

Anya slid down the trunk and landed on the ground like a cat, and Gwynn followed, trying to remain silent but failing. "How? How do you do that?"

Anya said, "When you were little girl, you had ballet class, yes?"

"Yes, and I hated it."

Anya laughed. "You are wonderful dancer. You should not hate it."

"I'm okay at the club, or even ballroom sometimes, but I was terrible in ballet."

"Remember learning to move en pointe?

Gwynn chuckled. "I remember trying to learn, but it was the most painful thing I had ever done back then."

"Is okay. It takes many years to become good at this, but is same idea when walking in crunchy environment."

"Crunchy?"

Anya shuffled her feet. "Yes, leaves are very crunchy. When dancing en pointe, do you remember how easy it is to fall?"

"Oh, yeah, I remember. And it hurt like crazy. If I have to walk en pointe to be quiet in the leaves, I'll just stick to being noisy."

"No, silly. You do not have to walk en pointe, but you must make similar movements. Short strides and landing only on toes or balls of feet is how you must do it. If you take long stride, both feet make noise pushing and landing. If you walk on all of sole of foot, is large surface area to make more crunch. Watch me."

Anya moved slowly with exaggerated short strides. Her feet rose and fell almost vertically, and she kept her heels elevated. "See? I am still making noise, but not as much. Everything that moves inside forest makes noise. Is sometimes good to try to sound like other animals."

"How do I do that?"

Anya said, "Remember sounds of bear? That is not good sound. Is too loud, but sound of deer is very good. Think about feet of deer."

"I think they're called hooves."

"Whatever," Anya said. "They are small like pointe shoes, and except when running, deer make very short strides. Also, they walk with rhythm. Maybe four or five steps, then stop to listen before moving again."

"I've never thought about that," Gwynn said.

"This is why I am here, so you can learn things you did not know. Also when deer is walking, is very difficult to hear other things moving. They pause to listen for threats moving in environment. You must also do this."

"Okay, I'll give it a try, but if you try to put me back in pointe shoes, I'm going to scream."

They practiced on the way back to the cabin, and by the end of the trip, Anya said, "Very good. You sound more like deer now instead of bear or maybe choo-choo train."

Gwynn slipped off her boots on the porch. "I was going to make tea for you, but since you called me a train, you can make your own."

When breakfast was finished, Anya said, "Is time to make telephone call and tell lie to Justice Department."

"Have you decided where we're going?"

Anya said, "Yes. We will tell to attorney general that we are going to is- land of Bonaire. Is plausible because I have company there, as you know."

"Okay, that covers the lie, but where are we actually going?"

"Athens."

Gwynn furrowed her brow. "Athens? Why? We've never been to Greece together."

"You are thinking of wrong Athens. I have house in city of Athens in state of Georgia. It was my father's house before he died."

"That's not far. Is it in a subdivision?"

"I do not know what this means," Anya said.

"Like a neighborhood with houses close together."

The Russian said, "No, is on piece of land two acres in size. Is easy to defend if someone comes to attack."

Gwynn pulled her sat-phone from her bag. "I'll make the call."

The first voice on the line was an extremely low-ranking civil servant whose job it was to play the role of first barrier between the attorney general and the telephone.

Gwynn played her part masterfully. "Good morning. This is Special Agent Gwynn Davis, formerly of Operation Avenging Angel. I need to make a position report. Agent Fulton and I will be in Kralendijk, Bonaire, for the next several days."

The woman stammered. "Okay, but why are you calling me with this information, Agent Davis?"

"You're my first step to the AG. Would you mind transferring me to her personal admin assistant?"

"Hold one moment, Agent."

Anya grinned and whispered, "You are good at this."

Gwynn took an abbreviated bow and mouthed, "Thank you."

"Attorney General's office. This is Mrs. Lewis. How may I help you?"

"Mrs. Lewis, it's Gwynn Davis."

The woman's tone turned pleasant. "Oh, hello, Agent Davis. How are you?"

"Doing great. I just want to make a relocation report for the AG's log since she's technically our task force commander."

Mrs. Lewis said, "I'm afraid you're a week behind. Task Force Avenging Angel is officially and eternally closed."

"Oh, I know, but Agent Fulton and I still think it's important for the department to know where we are, given our status and all. We'll be in Kralendijk, Bonaire, for the next several days and possibly longer."

"Okay, Agent Davis. I'll make a note. Thank you for calling."

"Wait! Before you go, I think it's a good idea if I speak with the director of the criminal division. Can you transfer me to his office, please?"

After reporting her lie to two more administrative assistants in the criminal division, she was finally connected to the director. When she told the lie for the last time, the director said, "Thanks for letting us know, but it's not necessary for you to make position reports. Your special status with the AG affords you the privilege of relocation at will."

Gwynn said, "I know, sir, but it just doesn't feel right to leave you out of the loop."

"Thank you for that, Agent Davis, but it's not necessary. Enjoy the island. It's gorgeous down there, but watch out for the donkeys."

"I've been watching out for jackasses my whole career, sir. Goodbye."

Anya giggled. "That was hilarious."

Gwynn said, "Thank you. I wanted to leave an impression."

"I think you did. We should pack and get going. It will take us five hours to get to Athens."

"I'm already packed," Gwynn said. "And as usual, I'm waiting for you."

"You are funny girl. My bag is already inside car. I did this while you were sleeping in."

The drive from deep in the mountains of East Tennessee to the flat terrain seventy miles east of Atlanta was like being transported from serenity to the real world, and they pulled into the driveway just after noon.

Gwynn said, "What a cute place. I love it."

Anya put on her mischievous smile. "Is only cute from outside. You will have very different description for inside of house. Is like you—beautiful on outside, but deadly beneath surface."

7

Podtverzhdayushchaya Informatsiya
(Corroborating Information)

The cell phone finally rang, but Johnny lay in a daze on his bed behind the still-locked door of his motel room on Chicago's notorious south side. The cacophony of street sounds played in his head like a relentless droning, replacing his sanity with chaos and confusion. The added sound of the cell phone blended so well inside his head that he made no move to lift the phone from the grungy nightstand only inches from his head.

Although the ringing of what he'd come to think of as the Russian Connection didn't stir him, the flashing light from his personal cell phone grabbed his attention. He rolled onto his side and extended a hand to grab his phone, but his delirium and weed-induced passivity landed his palm on the phone provided by the Russians. When the screen came into focus, his heart thundered, and the roaring inside his head morphed into a blood-curdling scream. Terrified, he thumbed the button and stuck the phone to his ear.

"Yeah."

The voice of the dwarf, Nikita Obrosov, pierced his senses. "This is how you answer telephone? Yeah?"

Relief flooded over Johnny like a warm blanket. "Sorry. I'm glad you called, though. I need to tell you about the count."

"What count?" Nikita asked.

"The money. Oleg told me to count the money, and I did. The amount isn't right."

Nikita said, "You are calling us liars?"

"No, no! Not at all! I mean, the count is high. There's one point five in the bag, and I was only supposed to get one million."

"This is interesting. Are you certain of this?"

"Yeah, I'm certain. I counted it several times. It's too much. How can I get the overage back to you?"

The dwarf grunted. "Wait one moment, and do not hang up."

The line turned silent as Johnny waited for the Russian to return to the phone. When the line came to life again, it wasn't the dwarf's voice booming through the speaker.

"Is Oleg. Nikita tells me you believe we have given you too much money. Is this true?"

Johnny swallowed hard. "Yes, it's definitely too much. I was only supposed to get—"

The Russian cut him off. "So, you're telling us that your information is not worth what we paid. Is this what you are saying?"

"No, my information is good. I mean, it's solid, but I agreed to one million."

Oleg cleared his throat. "Perhaps integrity is not only found inside Soviet Union after all. Keep this money you do not believe is yours. If your information results in the completion of our wishes, you may consider it very large bonus."

Johnny stared at the phone in disbelief before finally saying, "Thank you. I wasn't . . ."

Oleg said, "But of course, Amerikanets. If your information is worthless, you will join Yakov in Hell and we will take money back. This means do not spend it before you have delivered Burinkova into our hands. Tell to me that you understand this."

"I understand," Johnny whispered. "But I need money to live."

"Is okay to spend small amount of money for basic needs and maybe good bottle of vodka, but you must determine how much life is worth to you. As I have already said, your life has no value to us if you fail."

Before Johnny could respond, the line was dead and the screen went dark. The chemically-induced serenity he enjoyed before the call was long forgotten, and he was once again feeling the crushing weight of the one-point-five million dollars resting in silence beneath his temporary bed.

He splashed water on his face at the bathroom sink and studied his reflection. Driving his index finger into the mirror, he screamed, "You deserve that money! You deserve the retribution! And she deserves the pain that's coming, that little Russian bitch."

After pacing until his feet felt the burn of the threadbare carpet, he plugged in the Russian phone to keep its battery fully charged. Before laying it down, he turned the ringer all the way up and added the flashing light notification to reduce the chance of missing the next call.

Johnny tapped the screen of his personal cell, and a missed call appeared on the screen. He thumbed the voicemail button and stuck it to his ear. "Yo, Johnny Mac, I got it. Call me back."

The time stamp said the call had come in less than thirty minutes before, so he didn't hesitate to call back. The phone rang three times, and a man's voice filled Johnny's ear.

"Where you been, man? You gotta answer when I call. I'm doing this thing for you, so you gotta show me some courtesy and respect, man."

"Take it easy," Johnny said. "You're getting paid."

"Not yet I ain't, but that's gotta change."

"Don't worry. I've got your money. But you don't get it until I get the information."

The man said, "Well, it's time for me to get it. Your girls are going to Bonaire. That's an island in the Caribbean."

"Girls?" Johnny asked. "Plural?"

"Yeah, both of them. The Russian and the other one—Gwynn or whatever."

"They're together?" Johnny asked.

"Uh, yeah, they're together."

Johnny paused and whispered, "I wasn't expecting that."

"What did you say, man?"

Johnny planted himself on the edge of the bed. "How did you get the information?"

"It's what I do. Nobody's writing stuff down anymore. Everything's digital, man, and if it's digital, I can find it. That other one, Davis . . . that's her name, right?"

"Yes, it's Gwynn Davis."

"Yeah, man, she's the one. She reported to the Justice Department that her and the Russian were going to be in Kralendijk. That's the capital."

Johnny said, "And you're sure about this? If you turn out to be wrong, that's a big problem for me. And if it's a problem for me, it's an even bigger problem for you."

"You can cut the threats, dude. You ain't a cop no more. Just make sure you make the deposit into my account."

Johnny groaned. "No way. You said it yourself. If it's digital, somebody can find it. This is a cash deal, face-to-face only."

"Whatever, man. Just make sure I get my money before you get killed doing whatever you're doing. When and where?"

Johnny glanced at the clock on the nightstand. If it was correct, the sun would be coming up on the East Coast in minutes. "How about that coffee shop where we met last time?"

"Fine. When?"

Johnny checked his watch against the clock. "Ten o'clock tomorrow morning. That's thirty hours from now."

"Are you out of your mind, man? No way. I'm not waiting that long. You gotta do better."

Johnny sighed. "Listen, I'm out of town, and I can't take a plane back to DC. I have to drive."

"So, get to driving. Call me when you hit town, and it better be today, or you're on your own and I'm telling Davis and the Russian chick you're trying to buy info on them. Don't mess with me on this."

Johnny said, "Okay, okay. But I didn't get any sleep. I'm going to crash hard, so I can't promise I'll make it today."

"That's up to you, man. I get my money today or I drop a dime."

Johnny ran a hand through his hair. "Fine. I'll be there late afternoon, best case. I'll call when I'm an hour out."

"You better."

He set an alarm for two hours and curled up next to his duffel. To his great relief, his eyelids fell, and sleep took his exhausted mind and body.

When the alarm sounded, he slapped the phone until the noise stopped, and he stuck his head back into the pillow. Two hours later, someone pounded on his door. "Open up!"

He shook himself awake and pulled the curtain back far enough to see the sidewalk outside the door. A man in a tracksuit stood alone a few feet away from the door.

Johnny licked his lips. "Who's there? What do you want?"

"Open up. You gotta go. It's checkout time, so pay for another day or get out. It's up to you."

It can't be checkout time. I set the alarm for six, he thought as he fumbled for the phone.

When the screen said 10:47, Johnny panicked. "Okay. Give me two minutes and I'm gone."

"All right, mister. You've got your two minutes, but if you don't come out, I'm coming in. And you don't want that."

He shoved both phones into his pocket, grabbed his backpack and the duffel, and he was out the door in just over a minute. "I'm sorry. I overslept."

The man shook his head and stared at Johnny as he unlocked his car and climbed inside.

The gas needle was bouncing off the empty peg, and time passed as if everything were happening in fast-forward. He made it to a gas station that looked like the perfect place to get carjacked. Although he drew far more attention from prying eyes than he wanted, the experience of filling the tank and paying in cash went far better than he expected.

The road tugged at his exhaustion as the hours and miles ticked by. His watch told him that he'd never make DC before dark, even if the traffic was light, but his greatest fear was falling asleep at the wheel. He bought two enormous cups of coffee at his first fuel stop after the Murder-Mart stop he survived back in Chicago. The caffeine worked, but his bladder didn't cooperate. Extra unexpected stops on his eastbound trek ate up more time, but he had no choice. If he didn't stop, his body would relieve itself without his permission, and he couldn't speed because it would be impossible to explain the bag full of money if he were to be stopped by an officer.

At precisely seven o'clock, both phones rang simultaneously, and he made the only decision he could to stay alive. "Hello."

Oleg said, "This is much better way to answer telephone. Now, it is time for you to give us information. Where is she?"

Johnny watched his personal phone continue flashing on the seat beside him and said, "They're going to Kralendijk, Bonaire. Can you hang on for just a second?"

Without waiting for an answer, he grabbed his personal cell and shoved it to his ear. "I'm coming. I'm just outside Hagerstown on I-Seventy." He tossed the phone back onto the seat. "I'm sorry about that."

Oleg growled. "This other person you were talking to, is he paying you more than one and a half million dollars?"

"No, it was a guy I have to meet, and I'm late. I wasn't trying to disrespect you."

"This guy you are meeting, is he part of our thing?"

"Yes, kind of. He's a reliable informant."

Oleg laughed. "You still talk like police officer. That is going to get you killed one day. Do not ever make me wait for you again. You understand, yes?"

"Yes, I understand, and I'm sorry. It won't happen again."

"It better not," Oleg said. "Now, back to matter at hand. When will Burinkova be in Kralendijk?"

Johnny said, "I'm not certain. That's just information from one source, and I need to verify it before you act on it."

"So, you're giving to me unverified information?"

"No . . . well, yes. But I'll get confirmation tonight. I just don't want you sending your guys to the island if we're not sure they're going to be there."

"They?" Oleg asked. "Who is they?"

"Anya and Davis. It looks like they're traveling together."

Oleg let out a sigh. "And Davis is also responsible for our losses in this country, no?"

"No, not entirely," Johnny said. "It's Anya you want, right? There's no reason to go after Davis. She's not a threat."

"Perhaps she is not threat to you, but she cost us far more money than you can imagine. We want Burinkova, but if we get our hands on Davis, too, this is bonus for us . . . and maybe also bonus for you."

* * *

Johnny stumbled into the coffee shop an hour later, and his contact stared him down.

"You look like death, man. Where were you that it took so long to get here?"

Johnny collapsed onto a chair across the table from the ball-cap-clad tech wizard. He covered twenty-five hundred dollars with his hand and slid it across the table. "Here's your money, but I need secondary verification of their destination."

The man pocketed the cash without counting. "I gave you what I had. You don't ask the same doctor for a second opinion. I'm not chasing down corroborating information. That's on you."

Johnny met the man's gaze. "Ten thousand."

"Ten thousand what?"

Johnny checked across his shoulder and said, "Ten grand for corroborating information from a source other than DOJ email. Can you do it or not?"

8

Nedootsenennyy
(Underestimated)

Anya opened the door to what had been her father's house, and with a flourish, motioned for Gwynn to go first.

Gwynn accepted and stepped through the door. "Ooh, this place is cute."

Anya followed her. "Is not cute. Is dated, but is much better downstairs. You will see."

"You keep saying that. What's so special about downstairs?"

Anya pulled up the house's security cameras on her phone to make sure they were working as they should. "Cameras are all good. Follow me."

She opened the door to a hall closet and activated a switch inside. The back of the closet swung open to a descending staircase.

Gwynn said, "That's nifty."

Anya giggled. "I like this word, nifty. It means good, yes?"

Gwynn gave her a playful shove. "You're not fooling me, and I think you know that. You're English is better than mine when you choose. I've known you too long for the confused foreigner act to work."

Anya started down the stairs. "Is valuable tool. People believe I am not very smart when I struggle with language, and you know how much I love being underestimated."

They reached the bottom, and Anya pulled a string dangling from the ceiling to turn on a single bulb in the center of the room.

Gwynn scanned the subterranean room that looked like most basements she'd seen. "Okay, it's just a basement. It smells a little like mold, and those boxes look like they've been here for decades."

Anya smiled. "Yes, you are right, but just like my accent, this part of basement is only façade to make people underestimate."

A pocket door Gwynn hadn't noticed slid into its recess, revealing a short, dimly lit corridor, and Anya curled a finger. "Come on."

After the Russian entered a ten-digit code into a keypad, the bolts that kept the heavy door securely shut withdrew, and she pushed the door into the room beyond. The two stepped inside, and fluorescent lights came alive, filling the previously dark space.

Gwynn surveyed the roomful of state-of-the-art electronics, communication gear, and a wall covered in firearms of every imaginable style. "Oh, my God. This is amazing. It's like an operations center in an armory. I thought your dad was a psychology professor. Why would he need something like this?"

Anya grinned with pride. "Being underestimated is family tradition. My father was wonderful professor, but this was only one of his many skills. He was pilot in war and also government operative of sorts."

"I'm impressed. That would've made him a Cold War operative."

"It would," Anya said. "This is how he met and fell in love with my mother. Is similar to how Chase and I met and fell also in love."

"They say every girl wants to marry a man just like her father."

Anya frowned. "Who says this? Is not true. I did not know my father until after I met Chase. I have very old memory of maybe him singing to me when I was little girl, but I don't know for sure. Memories are strange things."

"I don't know who says it. It's just a saying. You fell for a guy who was a psychologist, pilot, and a spy. That sounds a lot like your father."

"Chase is not spy, and neither was my father. He was person who recruited and ran spies inside Soviet Union."

"Okay, but you get my point. They sound like they were cut from the same cloth."

"I think you are right," Anya said. "They are similar, but not same. My father and mother made together baby, and this was me."

Gwynn giggled. "That's how it works, but I'm not sure having a baby with Chase is in the cards for you."

Anya shrugged. "Imagine how beautiful our baby would be. If boy, he would be strong and tall, and if girl, she would be beautiful and graceful."

Gwynn nodded. "I have to admit it. The two of you would make beautiful babies, but we've got a lot to deal with right now. This isn't the time for that discussion."

Anya said, "Chase can no longer make baby. He had injury on mission, and now he cannot . . . you know."

Gwynn froze. "No, I *don't* know. He can't physically do it, or he just can't father a child?"

Anya giggled like an embarrassed teenager. "I am sure he can still do *that*, but no, he cannot make child." She cocked her head in silent thought for a moment, but Gwynn jumped in.

"Stop it, Anya. I know what you're thinking, and it's not nice."

"You cannot possibly know what I am thinking."

"Let me give it a shot," Gwynn said. "You're thinking maybe he can't, uh, perform, so he and Penny can't . . ."

Anya continued giggling. "No, this is not what I was thinking, but it is funny. Imagine being married to a man so beautiful but you cannot . . . well, you know."

Gwynn threw up her hands. "Nope. I'm done with this conversation. Let's get back to why your father needed an op center."

Anya said, "I think maybe he did not need op center, but his house was perfect place for it. I think this is why agency built it."

"Agency? Like the CIA?"

Anya shrugged. "I do not know. Perhaps he worked with CIA, but is more likely he was more like Chase and worked for someone outside of official government."

Gwynn sighed. "It's hard to believe agencies like that really existed."

"No, it is not that they existed. They still exist. You have been to Bonaventure. You have seen operation Chase runs, and he does not work directly for government."

"It all feels like something from the movies—like it can't be real."

Anya took her hand. "Is very real, and you and I are part of this world now."

Gwynn furrowed her brow. "What do you mean we're part of it? We work for the DOJ."

Anya smiled. "No, this is not true. You still have credentials and badge from DOJ, and maybe you are still having paycheck. I do not know. But we are definitely not working for government. We are very much on our own. If we fail, and it is discovered that we were doing this thing, government will call us rogue former agents and disavow any knowledge of operation."

Gwynn stared between her feet for a moment. "But if we get in trouble, they'll send HRT."

Anya shook her head slowly. "No, Gwynn. This will not happen. Hostage Rescue Team will not come for us." She lifted Gwynn's chin. "Look at me. I will do everything in my power to protect you, but what we are doing is very dangerous. Is not too late for you to go back to Washington, where you are safe."

"What makes you think I'm safe in DC?"

"They are not looking for you. It is me these people want. You are, to them, police officer doing job, but I am Russian traitor. Is impossible for you to understand. Is culture I do not have words to explain."

Gwynn squeezed her partner's hand. "Maybe this is a culture they can never understand. We're partners, and I'm not leaving your side. If they're coming for you, they're coming for us."

"I love you, friend Gwynn. I do not deserve friend like you."

Gwynn dropped Anya's hand. "Don't get mushy on me. We've got a fight to win. How soon do you think they'll come?"

"Is impossible to know, but I must prepare my people on Bonaire."

Anya pulled a chair away from her father's desk and lifted the receiver of the communication system.

Seconds later, a man's voice appeared on the line. "Island Adventures Bonaire."

"Hello, Michael. Is Anya Burinkova. I have for you information."

"Hey, Anya. Where are you? We all thought you'd be back by now."

She said, "I have some things I must take care of inside U.S., but I will be back soon. I am calling to warn you that people may come in search of me, and they are not good people. They are very dangerous. Is important you tell to them you do not know where I am or when I will return."

Michael said, "Whoa. Slow down. What people? And what do you mean, dangerous? What do they want?"

"I do not have time to explain details, but these men will probably be Russian like me. They will try to intimidate you. Is okay to pretend to be afraid. Just do not tell them where I am."

Michael let out a nervous chuckle. "If Russian thugs show up, I don't think any of us will have to *pretend* to be afraid."

Anya said, "Give to me just one moment. I have to think about something." While Michael waited silently on the line, Anya covered the mouthpiece with her palm and turned to Gwynn. "I have decision to make. Should I close business or try to find security team to protect my employees?"

Gwynn said, "Maybe both."

Anya removed her hand from the mouthpiece. "How many reservations do we have for next few days?"

Michael said, "We're booked solid through the weekend. There's at least one cruise ship in port every day until Monday."

She sat in silent thought for another moment and then said, "This is good. Give to everyone double pay until Monday, and I will send some people to watch for men who are coming."

"Double pay? That's awesome. They're going to love that."

Anya said, "I will call back soon with information about who will be coming to protect you."

He asked, "Do you want me to tell everybody what's going on? It would be pretty tough to hide a security team from them."

"Tell to them that security people are there to protect them from some people who want to stop our business on island. You can do this, yes?"

"Yeah, sure, but how dangerous are these guys? Will they try to hurt us?"

"I do not believe they will hurt you, but if they come, I need to know immediately. You have number for my satellite phone. If they come, call me instantly."

Michael said, "I gotta tell you, this is a little weird, but I trust you. When will the security guys get here?"

"I will call you back very soon with details, okay?"

"Whatever you say. You're the boss."

Anya said, "No, Michael. You are boss. I am owner. If anything happens that you are uncomfortable with, you have my permission to close business temporarily and continue to pay everyone. You understand, yes?"

He laughed. "No, I don't understand, but I'll keep you posted if anything weird happens down here. Oh, and hey . . . Are you in some kind of trouble? You're going to be okay, right?"

"Do not worry about me, Michael. I will be fine. I will be back on island before you know it."

She ended the call, and Gwynn immediately said, "You're calling Chase, aren't you?"

Anya drummed her fingertips on the desk. "Yes, I am. I cannot let anyone hurt people who work for me on island. They are good people."

Gwynn rolled her eyes. "They're also a good excuse for you to talk to Chase."

"This is also true, but you can listen to conversation and be chaperone."

She slid a second receiver toward Gwynn and dialed the number.

Chase Fulton answered almost immediately. "Yes."

Anya pulled the receiver away from her face and stared at it for a second. "This is not like you. You always answer telephone and say 'Hello, this is Chase.' You did not do this. Is everything okay?"

Chase said, "You're calling from Dr. Richter's op center."

"Yes, I am. Do you have maybe three minutes to talk with me? Is Anya Burinkova, by the way."

Chase couldn't contain his laughter. "Yeah, I figured that out. What do you need, Anya?"

"You know of Operation Avenging Angel I have been working with Department of Justice, yes?"

"Yeah, I know all about it. We lent a helping hand in the Dominican Republic."

"Good. You remember. Operation is now finished officially as far as government is concerned, but there are people who are not finished. I believe people are coming for me to make me pay for what we did to stop Russian Mafia inside United States."

Chase didn't hesitate. "Whatever you need, consider it done."

"You are wonderful friend, Chase. I love that you always want to protect me, but this time, is not for protecting me. I need team of maybe four people to guard my company and employees on Bonaire in case these people come after me there."

"No problem," he said. "We're between missions, and everybody's itching for something to do. A little island time might be just what my guys need."

Anya said, "It does not have to be your team. If you know contractor who can do this for me, I will pay."

"Payment isn't required, but we'll take good care of your people. When do you need us?"

"Thank you, my Chasechka. Is very kind of you. I would like to have team in place as soon as possible."

"You got it," Chase said. "I'll have Skipper book us a nice place to stay, and we'll head down this afternoon. Who is the on-site POC?"

"Point of contact is Michael. He is manager, and he is very good. There will be fifteen to maybe twenty employees."

"Got it. You're obviously in Athens. Do you need a couple of guys with you?"

Anya's eyes brightened, and Gwynn waggled a finger and mouthed, "No!"

The Russian stuck out her lip as if pouting. "As much as I would love to see you, I think I do not need anyone besides Gwynn, and she is here with me."

He said, "If you need me, I'm just a phone call away."

"Thank you, my Chasechka. Is beautiful thing to hear."

9

BESPOLEZNYY
(WORTHLESS)

Johnny McIntyre stacked banded cash in the bottom of his safe in the back room of his small, rented home in Arlington, Virginia, just across the Potomac from Washington DC. When the duffel was empty, he sat on the floor staring in disbelief at the largest pile of money he'd ever seen. Sweat rolled from his forehead as he lifted the top stack from the safe. Ninety-six hundred remained in the band after buying a two-hundred-dollar joint, more cups of coffee than he could remember, and enough gas to get him from Chicago back to DC.

A thousand bucks fit into his wallet, and two thousand more stuffed the money clip in his front pocket. He nestled the rest of the stack back inside the safe and secured the heavy door. Everything in his world felt foreign, even inside his own house. The sofa felt like it was made of cinderblocks. His favorite chair offered no consolation. And the bed he'd slept on for half a decade made him feel as if snakes were crawling all over his flesh. A barstool in his meager kitchen was the closest thing to familiarity he could find.

Through the years as a DOJ special agent, he'd studied case files from that stool with paperwork spread all over the countertop, but that night, nothing resembled casework, and his knuckles bled streams of crimson angst after he pounded on the impenetrable surface.

"Why? Why did she have to take everything from me? Why did I let that little commie tramp pull my whole life from beneath my feet? What's so special about her anyway? I could kill people indiscriminately if I wanted. I'd go to prison for doing what she gets praised for doing. She didn't work for it. She didn't earn it. I did!"

He leaned back, and the stool creaked under the stress. Tears of rage crept from the corners of his eyes, and he felt the bitter taste of acid in his throat. One more shot to the countertop split the flesh over his second knuckle, and blood poured from his wound. He didn't react to the pain. Instead, the fury inside him boiled ever higher until he could hear the thundering sound of his own blood coursing through his veins.

His cell phone yanked him from his hatred-fueled stupor. "Yeah, what is it?"

"Calm down, man. Are you all right?"

The voice of his source cracked inside his ear like limbs separating from a mighty oak beneath the stress of a tornado's wind.

"Do you have some verification yet?" Johnny demanded.

"I don't know. I've got some conflicting information. Meet me at the coffee shop in twenty minutes."

Johnny roared. "Just tell me what you've got."

"No way, man. Not on the phone."

"Fine, but I'm not driving back across the bridge. You come to Arlington."

"Okay, fine. Meet me at the Starbucks on North Glebe in half an hour."

Johnny threw the phone across the room and watched it collide with the refrigerator before sliding across the floor and beneath the table. A half-empty bottle of Jim Beam beckoned him from the opposite end of the counter, and he snatched the bottle by its narrow neck. Half a dozen swallows later, he felt the whiskey settling into his gut, and he couldn't wait for his body to metabolize the alcohol into his bloodstream.

Two minutes into what should've been a ten-minute drive to the coffee shop, an SUV swerved in front of Johnny and collided with an Arlington Transit bus. The bus took out four more cars before coming to rest on its side across three lanes of traffic. With horns blowing and furious drivers shouting obscenities, Johnny felt the effects of the Jim Beam warm his stomach.

Stopped and stuck with an overturned bus in front of him, and half a mile of furious drivers behind him, Johnny shifted into park and reached for his phone, but his hand came up empty. He dived onto the passenger seat and slapped at the floorboard, frantically grasping at nothing. As his heart rate thundered well beyond a hundred, he leapt from the car, leaving the door standing open, and sprinted away from the accident.

By the time he reached his house, his lungs burned as if he were breathing flames. He leaned against the door as he plunged a hand into his pocket for his keys, but just like the desperate grab for his phone, his efforts were rewarded with nothing more than a few coins and a ball of lint. He pounded his forehead against the door as he pictured his keys still inside his car a mile away.

The knuckles of his right hand wore the beginning stages of what would become scabs as the blood from pounding the counter slowly dried, but the scabs would have to wait. His fist had one more task before the blood could cease its relentless oozing.

Glass shattered, and shards flew inward as Johnny's fist exploded through the pane in the door. The razor-sharp peaks remaining in the frame sliced into his forearm as he stretched to unlock the door. When the knob finally turned, his arm looked as if it had been through a grinder, and blood poured from the new wounds.

Johnny powered through the door, crushing glass beneath his shoes, and he heard the tone he dreaded more than any other sound. He sprinted to the kitchen, where his cell lay broken beneath the table and the Russian phone on the counter rang incessantly. He grabbed it, shoved it against his face, and breathlessly said, "Hello."

He expected to hear Oleg's gravelly voice, but instead, Ilya Gorshkov's smooth baritone poured from the speaker. "What took you so long to answer, Agent McIntyre?"

Johnny caught his breath. "I was . . .I was in the other room."

"And you are out of breath from walking a few steps inside your simple little home?"

"No, I was . . . outside."

"Which is it, Amerikanets? Were you in another room or outside?"

He tried to control his breathing. "I was on my way to meet my contact to get verification for the information I gave you."

"Interesting," Ilya said. "You were going to meet this contact of yours, but you left behind the telephone you were instructed to keep with you always."

He gripped the barstool to steady himself. "There was an accident on the road, and—"

"Stop talking, you fool. I am quickly coming to believe you are of no value to us. Surely you remember what we do to people who have no value to us, yes?"

"Yes, I remember, and I'm doing exactly what you asked. My source has some new information. I was on my way to meet him so we wouldn't have to discuss it on the phone."

"This is very good," Ilya said. "When will you have this verification?"

"A few minutes after I meet him. Maybe half an hour."

Ilya said, "One half hour, and you better answer on very first ring. You understand?"

"I do. I understand. I'm sorry. It won't happen again."

Ilya's tone turned ominous. "If it does, I will have to assume my fear is correct and you are of no value to me or my associates."

With the phone line dead, Johnny crawled beneath the table and retrieved what remained of his personal cell phone. The screen looked as if it had eaten a bullet, and no matter how hard he pressed the button, it refused to come to life.

He leapt to his feet and sprinted back through the still-open door and down the sidewalk. When the accident scene came into sight, what he saw drove yet another dagger through his chest. A wrecker driver was raising the front of Johnny's car behind his tow truck.

He ran across several lanes of traffic, yelling at the top of his lungs. "Stop! That's my car!"

He pounded to a stop beside the driver's side door. "I'm Special Agent McIntyre with the DOJ, and this is my car. I need you to put it down."

The tow truck driver said, "You don't look like a fed. You look like a strung-out dude who hasn't slept in two weeks. How 'bout some ID?"

Johnny patted his pocket where his credentials pack would've been a year earlier, but in that moment, he found nothing. Dejected, he said, "How much?"

"How much what?" the driver asked.

"How much to unhook it? I need my car. It's a matter of life and death."

The driver laughed. "Dramatic much? If it was so important, why did you leave it sitting in the road with the door open?"

"Just tell me how much," Johnny said.

The driver shrugged. "Probably eight hundred, but you'll have to take that up with the impound yard. I can give you a lift if you want."

Johnny yanked his wallet from his pocket and thrust a fistful of bills toward the driver. "Here's a thousand. Take it and put my car down."

The man grabbed the cash and shoved it into his pocket. "Yeah, sure thing. I'll put it down, but it'll take another grand to unhook it. Otherwise, that offer to give you a lift to the impound yard ain't no good no more."

Johnny wanted to throw an elbow to the man's nose and step on his throat when he hit the ground, but that would not only send his car to the impound but also land him in the Arlington jail overnight. Instead of taking the driver down, he pulled the money clip from his pocket and pulled off ten more bills.

The driver laughed and pocketed the cash. "That's what I thought. Nice doin' business with you."

Johnny's car landed on the front tires with a thud, and the tow truck was gone seconds later.

With the street clear and traffic moving again, it took just over ten minutes to make it to Starbucks, where Johnny's source stood on the curb checking his watch.

"I'm here. I'm here. Sorry. There was a wreck."

"You got my money?" the man asked.

Johnny said, "That depends on whether you have verification of the destination you gave me yesterday."

"I've got a little bit of a discrepancy in the intel."

"What kind of discrepancy?"

"The info is still good based on another source over at Justice, but there's been a little movement at a house the Russian owns in Georgia."

Johnny scowled. "What are you talking about?"

"She's got a house. It belonged to some guy named Richter. He died a while ago, but your girl must've bought the place. Anyway, it's in her name now, and there's been some activity on the security cameras over there."

Johnny leaned in. "How do you know?"

"Simple. I'm good at what I do. I told you if it happens electronically, I can find it."

"All right. Give me the address."

The man grimaced. "Yeah, about that. What I do costs money."

Johnny yanked the money clip from his pocket. "I've got a grand. That's it. That's all I've got."

The man took the money and slowly counted each bill. "All right, then. Since we've got a relationship built on trust, I'll take this as a down payment, but you owe me another grand before this time tomorrow."

"Just give me the address."

The man motioned toward Johnny's car. "What happened to your bumper? It's all black and marred up."

"Never mind that. Just give me the information."

The source leaned close. "Look me in the eye, man-to-man, and tell me I'll have another grand in twenty-four hours."

"You'll have your money. Just give me the address already."

He rattled off the address and said, "You'd better get yourself a new cell phone. Yours bit the dust right after our last call."

The Russian phone vibrated in Johnny's pocket. He answered immediately and moved away from the table. "Hello."

"Very good, Special Agent. You answered promptly, just as I expect. You have for me verification of Anastasia Burinkova's whereabouts?" Ilya's tone was authoritative but not threatening.

"Unfortunately, I don't. It's possible she's in Athens, Georgia. It could be just a brief stop before heading for the islands, but to know for sure, I need to put eyes on the property."

Ilya said, "Is good. You are showing initiative. Why are you not already driving to Georgia?"

Johnny said, "I've got a few things I have to take care of here before I can—"

Ilya's harshness returned. "I gave to you one and a half million dollars, and you believe you have things to take care of that are more important than what I want?"

"No . . . no, sir. It's just that a window is broken at my house, and I have to get it fixed before I can leave. Otherwise, anyone will have access to my house."

"You will be in Athens, Georgia, by ten o'clock tomorrow morning or you will never again have to worry about piece of broken glass. I believe I have made myself quite clear, no?"

Johnny swallowed the confidence he'd had a moment before. "Yes, of course. I'll be there. You know, this would be a lot easier if I could call you instead of waiting for you to call me."

Ilya was silent for a moment before saying, "Okay. You may call on this number, but only on two conditions. First is if you see Anastasia with your own eyes. Second is if you have verified, confirmed sighting of her by someone you would trust with your life. You can follow these rules, yes?"

"Yes," Johnny said. "Thank you."

His first stop was the Apple store, where he replaced his broken phone with a new one. His second stop was in front of a row of townhouses where a major remodeling project appeared to be underway.

Johnny parked and approached a man in a yellow hard hat. "Are you the foreman?"

The man shook his head. "No, I'm the safety guy. Who are you?"

"I've got a broken pane of glass in my front door, and I need it replaced right now. How much would that cost?"

The man said, "What are you asking me for? I told you I'm the safety guy. I'm here to make sure these idiots who work for us wear their harnesses when they ride the boom lift. I'm tired of paying OSHA's fines. Your broken glass is *your* problem, not mine."

Johnny felt the minutes ticking away. "Point me toward a carpenter."

The man huffed. "Everybody with a tool pouch and a hammer is a carpenter, but you ain't goin' in there without a hard hat."

Johnny lifted the yellow hard hat from the safety officer's head and placed it on his own. "In that case, I'll bring this back after I find a carpenter."

The man protested, but Johnny was too many steps ahead for him to give chase.

He found the first man who met the description. "Excuse me. How much would you charge to replace a pane of glass in my front door right now?"

The man took a step back. "Do I look like a guy who needs another job to you? I'm trying to work here. I don't have time for—"

"Two thousand dollars if it's repaired within an hour."

The man leaned in. "Did you say two grand? What kind of joke are you trying to play? Nobody pays two grand for a piece of glass."

"Twenty-five hundred, but you have to come with me right now."

"I'm not getting in your car, but I'll follow you. Twenty-five hundred cash, right?"

"Yes, cash."

An hour later, Johnny's stash was twenty-five hundred dollars lighter, but his front door was whole again, and his headlights were aimed south for the six-hundred-mile drive to put eyes on the woman who'd cost him everything.

10

Propavshiy Bez Vesti Chelovek
(Missing Person)

Anya's phone rang, and she smiled as the number of the caller filled the screen. "Hello, my Chasechka."

Chase Fulton asked, "You're never going to stop calling me that, are you?"

"Probably answer to this question is no."

"That's what I thought," he said. "We've got boots on the ground in Bonaire, and we just left our first meeting with Michael. He's younger than I expected, but he's got a good head on his shoulders."

Anya said, "Thank you for doing this for me. I will, of course, pay at least for your expenses. You must let me do this."

Chase chuckled. "I'll make a deal with you. If you send me a bill every time I ask for a favor, I'll start sending you an invoice when you reach out."

"This is ridiculous thing to say. You always pay me when I help you with mission. Is unfair for you to work on mission for me without payment."

"That's what friends do," he said.

"Is this what we are, Chasechka? Friends?"

"Until I can come up with a better word for it, we'll stick with friends. Now, let's talk about what you're expecting from us down here."

She said, "That was impressive. You changed subject perfectly."

"Well, this isn't a social call. You clearly think the people who work for you are in danger, so we need to set some ground rules. Do you want an overt presence to scare away the bad guys? We're pretty good at looking scary."

"I think this is not what I want, but I am willing to listen to your argument if you think it is best. I believe covert presence is better. I do not want to frighten away these people. If they come, I want them to believe they are doing well right until moment I slit their throats."

"That changes things a little. If they show up, do you want us to deal with them, or would you prefer that we capture and hold them until you can get here?"

Anya thought for a moment. "I am not certain yet. Is very long way to island from Athens. For now, please protect people who work for my company and watch for Russian men you would call thugs. In Russian, this word would be . . ."

Chase said, "*Bandity*. Yes, I know. I speak your language better than you pretend to speak mine. We'll keep your people alive, and if your bandity show up, I'll give you a call."

"This is perfect preliminary plan. I made alliteration in English. You like?"

He ignored the quip. "If you need me and I don't answer, call the op center. Skipper and Dr. Mankiller are manning the phones around the clock. They'll be able to find me."

"This brings up point I need to discuss with Skipper. When she is looking for me, she always has magical way of finding me. I need to know how she does this."

"Give her a call," Chase said. "I can't promise she'll tell you how she does it, but it wouldn't hurt to ask."

"Thank you, Chasechka. Goodbye."

Anya slid the phone into her pocket, and Gwynn said, "I'm proud of you. You didn't flirt with him this time."

The Russian grinned. "Yes, I did, but was not flirting with words. It was flirting with tone of voice."

"Whatever," Gwynn said. "So, what do we do next?"

"We go for ride cart."

"What does that mean?"

"Come with me, and I will show you."

Anya led the way to the garage, where an all-terrain vehicle waited by the door. "This is cart."

Gwynn pushed the garage door button. "I think it's called a side-by-side, but I can go with cart if you insist. Where are we going?"

"We will do perimeter survey and find most likely place for bandity to try to get to us."

They climbed aboard the machine and pulled from the garage. After lowering the door, Anya drove across the open expanse behind the house and toward the tree line that delineated the property line.

Anya pointed into the trees. "Three hundred meters that way is stream of water maybe one meter deep and maybe three or four meters wide. Is obstacle too big to jump, so they will probably not come from this direction."

Gwynn said, "If I were hunting you, this is the exact route I would take."

"Why?"

Gwynn said, "Because it's the route you'd least expect."

Anya smiled. "This is precisely why I brought you here first. When second person comes, he will be professional, and he will think like you, but the first people will be arrogant fools. They will not do anything that makes their mission more difficult."

"I hope you're right," Gwynn said.

"I am still alive, so I am right more often than I am wrong."

They continued around the property until they came to the corner of the lot that met the road.

Gwynn said, "Let me guess. You think they'll drive right up the street and pull in the driveway, don't you?"

"They will only do half of what you describe. They will drive on road, but they will not put car in driveway. They will be lazy, but not *that* lazy."

When they finished the perimeter survey, Anya parked the side-by-side back in the garage and shut it down. "I must now call Skipper. You want to be also on phone call?"

Gwynn stepped from the cart. "Sure. Why not?"

Anya laid the phone on the kitchen table and called Skipper on speaker. "Op center."

"Hello to you, Skipper. Is Anya Burinkova."

"Hey, Anya. Chase said you'd be calling. How are you?"

"I am very good, and I am also very thankful you are willing to help until this is finished."

Skipper said, "Of course. That's what friends do."

"This is also what Chasechka told to me. Thank you."

"You've got to stop calling him that or Penny is going to make Chase stop taking your calls."

Anya said, "Is difficult for me, but I will try. I have favor to ask."

"Shoot."

"You always have way to find me even when I do not want to be found. How do you do this?"

Skipper said, "It's not that hard. I usually call your sat-phone. If you answer, I grab your location from the satellite data. I do the same thing if you don't answer. It's not as accurate, but I can usually get within twenty-five miles or so of your location."

"Why is this possible?"

"Satellites work on extremely precise timing. When more than one satellite links to your phone, I can triangulate your position by what's called an electronic resection. When you don't answer, only one satellite pings your phone, and the connection time is brief, so the location isn't very precise. It's as simple as that."

Anya said, "But technology to do this is not common, is it?"

"No, and it's not cheap, but in our line of work, I need to know where my team is."

"I do not believe this is only way for you to find me."

"No, it's not the only way, but it's the easiest. Your bone conduction audio device attached to your jawbone pings satellites from time to time. I can get within a hundred miles just using that technology. Is that all you needed to know?"

Anya said, "How can I turn off bone conduction device?"

"Well, uh . . . you can't unless you slice open your face and pry it from the bone. Without being inside your body, it can't recharge itself, so it'll die in a few hours."

"That sounds like terrible plan, but I must ask. How likely is it that someone other than you could find me using the bone conduction device?"

Skipper said, "The chances of anyone else knowing the precise frequency of your device and having the equipment to communicate with the satellites are astronomical. As far as I know, nobody except Dr. Mankiller and I knows the individual frequencies of the team's devices. It's not like anybody could stumble upon the discovery. The signals are minuscule. It would take a mole inside our team to divulge the information, and there's absolutely no chance of us having a mole."

Anya said, "This is very reassuring. Thank you."

"Sure. No problem. What else do you need?"

"I am afraid to tell to you what I would like to have."

Skipper said, "You're not getting Chase. He's spoken for, but other than that, I can't imagine telling you no, so let's hear it. If I can do it, you can consider it done."

"I would like to have real-time satellite imagery of my house in Athens."

"Like a live feed? Wow. You don't want much, do you, girl? It'll take some time. I don't know if there are any birds I can task, but I'll try. You have the ability to receive a live, secure feed there, right?"

"Yes, we have miniature version of your op center here."

"Yeah, I know. I've seen it. It's a little dated, but you should have the technology to receive the feed if I can grab a bird or two. I'll let you know, but it won't be quick."

"Thank you," Anya said. "This will sound like strange question from me, but can you think of anything I maybe have not considered?"

Skipper laughed. "Yeah, right. I'm never going to outthink you. You may not have the wherewithal to be an analyst, but nobody's better at tradecraft."

Gwynn covered her mouth to avoid having Skipper hear her laugh, but it wasn't enough.

Skipper said, "Hello, Gwynn. Take care of our girl. Chase would have a come-apart if anything happened to her."

Gwynn pulled her hand from her mouth. "I'll look after her, but it's nice knowing we've got a little backup if this thing goes south."

"Is this your first independent op?" Skipper asked.

Gwynn said, "If by independent you mean without the DOJ supporting me, then yes. I'll admit, I didn't feel so good about it until I knew you were on board."

"This is what we do," Skipper said. "Don't be afraid to ask. We can't help if you don't ask, but we can do a lot more than just help if you'll let us know what you need."

"Thanks, Skipper. I do have one question. Is Skipper you're real name?"

She laughed. "It might as well be. My real name is Elizabeth Woodley, but Chase gave me the name Skipper not long after he got to UGA. My dad was his baseball coach, so he hung out at our house quite a bit. After that, I guess you could say it just stuck."

Gwynn said, "Thanks again, Elizabeth. No, that just sounds weird. Thanks, Skipper. We'll be in touch."

Anya said, "Goodbye, Skipper. Do not forget my satellite, please."

11

UBIT' UBIYTSU
(KILLING THE KILLER)

Johnny McIntyre forced himself awake at the rest area off Interstate 85 near Clemson, South Carolina. He stretched and climbed from the back seat for the slow walk to the restroom. The reflection staring back at him from inside the mirror couldn't have been him. Even after splashing four handfuls of water on his face, he still didn't recognize the stranger in front of him.

Outside the confines of the restroom, he kept his hat pulled low in an effort to defeat the security cameras. Feeding spare change into the vending machine and sleeping in his car, instead of having breakfast at a diner after a night in a comfortable hotel, were but two more of the necessary sacrifices required to avoid tying himself to Anya's location. Plausible deniability reigned supreme in the mind of the former special agent, but that mind became less confident in its own sanity with every passing minute.

Back on the interstate, Johnny drove the remainder of the distance to the address his source had provided. The first pass by the front of the property showed nothing special about the basement rancher situated on a large lot. There were dozens of houses just like it throughout the area, so nothing about the property struck him as interesting.

Why would Anya want a simple little house in the middle of some podunk place in Central Georgia?

The arrangement of intersecting roads in the area gave him relatively good positions from which to stake out the property. If Anya was there, sooner or later, she'd have to come outside, and the mostly likely exit would be the garage since there was nothing within walking distance in the community besides similar houses.

The rear of the property presented some issues he wasn't prepared to deal with. A grove of hardwoods and pines with a stream dissecting the woodland made a decent barrier from the northern boundary of the lot. The primary advantage of the woods and stream was that it would be just as challenging to exit the property through the terrain as it would be to access it. Being a one-man stakeout operation, he was faced with the challenge of finding the perfect location to see without being seen.

After finishing his first circuit around the perimeter of the property, Johnny turned around and made the loop in the opposite direction. Perspective changes from every angle, and having a complete picture of his target area was critical to his operation. From the new direction, he noticed a small barn he hadn't seen on his first circumnavigation. It was diagonally across the street with knee-high weeds growing all around it. No tire tracks led toward or away from the structure, which was little more than an oversized shed that someone had obviously abandoned.

He found what had once been a driveway to the barn but had since become nothing more than part of the field. Johnny carefully drove the two hundred feet from the road to the dilapidated structure and parked, using the barn as cover between the car and the house Anya apparently owned.

Climbing from the car, he surveyed every direction and discovered that his position was even better than he'd initially believed. No houses were visible from behind the barn, and even better, his car was concealed from anyone passing on the road. It was as if the ramshackle building was a gift from above.

Confident in his position, Johnny slowly pulled against what had once been an operational door, but it was obvious its hinges hadn't budged in years. He gripped the handle and dug his heels into the ground. Heaving and lifting simultaneously, he finally broke the door free, and it swung outward several inches, but the success of moving the door came with a cost. Not only was the scraping of the hinges and frame noisy, but he'd also let out a grunt that probably could've been heard across the road.

A second tug against the handle resulted in far more motion than the first pull, but the movement was only Johnny's and not the door's. The handle separated from the ancient timber frame and sent him tumbling backward and head over heels toward his car. When he came to a stop against the front tire, he couldn't hold off his laughter. This ridiculous situation was his first moment of passing pleasure since he'd hefted the duffel from the floor in Chicago.

He gathered his wits, stood, and dusted himself off before squeezing through the narrow opening that seemed to be the only surrender the stubborn door would offer. Inside the shed, he could hardly believe what his eyes pieced together in the semidarkness. The outline of a car took shape in front of him, and he reached for his new phone with its flashlight function. His hand came back empty, and his heart sank into his stomach.

He forced his way back through the door and managed to move it a few more inches, making the passage slightly easier than before. Yanking open his car door, he snatched the Russian phone from the seat, but his personal cell was nowhere in sight. He dived toward the floorboard and ran a hand beneath both front seats. Finding nothing but spare change and a few petrified French fries, his mind reeled with disbelief and dread.

Johnny sat up and slammed his back into the seat. "Where are you? Why does this always happen to me at the worst possible times?"

The Russian phone must have a flashlight function.

The screen came to life at a touch, and he stared down at the display filled with Cyrillic characters instead of English letters.

"Why can't I catch a break?"

He struck the steering wheel with the same fist that had lost the battle with the countertop back in his Arlington house, and the blow reopened the day-old wound.

Johnny shoved the illegible phone into his pocket and headed back for the barn, believing his eyes would eventually adjust to the low light conditions inside. As he rounded the front of the car, his heel landed on something that couldn't support his weight, and he glanced down to see his brand-new cell phone, with its formerly pristine screen, spiderwebbed with cracks.

He growled at the world and his apparent curse as he lifted the destroyed phone from the ground. Shards of glass fell from the frame and puddled in his hand. In a fit of rage, he spun and threw the worthless hunk of Chinese plastic and circuitry through the air until it vanished silently into the overgrown field.

The instant the phone left his bloody hand, his mind exploded in disbelief at what he'd just done. Eating junk food from a vending machine and sleeping in his car were techniques he'd planned to avoid being connected with Anya, but now his blood flowed from battered knuckles, leaving DNA everywhere a drop met the earth. Aside from the blood, a demolished cell phone that could be traced directly back to him lay somewhere beneath three feet of grass and weeds in a field five hundred miles away from anywhere he should've been.

He leaned against the fender of his car and tried to calm his mind enough to think through his situation and stop the freight train barreling its way down the tracks and straight for his world. With deeper and deeper breaths came a clearer head, and he forced himself to walk through the basics of operational security.

Eliminating the expanse of DNA evidence of his location was key, so he wrapped his blood-covered hand in the tail of his shirt as he headed for the trunk of his car. When the trunk lid rose, revealing a beautiful first-aid kit gleaming in the corner of the space, at least an ounce of the dread he felt lifted from his shoulders, and he grabbed the kit. He planted himself on the edge of the truck, with the lid still raised above his head, and opened the plastic box. Gauze and tape were the first objects he found inside, and in that moment, he thought nothing could make him happier until his eyes fell on an elastic strap inside the top of the case. Bound by the strap was a penlight with a push-button on-and-off switch at one end.

He sent up a silent prayer—almost certain no one would hear or answer —that the battery inside the tiny light still had enough life in it to light his way inside the barn. Blood continued to drain from his hand and onto his shirt, but the wound would have to wait. Johnny slid the light from its binding and held it in the palm of his uninjured hand. He squeezed the tube and willed it to come to life with his thumb hovering over the switch.

Click.

A beam of beautiful, glorious light flowed from the device and illuminated the interior of the trunk. He quickly thumbed the switch to save the precious battery and slid the light into his shirt pocket.

Johnny wound the gauze around his hand until the blood was invisible, and he taped it in place with several wraps of the medical tape. Another glance into the open kit revealed a small bottle of hydrogen peroxide, and his forensic classes at the Federal Law Enforcement Training Center flashed through his head. He yanked the brown bottle from the kit and retraced his steps to the front of the car, studying every inch of ground beneath his feet in search of blood and pouring an ounce of peroxide on every drop he discovered. When he believed he'd found them all, he poured the remaining liquid on every spot he'd already treated as an extra measure of caution.

Investigating the interior of the barn couldn't be postponed, so finding the broken cell phone would have to wait. The door offered a small gift of an extra inch or two when Johnny squeezed back through the opening. He drew the penlight from his pocket and aimed it at the outline of the car. A touch of the button sent a narrow beam of light cutting through the darkness and falling on the canvas cover draped over what had to be a vehicle.

He tugged at the edge of the canvas, and the cover slid toward him with ease. It clearly wasn't tied down at any point, so he lifted the edge and shined the light beneath it. The beam reflected off the fender of an unmistakable sedan. He tossed the canvas aside, revealing an even larger swath of the car. It was a Crown Victoria, the epitome of a cop car from the previous decade. The layer of dust on the canvas said no one had moved it in ages, but beneath the cover, the car was in perfect condition.

To avoid leaving prints, he slipped his bandaged hand beneath the passenger-side handle and pulled the latch. The door clicked, and it swung open. The interior light came on, filling the interior of the sedan, but the beam of white light wasn't what caught his immediate attention.

The sound of a baby's toy rattle filled his head, and he struggled to make the sound fit inside his environment. The disconnect between the noise and the surroundings lasted only an instant before he knew all too well that the rattle never belonged to a baby—and it was certainly no toy. The fangs struck Johnny's arm as he fought to block the assault from the snake that had been coiled on the front seat of the car.

The pain was yet to come as adrenaline flooded Johnny's body and sent him fighting for his life. Retreating as quickly as his body would allow, he cleared the door of the car, but the snake came with him. The creature's fangs left Johnny's shirt sleeve, and the massive rattler fell to the dirt floor of the barn. It slithered into another coil and continued rattling more violently than before. Johnny found himself pinned against the wall of the barn with the threatening snake only inches away, poised and ready to strike again.

Think, Johnny, think!

He told himself to remain calm, but the words were wasted inside his skull. Terror had her relentless talons buried in his thundering heart, and Johnny instinctively reached for the 9mm he carried for so many years just behind his right hip bone. But the weapon wasn't there. That was one more thing the devious Russian had taken from him, and now he found himself unarmed on the threshold of death's door and face-to-face with an eastern diamondback, the deadliest snake in North America.

The snake was obviously determined to hold his turf, and Johnny had no ground to surrender. His back was pressed against the wall, and every decision he'd made in the previous week of his life replayed on his mind's silver screen.

In desperation, he kicked at the snake's head that seemed to hover in space. If he could make the snake retreat even a foot or two, maybe he could throw himself through the door and back into the light outside. The kick had no effect on the rattling killer, so Johnny forced his eyes away from it just long enough to take inventory of his surroundings. He silently begged for a weapon of any kind—even a stick would give him at least a chance. As he scoured the interior of the barn using the dim glow of the car's interior light, he saw the handle of a garden tool a few feet away, and he tasted the first nibble of hope.

He took a long, deep breath and slid the upper half of his body to the left, watching the snake's gaze as he moved. The slits of the demon's eyes moved as if somehow locked on Johnny's, and the threatening posture continued as the diamondback's forked tongue danced through the air in front of him, tasting Johnny's fear with every flicker.

Extending his arm farther than even he thought possible, the tips of his fingers finally touched the handle of the tool. Another inch, and he'd be able to grab it and shove whatever was on the other end of the handle toward the snake. Killing the killer would be the best possible outcome, but simply escaping was almost more than Johnny could let himself hope for.

He bent his body another inch as the snake took on an even more ominous posture with his head higher and his fangs glistening. Johnny felt his hand wrap around the handle of the tool, and an overwhelming instant of joy overcame him. In an instant, he yanked the wooden handle, praying it was a shovel he could use to behead the creature waiting to strike again.

His forceful heave did nothing to move the tool. It was frozen to the ground as if set in stone, and his attempt shook the rest of his body enough to send the treacherous beast at his feet into action. Every muscle of the snake's body tensed, driving his deadly fangs forward like lightning, but the strike aimed at Johnny's legs never found its mark. Instead, a second flash, even faster than the snake's advance, raced through the stream of light filtering through the narrow opening of the door, and a Russian fighting knife pinned the eastern diamondback to the dirt floor with less than an inch between the animal's fangs and Johnny's flesh.

12

ILI CHTO-TO YESHCHE
(OR SOMETHING)

Anya and Gwynn stepped into the barn with the beams of their pistol-mounted lights piercing the darkness. Johnny squinted and raised an arm against the blinding lights, and both women froze with their muzzles trained on the man against the wall.

In utter disbelief, Gwynn said, "Johnny Mac? Is that you?"

"Yes, it's me. Please don't shoot."

The women lowered their weapons, and Anya grabbed Johnny's arm. "You have been bitten. We must get you to hospital."

She holstered her pistol, withdrew her knife from the snake's body, and lifted the small wooden lever beside the door Johnny had battled moments before. The door swung open as if floating on air.

Johnny stepped over the dead snake that would've been his assassin if his former partners hadn't saved his life. "How did you do that?"

"Do what?" Anya asked.

"Make the door open so easily."

Anya patted the ancient wooden slats of the barn. "Is my building on my property. There are many rules of espionage, but near top of list is always have getaway car."

"That's your car?" Johnny asked.

Anya said, "Raise arm above head, and hold it there."

Johnny raised both hands in blatant surrender, and Anya laughed. "What are you doing? Were you bitten on both arms?"

He lowered his nonvenomous arm. "Sorry, I thought you were . . ."

Anya said, "Holding arm over head will make sure venom is distributed through body."

He froze. "What? Are you going to let the venom kill me?"

"No, of course not, but letting venom spread and dilute throughout body is best chance of survival. You are acting very strange, Johnny Mac. Is everything all right?"

"Well, no, not exactly. I mean, you just caught me sneaking into your barn, and you haven't even asked why."

The Russian stepped closer and examined Johnny's snakebite. "Is not necessary to ask. I know already why you are here. Now, we must get you to hospital. It was very large snake, so longer time we wait, more dangerous it will be for you."

Johnny said, "You know why I'm here? Listen, Anya. It's not what you think."

"Of course it is," she said. "Are you getting swimmy inside head yet?"

He shook his head. "No. I'm okay right now."

"This will not continue to be truth. You will become sleepy and weak. We can take your car if you think you cannot walk across street."

"No, I'm good. I can walk."

Gwynn glared at Anya every time their eyes met, but the Russian smiled and gave her a knowing wink.

A dozen feet before the road, Anya lunged forward and collapsed to the ground. On her way down, she grabbed Johnny, and instinctively, he made every effort to catch her. His attempt wasn't remotely successful from his perspective, but from Anya's, everything was falling into place— quite literally.

The two found themselves on the ground, and Anya giggled. "I am sorry. There was hole I did not see. Thank you for trying to catch me. Are you okay?"

Johnny helped Anya back to her feet. "Yeah, I'm all right. Are you?"

"Yes, is only small accident."

They walked Johnny across the road and into the garage, where Anya opened the back door of her Land Cruiser and Johnny slid onto the seat.

Anya closed his door and took Gwynn's arm. "You will drive to hospital. I will sit in back seat and take care of Johnny."

"But I don't know where the hospital is," Gwynn said.

Anya leaned close to her partner. "I will give directions as we go, and is okay. Johnny is not armed. I checked during fake fall."

Gwynn shook her head and whispered, "Of course you did."

Anya climbed in beside Johnny, and Gwynn took the wheel.

Johnny struggled with his seat belt, so Anya seized the opportunity. "Give to me. I will do it. What happened to your hand? You have bandage."

He shook his gauze-wrapped appendage. "It's a long story, but the most recent incident involved your barn door."

She said, "Door is tricky. You will probably be okay if hospital has antivenin for diamondback."

Johnny swallowed hard. "You mean they may not have antivenom?"

Anya patted his arm. "Correct word is antivenin, but is okay. Most people do not die from bite of that snake, but some do."

Gwynn called over her shoulder. "I still don't know where the hospital is."

Anya pointed toward the dash. "Press red button at bottom left."

Gwynn tapped the icon, and a red H appeared on the GPS. "Thank you."

Anya turned back to her patient, and Johnny tried to read the Russian's expression. He'd never felt more like a doomed mouse being toyed with by a sadistic cat.

She cocked her head and smiled back at him as if taunting him further. "Why do you not have gun, Johnny Mac?"

He recoiled. "What do you mean?"

Anya shrugged. "You are obviously here to protect us. This is why you were sneaking inside building to watch over Gwynn and me, yes?"

Johnny drew a breath of relief. "Yes, uh . . . of course that's why I'm here. I didn't bring a gun. I mean, I don't have a gun anymore."

"Then, how were you going to protect us?"

His brain whirred with excuses. "Yeah . . . I was . . . I just got here. I drove all night."

Gwynn's eyes loomed in the rearview mirror as Johnny stumbled through whatever he was trying to say.

Anya came to his rescue. "Is okay. You are probably feeling effects of venom. You will be sleepy and very weak, but we will take care of you. Give to me cell phone."

Johnny panicked. "Give you my cell phone? Why should I do that?"

Anya leaned even closer. "You will be very soon unconscious, and hospital will take away phone if you do not give it to me."

He subconsciously squirmed in the seat to confirm the feeling of the Russian phone tucked into his back pocket. "I'll hold onto it. I don't think I'm going to pass out."

Anya said, "Okay, is up to you. We will be at hospital in two minutes."

Anya made perfect use of those two minutes to stare, unblinking, at a man who'd once been her partner but lost himself when his ambition outweighed his competence.

For Johnny, those minutes were the longest of his life.

Gwynn pulled beneath the portico outside the emergency room and slid from the seat. She opened Johnny's door to see the man slouching against the seat belt.

Anya pointed toward the door. "Go find wheelchair and person to help us."

A man in scrubs met Gwynn at the automatic door. He was pushing a wheelchair and had a stethoscope hanging around his neck. "What do we have?"

Gwynn spun on her heel. "Male, approximately thirty-three years old, victim of an eastern diamondback bite about twenty minutes ago."

The man pushing the wheelchair said, "Nice. Are you a cop or something?"

Gwynn returned the man's gaze. "Or something . . ."

It took all three of them to get Johnny into the wheelchair as his condition worsened by the minute. In a daze, he squeezed his bitten arm against his body and moaned while saliva dripped from his lip as he tried to hold his head up.

Anya grabbed the handles of the chair. "I will push. You will show us where to go."

The man in scrubs made no effort to argue, and he jogged toward the automatic door. "Bring him this way."

Gwynn and Anya followed the man through another pair of doors, down a corridor littered with medical equipment, and behind a curtain into an exam room.

"Let's get him on the bed," the man said.

Seconds later, he and Anya had Johnny on his back on the hospital bed.

"You're pretty good at this," he said. "Are you a cop, too?"

Gwynn waggled a finger. "I never said I was a cop."

Anya said, "I am not police officer. I am merely woman who has sent many men to hospitals."

He tried to show no reaction but failed. Without a response, he started an IV and placed an oxygen canula beneath Johnny's nose.

With his initial work done, the man said, "You two can wait outside in the waiting room. The coffee isn't bad, and nobody's throwing up out there right now."

Gwynn asked, "Are you okay with leaving him back here?"

Anya stepped beside the bed and untied Johnny's shoes. "I will be okay with leaving him here after I have his shoes."

Gwynn sighed. "You always think of the best solutions."

The Russian grinned. "Is what I do. I am problem solver."

Handing the shoes to Gwynn, Anya slipped a hand beneath the patient and retrieved his cell phone and wallet. She pocketed the phone and waved the wallet. "We will give insurance information to person in front, yes?"

The man in scrubs said, "Yeah. Let them know he's in curtain six. And what's his name?"

Anya said, "His name is Johnathon McIntyre, but everyone calls him Micky."

The man scribbled the name onto a clipboard at the foot of Johnny's bed.

As they passed through the double pneumatic doors, back into the reception and waiting area, Anya held up Johnny's phone for Gwynn to see.

Gwynn frowned. "What is that?"

"Is Cyrillic Russian."

Gwynn groaned. "Why would Johnny Mac have a phone with Cyrillic on it? He can't read it, can he?"

Anya shrugged. "I do not think so, but it does not matter. It does not say anything important. Is only home screen. I will need a little time to read everything else, but I suspect this is probably phone given to Johnny by people who are coming to kill us."

"That's not encouraging," Gwynn said. "Will he be all right?"

Anya glanced back through the doors. "I hope so. He is worthless to us if he dies, but if he lives, he is Christmas and birthday presents rolled into one with big red bow on top."

"What do you mean?"

Anya led Gwynn away from prying ears. "If we can make him think we believe he is here to look after us, we can use him to lure killers into our trap."

"I didn't realize we had a trap."

Anya chuckled. "We do not *have* trap. We *are* trap."

Gwynn plucked Johnny's wallet from Anya's hand. "You get started on the phone, and I'll get our personal bodyguard checked in."

When Gwynn returned from the nurse's station, she sat beside Anya. "Did you find anything on the phone?"

"Nothing interesting. Is obviously burner. It has only calls and no messages. There is only one number in call history."

Gwynn let the information sink in. "So, Johnny's the mole, huh?"

Anya said, "He cannot be mole. He is no longer employee of DOJ, so he does not have direct access to internal information. He is link between people who are trying to kill us and another source we do not know."

"This is getting a little cryptic," Gwynn said.

Anya sighed. "Yes, I am thinking with mouth."

Gwynn giggled. "I think you mean you're thinking out loud."

"Yes, this is what I said. I am confused about one thing still."

"Do tell."

Anya stared at the ceiling for a moment. "Is curious that Johnny Mac would come here. If he has source inside Justice Department, that source would have told him we were going to Bonaire."

Gwynn gasped. "So, how did Johnny know we'd be here instead of on the island?"

"I do not know answer to this question yet, but it means whoever Johnny is getting information from has good information to give."

Gwynn waved Johnny's wallet. "He's got a wad of cash in here, and the bills are pristine, like they just came off the press."

Anya slipped several bills from the wallet and slid them between her fingers. "If counterfeit, is very good. I need a marker that will only write on—"

Gwynn held up a marker she lifted from the check-in nurse. "Way ahead of you."

Anya took the marker. "You will make very good spy one day." She drew a brown line across three of the bills. "These are not counterfeit. Where would Johnny get brand-new money?"

Gwynn said, "Maybe it was prepayment from the Russian Mafia for delivering us."

"No, this is not Russian thing to do. Giving to him money before he delivers us is not something Bratva would do."

"What other answer is there?"

Before Anya could answer, the cell phone vibrated, flashed, and rang. She jumped, surprised by the multiple notifications of an incoming call, and looked down at the phone. "This will be fun."

Gwynn stood wide-eyed. "What are you going to do?"

Anya pressed the button and held the phone to her ear. "Privet, comrade. Is Anastasia Burinkova. And what is your name?"

13

Razgovor
(A Conversation)

In Russian, the man's deep baritone remained steady and calm. "This is quite an unexpected turn of fate."

Even though the man couldn't see her, Anya smiled into the phone. "Is no turn of fate at all. Is precisely what I planned. Perhaps I have even saved you a very large sum of money."

"And what makes you say that, Little Sparrow?"

"You expected Johnathon McIntyre to deliver me into your hands, and for this, I am sure he was promised very handsome fee."

"Is he still alive?" the man asked.

"Probably not. Last time I saw him, he was drooling from mouth and bellowing in pain. He was foolish to believe he could follow me and hide without me finding him. And you are even more foolish for choosing him to do this ugly work for you."

He said, "You know there is a magnificent price on your head, comrade Burinkova."

"My head is far more expensive than you can afford."

He chuckled. "You have no idea what I can afford."

"Perhaps this is true," Anya said. "But no matter your fortune, it will be no good to you when I am standing in pool of your blood, watching your little life drain from your miserable eyes."

"Such big talk from one little girl. If you are so confident, then why are you hiding from me?"

"I am not hiding from you. I am lying in wait for you. I promise, though, I will not kill you quickly. I want both of us to be able to enjoy our time together."

"You do not frighten me, Little Sparrow. I am a powerful man with many powerful friends. This can only end one way, and that is with you dead and me spitting on your corpse."

"You are old man. I can hear this in your voice. You will send many men, but they will fail, and in the end, you will feel my blade. I can promise you this."

Anya's satellite phone vibrated in her pocket, and she withdrew it to glance at the screen. Chase Fulton's name appeared in block letters. "You will have to forgive me, but I have more important telephone call. You can hang up or simply wait. Either is fine with me."

She pulled the Russian phone from her ear, pressed the mute button, and answered her second call in English. "Yes, my Chasechka. What is it?"

"Guess who showed up in Bonaire."

"I do not know, but I have also news. Johnny McIntyre was special agent with me inside Department of Justice, but he made terrible decisions and ruined his career. He showed up here, spying on Gwynn and me."

Chase chortled. "I guess that didn't end well for him."

"He is in hospital and maybe will die."

Chase gasped. "What did you do to him?"

Anya said, "I saved his life, but maybe temporarily."

"Let's get back to that in a minute. I need to brief you on what happened here."

"Wait one moment," she said. "I want to have discussion with you and Gwynn inside car."

She muted the call and pressed the Russian phone back to her ear. In her native tongue, she asked, "Are you still here?"

The line was dead, so she hooked her partner's elbow and headed for the Land Cruiser. "I have on sat-phone, Chasechka, and I want you to hear." They climbed into the vehicle, and Anya pressed the speaker button. "Okay, we are inside car now. Tell to us what happened."

Chase said, "Hello, Gwynn. It's always nice to talk with you."

"Hey, Chase. So, what happened?"

He began the narrative. "It started with a couple of guys poking around. They didn't look like they fit in, so I put a couple of bird dogs on their trail, and we watched them overnight and throughout the morning. It turned out that our hunch was correct. Neither spoke Dutch or English very well, but they seemed pretty fluent in Russian."

Anya asked, "What did you do with them?"

"You know me. I'm a peaceful man, so I invited them to have a conversation with us. They apparently aren't the conversational type, so they turned our nice, quiet talk into a brawl."

"Are they still alive?"

"One of them is okay, but the other one is in quite a bit of pain. I've got some phone numbers for you, and Skipper is already tracing them. Let me know when you're ready to copy."

Anya pressed the button on the Russian phone to bring up the previous call. "Before you give to me numbers, let me give one to you."

She read off the number, and Chase said, "I don't think it's a coincidence that these phones and Johnny's are making and taking calls from the same number."

"Is no coincidence at all," Anya said. "I do not yet know who person is, but now I have heard his voice, so I will know who to gut like pig when time comes."

"I'm not envious of that guy," Chase said. "Speaking of guys, what would you like for me to do with these two lowlifes?"

She said, "There is Russian embassy in Havana."

Chase said, "Ooh, I like the way you think. Do you want me to see if either of these guys is interested in giving us a name or two?"

"Is waste of time, but you may try if you want. Perhaps you will get lucky."

He said, "I get the impression these guys aren't much more than peeping Toms. They clearly aren't well-trained fighters, and they're not much better at spying."

Anya froze. "Wait a minute. They were not good fighters?"

"No, not at all."

She said, "They are not alone. This is typical of Bratva. There will be at least two more men with them, and they will be the dangerous ones. If they know operation is a bust, they will flee."

"We can't have any fleeing," Chase said. "We'll get to work on finding their pals, and I'll call when we have something else to report."

"Be careful, my Chasechka. I do not want you to be hurt because of me."

Gwynn wondered if Anya's sentiment extended back to the moment she and Chase crossed paths for the first time, but she would never ask.

Anya pocketed the phone, and Gwynn said, "These guys are serious. They hit Bonaire fast."

"Yes, they did. That means there is mole inside DOJ who is probably reporting to Johnny, and he is passing information to Bratva."

Gwynn said, "I guess that means they'll send a hit team here now that they know where we are."

Anya nodded. "Yes, I answered Johnny's phone, and they know where he is. This means they know where I am, but maybe not you. I think maybe they are not aware that you are with me. This gives us wonderful advantage."

"I'll take every advantage we can get," Gwynn said. "But what are we going to do about Johnny?"

Anya let her gaze fall. "You probably think I want to do something terrible to him, but this is not how I feel. I am sad. I have been betrayed by many people in my life, but this one is maybe worst."

Gwynn sighed. "I get it. I think I feel the same way, but I can't really put it into words. I know he probably needed money, but there's no way he didn't know the Russians were going to try to kill you."

Anya laid a hand on Gwynn's. "Not just me, but also you. He did this to both of us."

She nodded slowly. "I know. So, what do we do with him?"

Anya drummed her fingertips on the steering wheel. "We will use him and give him opportunity to help us. If he refuses . . ." She froze, then turned back to face the emergency room entrance. "They already gave to him money."

Gwynn squinted against the sun filtering through the windshield. "What?"

"Money. They already gave him part of money they promised. I must talk to him."

She slid from the Land Cruiser, and Gwynn did the same, falling in locked step beside her partner. "What makes you think he's going to tell you about the money?"

"He will tell me because he is now more afraid of me than the other Russians."

"Interesting theory," Gwynn said. "We'll see how it plays out."

Anya gave her a wink. "As I said to you before, I love being underestimated."

The gatekeeper behind the check-in counter yelled, "Hey! You can't go back there. Stop!"

Anya ignored the woman as she shouldered her way through the double doors while Gwynn flashed her badge. Neither woman knew if the badge worked, but there was no question that Anya's shoulder did the trick.

They found Johnny in the same exam room, and Anya nestled onto the edge of the bed beside him. "How is arm?"

"It feels like it's on fire."

"Did they give to you medication for pain?"

Johnny nodded. "They did, but it doesn't seem to be working."

Anya leaned toward him and examined the two precise puncture wounds into which the snake poured its venom. "Look at me, Johnny Mac."

He swallowed hard and let his eyes meet hers. "Yes?"

She leaned even closer until her face was only inches from his. "No one has ever done for me what you did today."

He cocked his head in confusion. "What?"

"You came so far to protect me like knight in shining armor. Why would you do this?"

He lay motionless without offering any explanation, but the concern quickly vanished from his eyes.

Anya whispered, "This is wonderful thing for you to do, and I am flattered."

Although the pain meds hadn't met the overwhelming task of stopping the agony in Johnny's arm, it had taken a firm grip on the part of his brain that enjoyed having a beautiful, grateful woman only inches away. He stammered. "I just . . . didn't want anything to happen to you."

Anya gasped and pressed her lips to his. The kiss that followed left Johnny's brain producing chemicals more powerful than the doctors could inject into his IV.

When she pulled away, he lay there, basking in disbelief and an after-glow. "Why did you . . .?"

Anya stroked his face with the back of her hand. "Chivalry is not dead after all. Thank you, Johnny Mac. But I have only one question. How did you know where to find me?"

14

Kuklovod
(Puppet Master)

The snakebite victim closed his eyes and appeared to be instantly asleep. Whether it was the narcotics skating through his body or an Oscar-worthy performance on Johnny's part, Anya didn't care. Knowing she got the question in was enough to declare the small campaign a success, and it was one more rung toward the top of the Bratva's ladder.

Gwynn took Anya's arm and led her from the room. "Nice work back there. When I grow up, I definitely want to be you."

Anya cocked her head. "Is okay for you to also kiss him if this is why you want to be me."

Gwynn rolled her eyes. "No, thanks, but that was brilliant. Do you think he's faking being asleep?"

"I do not think this. I know it. I was watching his breathing rate, and it never changed. Breathing always changes at point of falling asleep. They did not teach you this at academy?"

"I'm sure they did," Gwynn admitted, "but I may have been daydreaming about catching bad guys during that class."

"Is okay. I sometimes dream in daytime, too."

"Really?" Gwynn asked. "Please tell me you dream about something other than being with Chase."

The Russian shrugged. "Yes, this is sometimes true. I pretend I am famous gymnast with many medals, or sometimes prima ballerina at Bolshoi."

Gwynn grimaced. "I didn't mean to conjure any bad memories."

"No, is perfectly fine. I could have been either of those things, but if that had been my path, I would have never met you. Not meeting you would have been one of greatest losses for me."

Gwynn stopped in her tracks. "Anya, that's amazing. Thank you."

"Is not necessary to thank me. Is only truth. Now, we must make plan to deal with Johnny Mac."

Gwynn sighed. "I hope you've got some ideas because I have no idea what our next move should be."

"Of course I have ideas. In Russian, word is *kuklovod*. It means—"

Gwynn cut her off. "Puppeteer, I know."

"Is close, but is better translation to *puppet master*. And that is exactly what we are. We will make our little marionette dance for us, and he will give to us everything we need to know."

"How do you know he has all that information?"

Anya said, "We need to know who is person, or maybe people, commanding this operation. We need to know who is inside DOJ making leaks of our information."

Gwynn raised an eyebrow. "I'm still surprised you think Johnny knows either of those little nuggets of knowledge."

"I had telephone conversation with man from only number on Johnny's phone. His voice was definitely voice of person in charge. If that person is making personal calls to Johnny, that tells me Johnny is working directly for this person without middleman."

"All right. That's a reasonable assumption, but how about the leak at Justice? How could Johnny know that one? He's been out of the loop for over a year."

Anya said, "Trust me. He knows. Here is story of what I believe to be truth. I believe somebody inside DOJ told Johnny about our plans to be in Bonaire, and he passed this intel to man on phone."

"That's possible."

"Is not only possible, is likely. Remember, someone sent men to Bonaire, and Chase captured two of them. No one sent other people here yet. So far, only Johnny has come. I believe he somehow found out we were coming here, and he came to check it out before reporting to Bratva."

"That's quite a theory," Gwynn said. "I guess it makes just as much sense as anything else, but now that you answered Johnny's phone, they know exactly where we are."

"You are very smart, friend Gwynn. I cannot decide if we should stay and fight or go somewhere else."

Gwynn clicked her tongue against her teeth. "We can't keep running just to see if we're being chased. I say we stay right here and let them try to hit us."

"I agree. Now we have plan. We must hope Johnny does not die . . . yet."

"You don't really think he's going to die, do you?"

Anya shrugged. "Was very big snake. Sometimes treatment doesn't work."

"As much as I want to kill him for what he did to us, I don't want him to die from the snakebite."

"Living or dead, he is not going anywhere soon, so we have time to find his other phone."

They drove back to Anya's property and pulled into the overgrown drive to the barn.

Anya parked the Land Cruiser beside Johnny's car. She stared down at her phone's screen and pointed into the field. "According to video, it should be four or five meters that way."

They stamped down the grass and weeds as they made their way down the imaginary line Johnny's demolished phone took to its resting place in the vegetation.

Gwynn bent and stood back up with a wad of black plastic that could've once been a cell phone. "This thing's had a tough life."

Anya lifted the phone from Gwynn's hand. "And according to information Skipper provided, it is only two days old."

They returned to the basement lair beneath the brick rancher and made a video call to Skipper at the Bonaventure op center.

Skipper looked back at them from the monitor. "Hey, guys. I guess you heard about the excitement in Bonaire."

Anya said, "Yes, I spoke with Chase, and he told me they captured two Russians snooping around."

"That's old news," Skipper said. "They found the two other Russians you warned him about."

Anya smiled. "This is very good. I hope no one was injured during the fight."

"There hasn't been a fight yet. The boys are planning to roll up the two other Russians tonight. Stuff like that is easier after the sun goes down."

Anya groaned. "Make certain they know these two men are extremely dangerous and will not give up easily."

Skipper laughed. "Come on, Anya. When was the last time you saw Chase Fulton underestimate an opponent?"

"I remember once when he did this."

Skipper crossed her arms. "Oh? Do tell. Just *who* do you think Chase underestimated?"

Anya widened her smile. "Me."

Skipper rolled her eyes. "Okay, I'll give you that one, but you can rest easy. The team is taking every precaution."

"You will tell me when operation is finished, yes?"

Skipper scribbled something on a pad. "Yeah, if you want, I'll patch you into the comms when the boys are getting ready to hit the Russians."

"Yes! Please do this. I can maybe offer advice on Russian countertactics."

Skipper said, "Thanks, Subject Matter Expert, but I'm pretty sure our guys can handle two low-level hitters from Eastern Europe."

Anya held up Johnny's broken phone for the camera to see. "Yes, I'm sure. Now, this is why we are calling. We need to know everything this phone knew before it was broken. You can do this, yes?"

"I can try," Skipper said. "Let's start with the SD card. You have a card reader, don't you?"

Anya worked the tiny card from its slot in the phone. "Got it. Yes, I have reader."

Skipper leaned toward the camera as if studying the card in Anya's fingers. "Stick it in the reader and tell me the IP address of the computer with the card reader."

Anya did as she asked, and Skipper pulled her glasses from the top of her head and slid them onto her face. "I'm in. The card is undamaged. I can get most of the information you want from the card, but I'd like to get my hands on that phone."

"I can ship phone to you and maybe have it to you overnight."

"No, that's not necessary. Just plug a charging cable into the computer and the port on the phone."

Anya waved the phone at the camera again. "It is badly broken."

Skipper huffed. "Would you plug it in, please? Just because it looks broken to you doesn't mean I can't work a little magic."

Again, Anya did as she was told.

Skipper's hands flew over the keyboard and mouse until that old familiar look came over her face. "Yep. These fingers have still got it. In less than fifteen minutes, I'll email you a full report of GPS locations, emails, calls, and texts made to and from that phone."

"You are amazing," Anya said. "Thank you."

Skipper winked. "You don't have to thank me. You're part of the family."

Anya bit her lip as the compliment washed over her. "Please tell boys to be safe."

"Tell 'em yourself. You'll be on the comms."

Just as she promised, Skipper delivered the twenty-five-page report with details of everything the phone sent or received and everywhere it had been.

"This is amazing," Gwynn said.

Anya peeked across Gwynn's shoulder at the report. "Skipper does amazing things."

"I can see that. We need a Skipper of our own."

Anya chuckled. "We have one. You are holding proof of this."

Gwynn continued reading the document until she'd flipped through seven pages. "Wait a minute. This isn't data from just the broken phone. It's information from his previous phone that had the same number. This is a gold mine."

They had a pizza delivered, and they studied every line of the report while downing the pie.

Gwynn wiped her mouth. "This is great pizza. Nice choice. Check this out."

Anya leaned in. "What is it?"

"It's the location of Johnny's previous phone."

Anya looked closer. "Chicago. Interesting. From there, it looks like he went back to DC and quickly came here."

Gwynn said, "You're right, but I think we need to find out whose phone numbers these are."

Anya rolled her chair in front of the monitor and keyboard and made some entries into the computer. After a strange sound Gwynn had never heard her make, Anya said, "There is something wrong with numbers. I don't think they are real."

"What do you mean?"

Anya pointed toward the screen. "This software should pinpoint any phone almost anywhere on Earth, but it can't find these phone numbers."

"Sounds like another job for Skipper," Gwynn said.

Anya lifted the phone to make the call at the same instant it rang. "Yes, hello."

Skipper said, "Hey, I've got some news."

"I was just about to call you."

Skipper continued. "I figured you were. It's about the phantom phone numbers, isn't it?"

"Is that what you call them?"

"It's my word for them," Skipper said. "But the actual term is ghost number. I've been running them through every piece of software I can think of, but I keep coming up empty."

"Do you have theory?" Anya asked.

Skipper said, "It's not much of a theory, but I suspect it's some type of spoofing software that routes calls and text messages through a couple hundred different cities before connecting to the actual number. It could take hours to get a good answer."

Gwynn asked, "What if we just called one of them and see who answers?"

"That's not a bad idea, actually," Skipper said. "But I'd like to do it a little more high-tech. I'll write a bot to call all the numbers simultaneously and track all the connections. It'll take me a couple of hours to write and debug the code, and the op in Bonaire will cut into that time."

Anya asked, "How long until the party begins in Bonaire?"

"That's the other reason I was calling. It's been dark for an hour, so the countdown has begun. We're T-minus-fifteen. Are you ready for the comms patch?"

"Yes, we are ready. I will play it on speakers here."

Skipper said, "I know you know how all of this works, but it would be best if you and Gwynn just listen. I can probably send bodycam footage along with the audio, but it might lag a little. Do you want to see the video feed?"

"Yes," Anya said. "That will be very helpful. Perhaps I will know one or perhaps both of these men."

Skipper said, "Oh, yeah, I forgot to mention. There aren't two men. There's only one."

Anya frowned. "This does not make sense. They would never send only one."

"This time, they did," Skipper said. "Because the other one is a woman."

Anya gasped. "A woman? This is terrible. They must not approach her until I have seen her on camera. This is crucial. You must make them understand."

"Calm down," Skipper said. "I'll tell them, but I can't let you be a distraction during the op. I'll silence your comms if I have to."

"We understand. We will be silent unless it is absolutely necessary for me to point out something dangerous."

Gwynn's cell phone rang, so she glanced at the screen. "It's a local Athens number."

Anya said, "Answer it. Perhaps it is free pizza."

Gwynn shook her head. "Hello?"

"Ms. Davis?"

"Yes, I'm Gwynn Davis."

"Ms. Davis, this is Janice Bell from the medical center. You're listed as the point of contact for Mr. Johnathon McIntyre. Is Mr. McIntyre with you, ma'am?"

Gwynn shuttered. "What? No, he's not with me. As far as I know, he's still receiving treatment for a snakebite in your emergency room."

"That's why I'm calling, Ms. Davis. It appears that Mr. McIntyre has gone missing from the hospital."

15

ODINNADTSAT' ALLIGATOROV
(ELEVEN ALLIGATORS)

Gwynn reverted to her persona as a federal law enforcement officer. "When was the last time you saw Mr. McIntyre?"

Janice Bell said, "I'm not certain, but it's crucial that we find him. He hasn't received his first round of antivenin, and his blood work came back with evidence of a massive dose of venom. Do you have any idea where we might find him?"

"I'm sorry, I don't know where he is, but I do have a couple of questions. First, are there security cameras in and around the emergency room?"

The nurse said, "We don't have cameras inside the treatment and triage rooms, but there are cameras on the exterior of the building. They mostly show the parking lot and people smoking."

"May I have a look at the footage for the window of time in which Mr. McIntyre went missing?"

"I've already reviewed the footage, and he didn't leave through the main entrance or the parking lot."

"I understand," Gwynn said, "but I'd still like to take a look if you wouldn't mind."

"I'm sorry, but we can't release that footage to anyone except law enforcement."

Gwynn smiled for the first time in the conversation. "Then, we're in luck. I'll be there in twenty minutes."

She hung up without waiting for Janice's response, and Anya said, "This does not sound like good thing."

Gwynn ended the call and said, "Johnny's missing from the hospital, and we have to go down and take a look at the security footage."

It was Anya's turn to smile. "Plan is working perfectly."

"What plan?"

"I left telephone tucked beneath Johnny's hip on hospital bed while I was making him forget his name."

Gwynn laughed. "You have that effect on men, but I still don't understand the plan."

"You have also this effect on men, but you have not been trained how to exploit it completely. Women are most powerful force on Earth. We can make men do almost anything we want simply by feeding their caveman ego."

"I don't know about that, but men don't always do their thinking with their brain. Let's get back to this plan of yours that you failed to brief me on."

Anya shrugged. "I did not know if plan would work. This is why I did not tell to you until now. Johnny did not escape from hospital. He was taken."

"Keep talking."

Anya said, "He was in too much pain and on drugs of narcotics. He cannot drive, and he probably cannot walk very well."

"Why can't he walk?" Gwynn asked.

Anya reached into her pocket and pulled out her evidence. "I have his shoestrings. If person runs without shoestrings, shoes will come off and person will have bare feet."

"You're something else."

Anya said, "I think this is compliment from you, yes?"

"Yes, it's a compliment. Now, let's go take a look at that security footage."

Janice Bell wasn't hard to find. She was standing next to the intake nurse behind the reception counter.

Gwynn pulled her credentials from her pocket and held them up. "I'm Special Agent Davis, and this is my partner, Special Agent Fulton. We spoke on the phone a few minutes ago about reviewing the security footage during the time Mr. McIntyre disappeared."

"You're a cop?" Janice asked. "Why didn't you say that earlier? And should we consider Mr. McIntyre to be dangerous? Is he a criminal of some kind?"

Anya jumped into the conversation. "It should not matter to you if he is dangerous. He is no longer here, so you are in no danger."

"You're not American, are you?"

Anya pulled the tiny plastic American flag she always carried in her pocket and spun it between her fingertips. "I am now. Where can we see security camera film?"

"Follow me," the nurse said. "I'll take you back to the security office."

An overweight rent-a-cop behind a cluttered desk licked chocolate from his fingertips over an empty Krispy Kreme box. "Oh, hey. I wasn't expecting visitors."

Gwynn produced her cred pack again. "We're here to see the security footage for the past two hours."

"And what is it you're looking for?" the guard asked.

"We'll know it when we see it," Gwynn said. "We're looking for a patient *you* lost."

The guard stared with disappointment into the empty box in front of him. "All right. Come with me, and I'll set you up in the office next door. You need to know that I'm not responsible for patients who get up and walk out AMA."

Anya frowned. "AMA? What is this?"

"Against medical advice," the man said. "I'm here in case there's a disturbance or somebody gets violent in the ER—not to babysit patients."

"We're not blaming you," Gwynn said. "Of course you can't be responsible for people who change their minds. We're more interested in seeing who came *into* the ER in the last two hours."

The guard motioned toward a workstation. "Suit yourself. There's the monitor. The software is pretty self-explanatory, but if you need any help, let me know."

Gwynn slid onto the chair and took the mouse in her hand. "He was right. This is the simplest video software program I've ever seen."

Anya pulled up a chair beside her, and Gwynn played the video at three times its actual speed. They studied the screen carefully and paused every time anyone approached the doors to the ER who didn't appear sick or injured.

Twenty minutes into their search, Anya jabbed a finger at the monitor. "There! Stop video."

Gwynn froze the frame and zoomed in on a pair of clean-shaven men in dark tracksuits and sunglasses.

Anya stood. "I will be back in two minutes. Do not move from that spot on video."

She vanished and returned well within her predicted time frame with the reception nurse in tow.

Gwynn rolled from in front of the monitor and pointed toward the two men frozen on the screen. "Do you remember these two men from about an hour ago?"

The woman leaned close. "Oh, yeah. I remember them. I asked if I could help them, and they ignored me."

"Where did they go?" Gwynn asked.

"I don't know. The last time I saw them, they were headed down the hall toward radiology."

"And you didn't see them after that?"

"No, I told you that was the last time I saw them, and I say good riddance, as far as I'm concerned. Those two were up to no good. I'd bet my paycheck on it."

"I think you'd win that bet," Gwynn said. "Since you haven't seen them again, that would mean one of two things. They're either still inside the hospital or they left through another exit. Would you agree?"

"Yes. This is the first time I've left the desk since I got to work. If they had come back through the ER, I definitely would've noticed."

Gwynn said, "I have a bizarre question. Do you happen to have a floor plan of the first floor?"

"Sure. They're everywhere."

Gwynn said, "I'm not following."

"We're required to post them all over the hospital. There's one right outside this door."

They followed the woman through the door and into the hallway, where she pointed at an emergency evacuation plan complete with the "You Are Here" arrow.

Gwynn snapped a picture of the placard with her phone. "We'll need to check every exit on this floor. Would you mind if we did that on our own, or do we need an escort?"

The woman pointed back toward the reception area. "Do you see that waiting room full of people? Do you really think we have enough personnel to provide you with an escort? Go where you want. Just tell Porky Pig next door what you're doing. You never know when he's going to burst into action and actually do something resembling his job description around here."

That got a good chuckle from both women, and Gwynn said. "We'll be sure to keep him posted on our whereabouts."

"Here's a friendly little tip for you. If you bring donuts next time, he'll give you free run of the place."

"We'll keep that in mind," Gwynn said. "Thanks."

They began their search in the treatment room that had been Johnny's, but it was occupied by a teenager who appeared to be missing three fingers. The boy stared up at them and then down at his hand. "Lawnmower."

Anya slipped off the shoe and sock and held up her four-toed foot for him to see. "Makarov pistol, underwater, fired by American spy. My story wins."

The boy's eyes grew enormous. "Are you serious?"

As she slid her sock and shoe back on, she said, "I am always serious."

"Did you kill him?" the boy asked.

"No, I fell in love with him, but I do not recommend that you shoot women in their feet, hoping for same result. Take care of hand. American girls dig scars."

The closest door was an emergency exit. Anya pressed her hand against the bar, but Gwynn stopped her. "It says an alarm will sound if you open the door."

Anya said, "Yes, I saw sign, but I think sign is not correct and no alarm will sound." She pressed the bar, and the door swung open to a cluttered alleyway behind the hospital.

"Why didn't the alarm go off?" Gwynn asked.

Anya hooked her finger around a small wire leading from the bar of the door. "Someone cut wire. Is tradecraft. Disabling alarms—and sometimes bombs—is important skill for people like us."

They walked through the open door and examined the alley.

Gwynn said, "This is a pretty good egress route, and I don't see any cameras."

As she walked away, Anya said, "I see something much better than camera."

Gwynn followed her partner to the end of the alley that opened up to a four-lane road.

Anya stepped onto the sidewalk of the busy street and took a knee beside a man with a shaggy beard and a cardboard sign lying on his lap. "Hello, sir. My name is Anya, and I have question."

He growled. "Does this look like an information booth to you?"

She pulled two twenties from her pocket and slipped them into the man's hand. "How long have you been here?"

The man slid the bills together, seemingly savoring the feel of the cash in his palm. "'Bout a month, I guess."

Anya said, "Have you been sitting here on this corner all day?"

He shoved the money into a pocket. "No. I had a meeting earlier with the mayor about urban beautification, and then I had to spend some time with the Pope. Do I look like I've been anywhere besides right here? I told you I've been here a month. That includes all day today. Thanks for the cash, lady, but what do you really want?"

"I want to know if you saw two men in black tracksuits with a third man dressed in either a hospital gown or jeans and a brown T-shirt."

"What's it worth to you?"

"I have two more of those twenties."

The man held out a palm. "Hand them over, and I'll tell you."

Anya didn't move. "You will answer question first, and I will give to you money after."

The man wiped a dirty hand across his tangled beard and mustache. "The third guy . . . he didn't have no shoelaces."

Anya smiled, and two more twenties made their way into the man's hidden pocket. "How long ago?"

He held up a hand against the sun. "Oh, maybe forty-five minutes ago. The bus runs every fifteen minutes, and I seem to remember three of them after your guys left."

That won the man another twenty, and Anya asked, "Did you see them get into a car?"

"No, weren't no car. It was a black SUV, like a Chevy Suburban or something."

"And which way did they go?"

He held out his hand again, and Anya papered his palm. Without counting the bills, he shoved them away as if they were priceless treasures. To him, they probably were.

He stuck a crooked finger through the air. "They left that way, but they turned around and went back the other way after pulling away from the curb."

Anya stood. "Thank you, sir. I hope your life gets better soon."

He looked up at her through squinted eyes. "Five boys can't kill eleven alligators."

Anya stared back. "What?"

"Five boys can't kill eleven alligators."

"What does that mean?"

He stuck out his hand again. "I'll tell you, but it ain't free. Nothing's free in this world."

Anya laid the remaining cash onto his waiting hand, and he said, "That was the license plate. Five, B, C, K, eleven, A. Five boys can't kill eleven alligators."

16

BARMENY I NISHCHIYE
(BARTENDERS AND BEGGARS)

As they rounded the front of the hospital, back toward the parking lot, Gwynn said, "You should really teach a class at the police academy."

"What do you mean?"

Gwynn motioned behind them. "What you just did back there . . . nobody teaches that stuff."

Anya said, "I was taught this from KGB and SVR. American bartenders and beggars see everything."

"Yep, you should definitely teach a class."

Anya stopped and turned to her friend. "I have been teaching this class for more than two years, and you are my best student."

"I'm your only student."

Anya shrugged. "So, this means you are also my best student."

Inside the Land Cruiser, Anya dialed Skipper's number in the op center. "I have for you license plate number. You can run it for me, yes?"

Skipper said, "There's nothing like getting straight to business, is there? Send me the number."

Anya said, "Five, Bravo, Charlie, Kilo, one, one, Alpha."

Skipper stroked the keys. "This is interesting. It comes back as a Chevrolet Suburban registered to a labor union based in Chicago. Does that make any sense?"

Anya said, "Yes, this makes perfect sense. Can you find this vehicle?"

Skipper chuckled. "You don't ask for much, do you?"

"I will do for you something wonderful someday."

"You already do," Skipper said. "You keep my boys alive when they get a little overzealous in the field."

"They are also my boys. I love all of them as if they were my own brothers . . . except for Chase. Thinking of him as brother is weird."

Skipper said, "Yeah, that's enough about that. Let's get back to your Suburban. If it has OnStar, and their subscription is up-to-date, I can find it. Give me a minute."

She worked the keyboard and mouse like a concert pianist before saying, "Well, that was a dead end. Their OnStar subscription ran out eleven months ago, but I'm not finished looking."

Anya and Gwynn waited patiently until Skipper said, "Got 'em! They have Dog Star."

"What is Dog Star?" Anya asked.

Skipper said, "It's a subscription satellite radio service. It's cheaper than XM and some of the others, but there aren't as many channels. I can track them as long as they've got a clear view of the sky."

"Where are they now?"

Skipper studied the screen. "Their last satellite ping was just outside a house about a mile from yours."

Gwynn said, "But you don't see them now?"

Skipper groaned. "They probably went inside a garage or carport where the satellites can't see the vehicle."

"Give to me address," Anya said.

Skipper read off the address and said, "Systems like this aren't designed to be pinpoint accurate. They could be anywhere within a one-hundred-foot radius of that address, so I don't recommend storming in there with guns blazing."

Anya threw a hand over her heart. "This hurts my feelings. I am always subtle."

"Yeah, right," Skipper said. "Subtle is exactly how I'd describe you. Be careful, please."

Gwynn said, "I won't let her get out of control yet, I promise."

"Thanks for that," Skipper said. "Let me know if I can do anything to help."

Anya said, "You have done already everything we could want. Thank you. We will call when we have Johnny back in our hands."

"What do you mean, back in your hands?" Skipper asked.

Anya brought the analyst up-to-date on their situation and then asked, "Have the boys captured the two remaining operatives in Bonaire?"

"They're working on it," Skipper said, "but I'll call as soon as they get them rolled up."

Anya ended the call. "Let's go find Johnny Boy."

Gwynn giggled. "Is Johnny Boy your pet name for him now that you made out with him in the hospital?"

"We did not do this thing you call 'making out.' I only kissed him. He was too shocked to make also kiss in return." She lowered her gaze and continued. "I have for him name, but is not pleasant name. He is traitor, but he is still useful to us. This is basics of plan. We will use him to get who and what we want, then I will call name to his face before—"

Gwynn held up a hand. "Don't say it. I don't even want to think about it. Johnny was always a bureaucrat, but I never thought he'd turn into a snake."

Anya slowly shook her head. "He is worse than snake. He is *khudshiy predatel'*, but I do not know English word for this name."

"I've got a few English words for him," Gwynn said. "I've never been betrayed like this. It's going to be impossible for me to play along with your game of pretending that he was here to protect us."

"You must do this. It is only way we will be able to use him to find his masters."

"I don't know," Gwynn said. "My acting skills aren't as good as yours."

"Is okay. Just remember we are doing what is necessary to achieve our goal of beheading Bratva. Johnny is our roadmap to that head. We don't have to like the road, but he is what we have until something better comes along."

"We don't actually have him at the moment," Gwynn said.

"Yes, but we will have him again if he does not die from snakebite."

"Is he really in danger of dying if he doesn't get the antivenin?"

Anya said, "Yes. It was very large snake with much venom."

Gwynn let out a long breath. "In that case, I guess we should go find him before he makes an appearance at the Pearly Gates."

They found the address Skipper provided, and Anya eyed the house carefully as they made their first pass. "This is very good. There are no other houses within five or six hundred meters, so the Suburban must be inside garage."

"We could wait until dark and do a little snooping," Gwynn said.

"I am afraid Johnny will not live until dark. We must go now. You have gun, yes?"

Gwynn patted her concealed holster. "I never leave home without it."

"Good. Hopefully, we will not have to kill anyone here. That would be difficult to explain."

Gwynn chuckled. "Killing someone anywhere is tough to explain."

Anya smiled. "Not always."

Gwynn rolled her eyes. "Not everyone is a trained Russian assassin."

"This is true, but I suspect there will be at least two people inside house who are also Russian and trained. They will not be as trained as me, but they will put up very good fight."

"Thanks for the warning," Gwynn said. "Let's make it happen."

Anya cranked the wheel and spun the heavy Land Cruiser through a one-hundred-eighty-degree turn. She left the edge of the road just as the tree line gave way to the open yard of the target house. "Hold on. It will be bumpy."

Gwynn held the handle above the door with one hand and the dash with the other as the SUV bounded across the yard. "Are you going to ram the house?"

"No, but I am going to lock door."

Gwynn continued holding on as they roared toward the home. Anya hit the brakes hard and slid the SUV to a stop with the right front fender barely touching the front door. The rear bumper came to rest inches from the garage, making an exit impossible.

Almost before the SUV stopped, Anya threw open the door. "Let's go!"

Gwynn sprang from her seat and launched herself across the center console, following her partner from the vehicle since exiting through her side wouldn't be possible.

They sprinted in locked step around the house until the back door came into sight, and Anya extended a hand to have Gwynn back off. As soon as there was adequate space between them, the Russian launched herself through the air and landed a boot just beneath the doorknob. The flimsy residential door lock exploded from the jamb, sending splintered wood in every direction.

Gwynn watched her idea of a surprise attack shatter with the remains of the door.

The interior layout of the house was nearly identical to Anya's, so getting lost wasn't a concern. No one offered a gunfight when the two women landed inside the kitchen through what had been the house's back door, so they continued through the house, searching each room as they moved.

Anya continued the dynamic approach to clearing the house, and her bull-in-a-china-shop technique paid off on the second door she kicked open. One of the men they'd seen in the security camera footage from the hospital raised a pistol and fired two rounds in rapid succession.

An instant before he pulled the trigger, Anya dived to the floor and kicked Gwynn back into the hallway. The two 9mm Makarov rounds pierced the sheetrock and tore through the walls where the two women had been standing a fraction of a second earlier.

Three pistol shots roared from the hallway behind Anya, but she was too focused on the gunman in front of her to deal with anything behind her. She grabbed the base of a floor lamp and hurled it toward the shooter. While he was dodging the incoming missile, Anya sprang to her feet and seized the man's gun hand. With a powerful turn of her hips, she lifted the shooter from his feet and threw him onto his back at the foot of the bed. The sickening sound of several of the bones in his hand and wrist crumbling filled the air an instant before he bellowed in agony.

In one fluid motion, Anya stripped the pistol from the man's demolished hand and landed a perfectly executed strike to his temple. She sent a boot heel to the man's face, ensuring he wouldn't rejoin the fight anytime soon.

With the unconscious man's pistol in her hand, Anya stepped back toward the door, where she found Gwynn kneeling in the hallway with her Glock still trained on the corpse of the second man from the hospital video. He was slumped at the end of the hall with blood pouring from his chest and nose.

"I thought we agreed to kill no one," Anya said.

Gwynn didn't take her eyes off the body of the dead man at the end of the hall. "I guess I didn't have all the facts when I made that agreement. Consider our terms to be renegotiated. He had me dead to rights, but I pulled the trigger before he could."

Anya stepped around her partner and laid two fingers against the man's neck. "You may relax. He will not try to kill you—or anyone else—ever again."

Gwynn lowered her pistol. "Did you kill your guy?"

"No. I did not renegotiate agreement. He is only unconscious with maybe some broken bones in hand and face. We must now find Johnny."

They searched both bodies and retrieved a pair of cell phones and almost three grand in cash, but neither man had any identification on him. They bound the unconscious man's hands and ankles with shoelaces just in case he returned to the land of the living sooner than expected.

After clearing the remainder of the house, they found Johnny, still in his hospital gown and lifeless in the back bedroom.

Gwynn gasped. "Please tell me he's not dead. I want to be the one to kill him when this is over."

Anya pointed toward his chest. "He is breathing, but barely. Help me get him to car. We must return him to hospital right now."

Gwynn huffed. "I say we wake him up and make him walk to the hospital."

"This is not possible. You must cooperate with me. We cannot let him die."

"Fine, but I'm taking his feet. You get the other end."

They carried Johnny to the Land Cruiser and laid him on the back seat with the seat belts woven around his body.

Gwynn said, "What are we going to do with the guys inside?"

"This is problem for Bratva, not for us, but we must move the man who is still alive."

"Move him? Where?"

"I want him to wake up with his head lying on his dead partner's lap," Anya said. "This will give maximum psychological effect."

Gwynn closed her eyes for a moment, imagining what it would be like to wake up lying on the corpse of your former partner.

They moved the man who gave no signs of regaining consciousness anytime soon.

Anya wiped her prints from the Makarov pistol and placed it back in the hand of its owner. "I think maybe he will be confused when he wakes up. Maybe he will even think he shot his friend."

Gwynn studied the macabre display at her feet. "Nobody who knows me would ever believe that I, of all people, would be involved in a situation like this. I was a nerdy schoolgirl 'til I met you. Now look what I've become."

Anya took a knee beside her friend. "I am sorry to have done this to you. Your life would be better without me."

"Don't say that. You didn't do this to me. This is what I signed up for. I never wanted to be the kind of fed who spent her whole career on boring white-collar crimes. Thanks to you, I get to kill Russian Mafia thugs and clean up the world, one scumbag at a time."

"This is one way to look at it," Anya said, "but I am still sometimes sorry for showing you the ugliest side of humanity."

"It comes with the job, partner. I see and do things like this so three hundred million innocent Americans don't have to."

Anya stood and offered a hand. "We must take Johnny back to hospital. If you touched anything, we must wipe off fingerprints before we leave."

"All I touched was my gun and this guy's clothes, so we're good to go."

"Did you load pistol?" Anya asked.

"Do you mean *re*load after shooting?"

"No, did you load bullets you fired into this guy?"

Gwynn palmed her forehead. "I'm such an idiot sometimes. Of course my fingerprints are on the shell casings." She lifted the three empty casings from the floor of the hallway and pocketed them before heading for the Land Cruiser.

Anya parked beneath the portico outside the entrance to the emergency room, and Gwynn walked inside with her badge and credentials in hand. She approached the reception desk and asked, "Is Janice Bell available?"

The lady behind the desk said, "No, ma'am. I'm sorry, but she's gone home for the day. Is there something I can help you with?"

Gwynn said, "I'm confident someone briefed you on the missing patient from earlier today."

"Yes, it's in the log. Has he been found?"

"You could say that. He's outside in my vehicle, but we need a wheel-chair or a gurney to bring him in."

Seconds later, two orderlies in scrubs appeared, pushing an empty hospital bed. They loaded Johnny onto the bed, then rolled him through the waiting area, past the double doors, and into the real emergency room.

Once they were situated in a curtained exam room, Gwynn handcuffed Johnny's left wrist to the bed. "Is your security officer here twenty-four seven?"

One of the orderlies said, "Yes, they're always here, but don't expect to be impressed."

"We already met one of them this morning."

The orderly extended his arms as if mimicking the security officer's belly. "Big guy? Smells like donuts?"

"That's the one," Gwynn said. "Is he still on shift?"

"Yes. They work twelve-hour shifts. He'll get relieved at six and come back at six tomorrow morning with a big box of pastries that he'll never share."

Gwynn found her way to the security officer and stuck her head inside the office. "Hey there. We found your missing patient."

The officer laughed. "He wasn't my missing patient. I told you I'm not responsible for runaways."

She tossed a business card onto the man's desk. "That's my cell number at the bottom. I cuffed your patient to his bed in exam room four. Call me before anyone takes off the cuffs. Otherwise, if he escapes again, it *will* be your problem."

He lifted her card and examined it closely. "Your cell number, huh? Maybe you'd like to get some dinner. I know this great place downtown that—"

"Sorry. If I had time for dinner, I'd have time to babysit the patient. Call me if he does anything strange. We'll talk about dinner later if things cool down on the case I'm working."

The grin on his face looked as if he'd just been awarded a lifetime supply of all the donuts he could eat. "I'll look in on your guy. Is he dangerous?"

"He's a delirious rattlesnake victim. He's no threat, but don't let him run again. Oh, one more thing. I recommend that somebody put a catheter in him. You don't want to have to escort him to the bathroom every time the need arises."

"I'll see that it's taken care of"—he examined her card again—"Special Agent Davis."

She gave him a wink. "You can call me Gwynn."

17

Shkola Ubiyts
(Assassin School)

Anya Burinkova slid behind the wheel of the Land Cruiser and turned to Gwynn in the passenger's seat. "Do you really believe Donut Boy will keep Johnny inside hospital this time?"

Gwynn giggled. "Donut Boy? I like it. I think he wants to be my Donutechka, but that's not happening."

"Is okay to make him believe is possible, though. I told you before, women are most powerful force on Earth."

"Yes, you did," Gwynn said. "I'm learning. Now, the answer to your question is no. I don't think the 'tier-one security force' in this place will keep anybody anywhere, but I also don't think Johnny will run on his own, and we did eliminate the guys who rolled him up. Until they send more guys, Johnny will remain cuffed to that bed."

"Is very good theory. When are they giving him antivenin?"

Gwynn said, "I didn't ask, but I don't care as long as they keep him alive so I can kill him later."

Anya stared back at Gwynn. "You are terrifying woman. When you find person to be your husband, I will tell him to be very afraid of you."

"Oh, listen to you, Mrs. Gut You Like Pig. You're the dangerous one."

Anya smiled. "Perhaps. Maybe we are both frightening, and this is why we have no husbands yet."

"Let's change the subject. We need to go back to the house where the two Russians are."

"Why?"

Gwynn sighed. "I thought of something I should've considered before we left. My pistol is government-issue, meaning they have a ballistic record of barrel. We have to harvest those three bullets I put inside Boris, or Dmitri, or whatever his name was."

Anya pulled the vehicle into drive. "I should have thought of this also. You will make very good assassin one day."

"No, thank you," Gwynn said. "I'll stick to my lawyer-with-a-gun gig."

"Sometimes, is same thing."

* * *

Anya pulled the Land Cruiser onto a leaf-covered dirt road behind the house and stopped. "We must walk now. We cannot risk having our car identified by anyone who might drive by. At some point, police will come and have questions."

"I get it," Gwynn said as she slid from the seat.

Anya opened the rear hatch and shouldered the medical bag from inside. They crossed the thousand feet between the tree line and the house in minutes and stepped through the demolished rear door.

When Gwynn stepped into the hallway, she gasped and covered her mouth. "Oh, my God. Somebody shot the other guy."

Anya stepped around her and studied the gruesome scene spread out at the end of the hall. "It was not someone else. He shot himself. Look where gun is lying."

Gwynn took a mental picture of the horrific tableau and mentally pieced it together in slow motion. "You're right, but why would he kill himself?"

"Is very simple. Killing himself was much better than what Bratva would do to him for failing."

Without another word, Gwynn opened the med bag, retrieved gloves, booties, and a pair of long forceps. "I am *not* looking forward to this."

Anya said, "I will do it if you cannot."

Gwynn shook her head. "No, I made the mess, so I'll clean it up." She worked tirelessly for several minutes, pressing the forceps through destroyed tissue until she retrieved two of the three bullets she fired. Finally, she stood and pulled off her mask. "I am so glad I didn't go to medical school."

Anya said, "When you fired third bullet, was he leaning forward or backward?"

Gwynn stared at the ceiling for a moment. "It all happened pretty quickly, but I think the two I put in his chest forced him back against the wall, and he may have been leaning forward a little bit for my third shot."

"Pull his head forward and look for exit wound."

Gwynn sighed. "Why didn't I think of that?"

Anya said, "Because you are not assassin . . . yet."

Gwynn slid a gloved hand behind the man's head and pulled him forward. "Oh, yeah. That's definitely an exit wound. I could've probed all day and never found the bullet."

Anya pointed to the wall behind the corpse. "There is small hole in Sheetrock."

Gwynn eased the man back in place and stood. "Yep, there it is."

A few seconds later, she held up the projectile in the jaws of the forceps. "Look what I found."

Anya motioned toward the other dead body. "We must now replace your bullets with his."

"What?"

Anya said, "Someone will do autopsy, and if there are no bullets inside dead body, many questions will be asked. I do not like questions like these."

"I get it, but how are we going to . . . I mean, are we going to shoot him again with that guy's gun?"

"Not exactly," Anya said. "Come with me, and I will teach you trick of assassin."

She followed Anya into the garage. "What are we looking for?"

"We need tall trash can."

Gwynn said, "There's a bucket. Will that work?"

Anya pulled on a pair of gloves and lifted the five-gallon plastic bucket. "We need now large book, like maybe phone book."

Gwynn pulled a handful of *National Geographic* magazines from a shelf. "How about these?"

Anya held out the bucket. "Put five of them in bottom."

Gwynn dropped the magazines into the bucket. "When are you going to tell me what we're doing?"

"Trust me. Is more exciting if you do not know."

Their next step was the bathroom, where Anya placed the bucket beneath the bathtub faucet and turned on the water. Soon, the bucket was full, and she slid it to the center of the tub. "Now, we need gun."

Gwynn retrieved the dead Russian's Makarov and handed it to her partner.

Anya pulled a towel from the linen closet and wrapped it around her arm before gripping the pistol. She held the muzzle over the bucket and fired a shot into the water, then she tilted the bucket slightly and searched for any evidence of a leak. Finding none, she pulled the trigger twice more, sending two more bullets into the water-filled container.

When the ringing echoes of gunfire finally ended, she tossed the towel from her arm and poured the contents of the bucket into the tub. The soggy magazines hit the porcelain with a thud, and the water swirled around the drain. One by one, she lifted each magazine until she found an entry wound but no exit. Thumbing through the pages, she let the first bullet fall from its entrapment, then she picked up the bullet and dropped it into Gwynn's gloved hand. "There is one. Two more to go."

Gwynn shook her head. "You're amazing. You know that, right?"

"Yes, of course, but is always nice to hear."

She recovered the two remaining bullets and piled the magazines back into the bucket. "Is now time to give implant surgery. It would be best if you do it because you know where each bullet was inside body."

Reversing the procedure she used to extract each of her bullets from the dead man, Gwynn carefully placed each nine-millimeter Makarov round exactly where the bullets from her Glock came to rest, including the third round in the Sheetrock wall.

When she was finished, she pulled off her gloves and pocketed the forceps. "If my tally is correct, I can name about twenty felonies I've committed today. This isn't the most shining day of my career."

"Do not worry. In twenty minutes, there will be nothing left to connect us to any of this. You will take bucket and magazines into car, and I will meet you there. We will get rid of them far away."

"Wait," Gwynn said. "What are you going to do?"

As if it were an everyday occurrence, Anya said, "I am going to build bomb. Now, go."

Gwynn carried the med bag and bucket back across the open expanse and into the tree line.

A minute later, Anya halted her sprint beside the driver's side door. "You are ready to go, yes?"

Gwynn pulled on her seat belt. "Absolutely."

As they pulled back onto the paved road, the house where they'd been only minutes before exploded in a massive ball of orange flames and a plume of black smoke.

Gwynn jerked to see the explosion. "Should I expect bombmaking to be part of my assassin training?"

Anya didn't glance at the fire. "Making bomb inside house with natural gas is simple. It takes only steel wool or Brillo pad with alcohol inside dish in microwave oven. All that must be done after is turn on gas, set microwave, and wait."

"And you learned all of this from your training back in Russia?"

"Not all, but most. Learning should never stop. There is always new technology and better tradecraft to learn."

Gwynn said, "I don't think we have assassin training programs in this country."

Anya laughed. "Oh, you beautiful naïve girl. America has best killing schools in all of world." She paused and thought for a moment. "No, maybe this is not true. Maybe Israel has best, but America is very close second."

Gwynn glanced one last time at the burning house. "If you knew you were going to burn the house down, why did we go to the trouble of harvesting and replacing my bullets?"

"Sometimes fire department is very efficient. Maybe they will put out fire before it reaches bodies."

Gwynn sighed. "I guess it's true that the devil is in the details."

Anya rolled to a stop at an intersection. "Devil is inside everything. Working to keep him out of details is how people like me—or us—stay alive to work one more day."

Gwynn glanced back, but only the plume of smoke was still visible as they pulled through the intersection. "I guess that makes you the assassin philosopher."

"No, I am small, sharp tool used by people in power to do what they cannot bear to do themselves."

"Maybe that describes most of us."

Anya turned to face her. "Perhaps it describes all of us."

They rode in silence for half an hour until Anya pulled into a small parking lot behind a nondescript, one-story building.

"What's this place?" Gwynn asked.

"Is place where we put things to never be found again. Bring bucket and follow me."

Anya pressed a series of keys on the cipher lock by the back door, and the bolt slid open. She led Gwynn into a short corridor and through a second door to a descending staircase.

"From outside, you'd never know this place has a basement."

"It has actually two basements. My father owned this building before he died."

"So, is it yours now?" Gwynn asked.

"No. Father left it to Chase, but I have combination to door."

They pushed their way through a heavy steel door and into an industrial space with several pieces of old machinery.

Gwynn asked, "Do you know what all this stuff does?"

Anya reached for the bucket. "I know only some, but this is my favorite."

Gwynn turned to see Anya sliding open a metal door about the size of an automobile window. Slowly, the sounds of machinery grew until the interior of the contraption in front of them came to life. Wheels with teeth turned against each other and interlaced like gears. Anya tossed the bucket and its contents into the machine, and the teeth tore at the plastic and paper like a ravenous dog.

In seconds, everything Anya had thrown into the trash eater was gone, and she turned to Gwynn. "What about pistol?"

"What about it?"

"Do you want to keep it?"

Gwynn subconsciously reached for the weapon. "Of course I want to keep it. Besides, it's still government property. I have to turn it back in when I retire or they issue me another."

Anya bowed her head for a moment. "We should have talk."

"About what?"

"About what happens after this mission."

A weary look came over Gwynn's face. "Okay, what about it?"

Anya motioned toward a pair of metal chairs, and they took a seat. "First, you already know that we may not survive this mission. We are dealing with very dangerous people with more money than anyone you know. They will continue to send people to kill us until we kill all of them, or they kill us."

Gwynn said, "I knew all of this when I came on board."

"Yes, but what you did not consider is what will happen when this is finished, if we are alive. I do not think you will again become lawyer with badge and gun."

"Why not?"

Anya sighed. "Is difficult to explain, but during this mission I will teach to you many things—things police officers cannot do. Once you learn these things, and when you have been forced to do things you could never imagine, it will be very difficult for you to live inside world of rules and regulations."

"But what else am I supposed to do?"

Anya pointed at the machine that had just eaten everything they threw in. "You said you were making count of felonies today. We just destroyed evidence of manipulating a murder scene, and you shoved bullets inside a dead man's body."

Gwynn's expression fell. "Oh, Anya. I didn't . . ."

"Yes, I know. You did not think of this, and it is my fault for bringing you into this terrible world."

Gwynn said, "You didn't bring me. I came willingly."

"You came willingly into something you did not understand."

Gwynn reached for Anya's hand. "I told you that we started this together, and we're going to finish it together. Whatever that means, and whatever that costs, I'm willing to pay the price." She stood, drew her pistol, and tossed it into the mouth of the machine. "Come on. Let's finish this damn thing."

After shutting down the machine and collecting a bag of fine powder from the belly of the grinder, Anya tied the bag and headed for the stairs. Once outside, she tossed the bag into a dumpster on the adjoining property and climbed back into the Land Cruiser.

Just before pulling out of the parking lot, a chirp sounded, and both women reached for their phones.

Gwynn said, "It's not mine."

Anya pressed the button to hear her voicemail, and a man's stern voice filled the interior of the vehicle. "Anya, it's Chase. Call me as soon as you get this message. We have a serious problem."

18

Drugaya Anya
(Another Anya)

Anya crushed the brake pedal, bringing the Land Cruiser to a screeching halt. "This does not sound good."

Gwynn tugged her seat belt to release the tension after the violent stop. "Don't just sit here in the street. Pull over and call him."

Anya hit the accelerator almost as aggressively as she'd stomped the brake and then roared into an empty parking lot behind a vacant building.

Before they'd rolled to a stop, Chase Fulton's phone was ringing almost two thousand miles away in the Leeward Antilles. "Anya, listen. We've got a serious problem."

"We have also problem in Athens. I will tell to you after I hear yours."

"It's not just mine," Chase said. "I'm afraid it's about to be yours. As I told you before, we found the two Russian hitters. We tried to roll them up, and—"

Anya belted out, "What do you mean, you tried?"

"That's what I'm telling you. We tried. We nabbed the guy, but the woman escaped."

"You are still searching for her, yes?"

"No, we're dealing with part two of the problem. By all indications, she already left the island."

"How did she leave? On airplane or boat?"

Chase growled. "If you'll stop interrupting me, I'll tell you everything I know."

Anya silently waited for him to continue.

He said, "At this point, we believe she left by airplane, but we're not a hundred percent certain. The one thing we do know is that she—or someone—crippled our jet on the tarmac."

Anya opened her mouth to ask another question, but Gwynn held up a finger, and Chase continued. "Somebody hit the nose gear with a vehicle, so we're dead in the water until we can get the mechanic and the parts from the States."

He paused, giving Anya a chance to jump in, but she resisted the urge.

He said, "Cotton, our mechanic, is working on getting the parts together, but it'll be at least three days before the plane is airworthy again. Okay, it's your turn."

Anya didn't hesitate. "You have interrogated the man, yes?"

"Kodiak and Mongo are working on him now, but so far, it appears he's more afraid of whoever he's working for than he is of us. We're not getting much out of him."

"This is also part of problem here. We killed one of killery here, and the other one killed himself."

Chase let out a low whistle. "I thought you said they would send low-level hitters first."

Anya said, "They did. Next ones will be very serious."

"I'm starting to believe the woman who got away down here was pretty serious."

"Send to me her picture," Anya said.

"We don't have any clear shots of her. We've got her on video for about nine seconds, so that's the best I can do. Skipper's analyzing the video and working on finding any planes that departed Bonaire in the last hour."

Anya said, "I would like to see video. Perhaps I know this person."

"She's fresh," Chase said. "She reminds me a lot of you when we first . . . met."

Despite the weight of the conversation, Anya laughed quietly. "We did not *meet*, my Chasechka. I *caught* you. That is not same thing as meeting."

"Let's count toes and see who wins."

Anya gasped. "Chasechka, I cannot believe you would say this to me. Just because you shot off my toe does not mean you caught me."

"Believe what you want," he said. "But let's get back to business. We still have the two original guys we grabbed down here, as well as the hitter. With the plane out of commission, what do you want us to do with them?"

Anya said, "I have airplane. I will come get you."

"Your plane won't carry all of us. I can arrange something if you need us off the island in a hurry."

"This is not necessary," Anya said. "Where are parts for your airplane?"

"Savannah, Georgia."

"And where is mechanic?"

Chase said, "St. Augustine."

"Give to him my number. I will pick him up and take him to Savannah. He can inventory parts, and we will be on Bonaire by tomorrow afternoon with everything you need."

"I'm not sure you need to take a break to come rescue me while the whole Russian Mafia is chasing you down."

"I am not concerned about them right now. They will never suspect I will return to Bonaire, so is maybe safest place on Earth for me."

"Whatever you say. I sent the video clip, and I'll text you Cotton's number. I'll tell him what's going on and have him call you."

Anya said, "Gwynn and I will see you tomorrow afternoon."

After Anya hung up, Gwynn said, "This is getting serious a lot faster than I expected."

"Yes, it is, but we will win."

"I like the confidence," Gwynn said, "but I'm not so sure that Chase's team is—"

Anya cut her off. "Do not blame them. I told them to expect not-so-good team of hitters. I did not prepare them for truth, so is my fault, not theirs."

"You don't have to defend them. I know they're hardcore, but letting the woman escape is a pretty big screwup in my book."

Anya looked away. "Yes, is definitely big screwup. This can mean only one thing."

"What's that?"

The Russian turned back to her partner. "This woman is not *fresh* like Chase said. If she can escape from them, she is experienced, well trained, and extremely dangerous."

Gwynn bit her lip. "Are you saying she's another Anya?"

"I am saying she might be better than me."

Gwynn scoffed. "Nobody's better than you."

"I will tell to you again. You are beautiful, naïve girl. There are many who are better than me. I have only one advantage. I am more experienced than most. This does not mean I am more dangerous. It only means I have seen more terrible things and made many more mistakes."

Gwynn said, "After what we did in that house, I think I can check off one more terrible thing I've seen."

Anya focused on her partner. "Do not let yourself believe you have seen worst. Before this is over, we will both see and do many things that are more terrible than pulling bullets from bodies."

Gwynn swallowed hard. "I'm not sure I'm ready for that."

"Only psychopath is ready for that," Anya said. "There is no way to prepare for what is coming."

The phone chirped before Gwynn could respond.

"Hello, is Anya Burinkova."

"Hey, Anya. It's Cotton Jackson. I'm Chase's A and P mechanic. He told me to give you a call."

"Yes, Cotton. I remember you. We have met."

"Oh, trust me. I remember. You're tough to forget."

"Thank you. I will take you to Savannah from St. Augustine to collect parts for Chase's airplane, and then we will fly to Bonaire. You are ready now, yes?"

"Yes, ma'am, I'm ready, but I'm not in St. Augustine. I'm already at the Gulfstream shop in Savannah. I've got all the parts palletized and ready to go. What kind of plane do you have?"

"Is only small Citation jet. There is no way to put pallet inside. You will have to break it down to individual parts. We will be there in one hour. You can have parts ready to load in this time, yes?"

"Yeah, I can get that done. When you get here, taxi to the Gulfstream ramp, and I'll have a lineman tell you where to park so we can load up."

Anya said, "Okay. You have passport, yes?"

Cotton chuckled. "Yeah, I've got a passport and a toothbrush. I've also got about a thousand pounds of tools and parts. Are you sure you can haul everything?"

"Yes, I am sure. We will see you in one hour. Goodbye."

She hung up, and Gwynn said, "It sounds like we're going to Savannah, but we drove here from the mountains. Where's your plane?"

Anya smiled. "It is here at airport in Athens. It is inside hangar that used to be my father's."

"You're just full of surprises, aren't you?"

Anya shrugged. "You should not be surprised that I am well prepared."

* * *

The approach into Savannah/Hilton Head International was a blind carnival ride. A line of thunderstorms barreling its way from the northwest had the airport covered in low clouds and whipping wind.

Gwynn gripped her seat. "I don't know about this. I've never flown in weather this bad. Are you sure we can get in?"

Anya's tone dripped with confidence. "Do not worry. Airplane is very capable, and I am good pilot. We will make one try. If we cannot get in, we will turn for alternate airport in Florida and wait for storm to pass."

"I wasn't questioning your ability. It's just weird to be in the cockpit and not be able to see anything outside."

"Is okay. I have very good instrumentation, so I do not need to see outside."

"Whatever you say. I'm starting to think the Russian Mafia has some control over the weather."

Anya continued the approach with her attention on the instrument panel. "This would not surprise me. They are very powerful."

The air traffic controller said, "Citation Five-Two-Five Alpha Bravo, you are five miles from MIZLU. Turn left heading zero two zero and maintain two thousand until established on the localizer. Cleared ILS zero one approach."

Anya replied with only a hint of an accent. "Left zero two zero. Two thousand until established. Cleared ILS one, five Alpha Bravo.

The controller said, "Five Alpha Bravo contact Savannah Tower on one two five point niner seven. Good day, ma'am."

"Tower next on twenty-five ninety-seven. Good day."

Anya set the tower frequency and said, "Savannah Tower, Citation Five-Two-Five Alpha Bravo outside MIZLU on ILS one."

The tower controller answered promptly. "Citation Five Alpha Bravo, Savannah Tower. Wind three four zero at one four gusting to two eight. Cleared to land runway zero one."

Anya said, "Copy wind. Clear to land. Citation Five Alpha Bravo."

Gwynn's brain reeled, wondering if she would ever understand the language of air traffic controllers.

The turbulence continued shaking the small jet violently as they descended on the approach.

Anya said, "Look for airport, and tell to me when you see it."

"I don't see anything," Gwynn said.

"You will. Look first for ground and then for airport. It will be okay. Put gear down, please."

Gwynn reached for the landing gear lever and lowered it just as Anya had taught her during their last flight. She said, "Gear down. Three green."

Anya held the yoke with her left hand and the throttles with her right. "Thank you. It will maybe get even bumpier on our way down. Make sure seat belt is tight."

That did little to comfort Gwynn, but she tugged on the seat belt until she could barely move. A few seconds later, she almost screamed, "I can see the ground."

Anya never flinched. "Very good. Now look for airport ahead, and tell to me when you see it."

The seemingly unimportant task gave Gwynn's brain something to do instead of panic. A minute later, she said, "I see runway lights."

At the same instant, a mechanical voice said, "Minimum . . . minimum."

Anya looked up from the panel to see the same runway lights Gwynn saw a few seconds earlier. One final scan across the panel told her the airplane was doing everything perfectly. She glanced at the three green landing gear lights and then at the enunciator panel. "Three green, no red, clear to land."

Gwynn said, "I don't know what that means, but I like the sound of 'clear to land.'"

Anya didn't acknowledge her comment as she let the main gear kiss the runway as gently as possible. She turned left and called the ground controller, who gave her taxi instructions to the Gulfstream ramp. "See? I told you everything would be okay."

Gwynn let out a long sigh of relief. "Every day, I want more and more to be like you when I grow up."

Anya giggled and pointed across the ramp. "Look at rain coming. We made it just in time."

A lineman directed them to a spot just outside a massive hangar with "Gulfstream" painted across the front, and Anya shut down the engines and electronics.

Gwynn said, "We may have made it to the ground before the rain got here, but we're going to get soaked when we get out of the plane."

"I will make with you bet that we will not get wet at all when we walk off plane."

Gwynn cocked her head. "How's that possible?"

Before Anya could convince Gwynn to take the bet, a lineman connected a tug to the front landing gear, and in seconds, he pulled the jet and its occupants inside the waiting hangar.

* * *

It took Cotton and three other men less than twenty minutes to load everything into Anya's Citation, and twenty minutes after that, the storm had passed.

The tug pushed the plane out of the hangar and back onto the ramp.

The lineman asked, "Do you need fuel, ma'am?"

Anya said, "No, we are too close to maximum gross weight."

As they climbed aboard, Gwynn said, "I think I'd rather sit in the back this time. Cotton can sit up front in the scary seat."

After a fuel stop in The Bahamas, they continued and landed in Bonaire under a perfect blue sky. A tall man, wearing a colorful knitted cap over long dreadlocks, strolled across the ramp toward the Citation.

When she stepped from the plane, Gwynn said, "Who is that guy?"

Anya squinted against the sun and then sprinted toward the man. She threw her arms around him and yanked the ridiculous hat from his head.

Gwynn stepped beside them, and Anya said, "You remember my Chasechka, yes?"

She extended a hand. "Of course I remember. Hello, Chase."

He pushed her hand away and wrapped her in a hug that wasn't exactly like the one he gave Anya. "It's good to see you again, Gwynn. Thanks for coming to our rescue."

Gwynn waved him off. "No problem, mon."

19

DVE SEKUNDY
(TWO SECONDS)

"Welcome to our temporary home," Chase said as he opened the front door for Anya and Gwynn.

"You did very well," Anya said. "There are maybe three or four houses on all of Bonaire with this much privacy. You are very smart, my Chasechka."

He said, "I can't take the credit. This is all Skipper's doing. She'd make a heck of a travel agent if the intel analyst gig ever fell apart."

"You have Russians here, yes?"

He motioned toward the rear of the house. "The two Peeping Toms are in the room on the left, and the hitter is in the shed out back."

"You are keeping him inside shed?"

"No, that's just where we're interrogating him. I didn't want to get blood on the floor."

"This is good thinking," Anya said, "but I have better idea. Bring him inside, and put him in next room beside other two."

Chase grimaced. "Ouch. I know what that means. I'll see if I can find some plastic to cover the floor."

Anya jerked. "Ooh, I have even better idea. Wait, please." She walked down the hall and pointed to the door on the left. "This is where first two are?"

Chase nodded, and Anya said, "This bathroom is very convenient. Bring man you call hitter into house and put him inside bathtub. This will make very easy cleaning up, and if he is experienced *ubiytsa*, putting him inside bathtub will be very frightening for him."

Chase chuckled. "You're one sick puppy, you know that?"

Anya tilted her head and smiled. "Aww. You know how much I love when you call me pet names."

Chase rolled his eyes. "There's a better bathroom and two pairs of coveralls all the way in the back. You'll probably want to put your hair up."

Anya eyed Gwynn. "You are coming, yes?"

"Oh, yeah," Gwynn said. "I wouldn't miss this for the world. If you plan to pull teeth, let me do it. That's my favorite."

Chase turned to Gwynn. "I can't believe she's turning you into a creative interrogator."

She laid a hand against his bicep. "She's not turning me into one. She's uncovering the one that's been inside me all along."

"That's even scarier. I'll go get your guy."

Gwynn and Anya emerged from the back room, both clad in coveralls and sporting ponytails. A few seconds later, Chase, Mongo, and Kodiak came through the back door, hauling a sweaty, disheveled man in his thirties, his hands bound behind his back. Mongo—all six feet eight inches and three hundred pounds of him—escorted the man into the bathroom and deposited him into the tub.

Anya asked, "Are other two men awake?"

Mongo said, "Hey, Anya. It's nice to see you. If they're not awake, I'll rattle their cage. I'm sure they don't want to miss the show."

"Is nice also to see you, Marvin."

The big man blushed. "You know, since my mother died, you're the only person left on Earth who calls me by my real name."

She patted his enormous chest. "This makes me special. Thank you for waking up other two."

The giant burst through the bedroom door like the freight train he was, and both men recoiled. Mongo growled, "Hello, boys. I just wanted to make sure you didn't need your pillows fluffed or perhaps a spa treatment." Neither man made a sound, and Mongo shrugged. "Guess not."

He stepped by the two women. "They're wide awake. Let me know if you need any help."

Anya said, "Thank you. Did you get anything from him yet?"

"Just his name."

"I do not care about his name. He will not live long enough for his name to matter."

She and Gwynn stepped into the bathroom and closed the door behind them.

Anya approached the man kneeling in the bathtub and leaned down to look into his eyes. Without a second of hesitation, the man lunged forward with a noble attempt at a headbutt, but Anya threw an abbreviated punch to his throat before his forehead could strike her nose. The man gagged and sputtered for several seconds before Anya grabbed the back of his head and slammed his face into the faucet. The man struggled against his restraints and twisted like a dawning tornado.

Anya said, "Tie his feet."

Gwynn pulled a length of cord from the pocket of her coveralls and bound his ankles.

After yanking him backward, Anya folded him in half, and the man let out an animal's cry.

In her native Russian, she hissed, "Oh, this one likes pain. I am going to enjoy this. Do you understand English?"

He fought to compose himself and spat in Anya's face.

Instead of reacting with physical violence, she licked her lips, smiled, and spoke in Russian. "You taste like fear and desperation."

The blood pouring from his nose curved around his lips and fell in droplets onto his shirt.

Anya drew one of the three knives she had tucked away inside the coveralls, and the man jerked backward. She tapped the point of the blade against his upper lip, allowing a drop of blood to glide down the steel. Holding the blade a foot in front of his eyes, she said, "You are making your shirt bloody, so I will help you take it off."

In blinding motions too fast to see in detail, she cut the man's shirt from his torso without leaving a scratch on his skin. A liquid stain formed on the front of the man's pants as he came to realize the peril he was in.

In trembling Russian, he asked, "What do you want?"

Anya smiled up at Gwynn. "I told you this would be easy. He is volunteering to give to us whatever we want, and I did not cut him yet."

Gwynn huffed. "I don't like the easy ones. They're no fun."

"What do you want, you crazy *suka*?"

Anya frowned. "This is terrible name to call me unless you were talking to my friend. If you were talking to her, this is very bad decision for you." She raised her knife above her shoulder, spun it in her palm, and landed the pommel against his cheekbone with enough force to split the skin and add to the already impressive blood flow from his nose.

She moved to within inches of his face. "You will not call either of us any more names. You understand this, yes?"

The man narrowed his gaze and snarled, and Anya raised her knife again.

"Okay, okay," he said. "What do you want?"

"I want you to look at me. I want you to memorize every detail of my face. You can do this, yes?"

He didn't answer, so she placed the tip of her blade between his legs and applied enough pressure to split the material.

He worked to pull his hips away, but she never softened the pressure. "You can memorize my face, yes?"

"*Da! Da!* Yes."

"Good. I am Anastasia Burinkova. I am woman you were sent to kill. They showed you pictures of me, yes?"

"No, you've got it all wrong. We weren't sent to kill you. We were supposed to bring you back with us."

She ignored him and said, "Your face is a mess. I will wash it for you."

He yelled in protest, but Anya had him on his back and staring up at the faucet before he could resist. She spun the hot water knob, and a flood of water poured over his face. He spewed and fought for air until Anya shoved a fist beneath his chin, forcing his head to remain still. Once the cold water turned warm, she smiled and replaced her fist with her blade. As the water turned from warm to scalding hot, the man kicked and jerked, desperately trying to escape. The commotion sounded like a wild bull fighting to escape from his stall.

After half a minute of unbearably hot water splashing the open wounds on his face, Anya spun the knob and stopped the flow. "You look much better now, but that cut will need probably stitches. You want me to give to you stitches, or do you want my friend to do it? She is not very good at it, but she likes to practice. Is up to you."

He fought to catch his breath and spit out the water. "Please. Just tell me what you want."

"I think we will play guessing game," Anya said. She laid the razor-sharp knife against the man's shoulder. "You will tell to me what you think I want to know. If you are correct, there will be no pain. If you are incorrect, I cannot make same promise. Is now your turn to talk, and you have two seconds to begin."

Anya pretended to look at her nonexistent watch and allowed two seconds to pass without the man saying a word. "Time is up." The tip of her blade found the upper part of his humerus bone, and the man roared in pain. She withdrew the blade and shoved a hand towel toward her victim. "Here. Hold pressure on wound. Oh, I forgot. Your hands are tied. Too bad. Wound is above heart, so maybe you will not bleed to death."

After dropping the towel, she placed the tip of her blade against his other shoulder. "Your two seconds begin again now." Again, her eyes fell on the imaginary watch, and she pressed the blade.

Before the steel pierced flesh again, he yelled out, "My name is Mikhail Viktorovich Tornovich."

Anya's mouth fell open, and she took a step backward in utter disbelief.

Gwynn planted a hand against Anya's back. "Are you okay?"

Before answering, Anya delivered a crushing elbow shot to Mikhail's temple, and the man fell limp inside the porcelain tub.

She opened the door and led her partner into the hallway. "Chase, where are you?"

"In the kitchen. Is everything all right?"

As if floating across the floor, Anya moved to the kitchen and sat on a stool at the end of the counter.

Chase said, "Are you all right? You don't look so good. What did he do?"

Anya sat in silence, so Gwynn said, "The guy in the bathtub said his name was Mikhail Viktorovich Tornovich, and as soon as he said it, Anya froze."

Chase bent down to peer beneath the cabinets and into the living room. "Mongo, what did the guy tell you his name is?"

Mongo turned down the volume on the television. "Tornovich. And I think he said his first name is Mikhail, but I can't be sure. I was busy trying to twist his hip out of place."

Chase laid down the apple he'd just pulled from the bag. "That sounds pleasant."

Anya stared up at Chase as if she'd just seen a ghost.

He turned to Gwynn. "I guess you don't know the history, huh?" She shook her head, and he said, "A communist named Colonel Viktor Tornovich was Anya's Russian handler. He trained and dispatched her on the mission to find me. Her orders were to either flip me to spy for Russia or kill me. I think that's the only mission she's ever failed to complete."

Gwynn squinted. "I don't get it. The guy in the bathtub isn't old enough to have done any of that. He's probably younger than us."

Anya took Gwynn's hand. "Not him. His father."

Gwynn covered her mouth. "Are you serious?"

Chase nodded along with Anya and said, "I killed the colonel in Virginia when he came looking for his missing lamb. If I remember correctly, I set him on fire and shot him in the head, in that order."

"Unbelievable," Gwynn said.

Anya shook her head. "No, is very believable. Is small community and makes perfect sense that Colonel Tornovich's son is working for Bratva."

Gwynn glanced between Chase and Anya. "So, what do we do now?"

Anya stood. "We pull everything he knows out of his head, piece by piece, and send him to meet his father in Hell."

"Do you have any pliers?" Gwynn asked.

Chase pulled a tool from his pocket. "I've got a Leatherman. Will that do?"

Gwynn slid it from his hand and opened the needle-nosed pliers. "Perfect."

Anya stood from her stool. "Mongo, we need you."

The giant rose to his feet. "At your service, ma'am."

"Will you please bring man from bathtub into room with the two others?"

"Anything for you. But do I have to be gentle?"

Anya almost smiled. "Please do *not* be gentle."

With one enormous hand, Mongo gripped Mikhail's ankle, dragged him from the tub and down the hall, and finally deposited him facedown in the bedroom. The other prisoners stared down at their countryman with shock and disbelief painted all over their faces.

Anya placed a knee on Mikhail's back. "Does everyone understand English?"

The younger of the two men said, "Me, not so good."

Anya said, "This is okay. Your comrade will explain to you if you do not understand." She grabbed Mikhail's left ear in a viselike grip and stretched it outward. "You will tell to me name of woman who was with you. Two seconds begins now." Wasting no time pretending to check her watch, the two seconds passed, and she sliced the man's ear from his head.

The two other men yelled, and one choked back the contents of his stomach.

"I will have her name, or you will have no ears. Two seconds."

Writhing in agony, Mikhail screamed, "*YA ne mogu.*"

Anya drove her full weight onto his back with her knee. "Yes, you can, or I will carve you into pieces and feed to sharks."

He sobbed and pleaded in Russian. "Please. Do not do this. You do not understand what you are asking me to do."

"I understand perfectly," Anya hissed. "Your father raped me more than one hundred times, and I was only one of the dozens of innocent girls he did this to."

"I am not my father. Please."

She continued. "Your father had only one life to give, and the man I love took it from him. One life is not enough payment for the things he did to me and other girls. You must now pay for sins of your father." Anya repositioned herself, keeping full pressure on Mikhail's spine beneath her knee, then slid her knife above his ear. "Give to me her name."

He hesitated, but one of the men tied to the bedpost yelled, "Her name is Gladiatorsha."

20

Gladiatorsha
(Lady Gladiator)

Still pressing the blade of her knife against Tornovich's head, Anya looked up at Gwynn. "Tell to Chase the name Gladiatorsha."

Gwynn sprinted from the room and found Chase still in the kitchen. "Anya got a name out of them. They said the woman's name is Gladiatorsha."

Chase yanked his phone from a pocket. "I'll get Skipper on it, but that's not a real name. It means 'female gladiator' in Russian."

Skipper answered almost before the phone rang in St. Marys. "Op center."

Chase said, "I need you to run the call sign Gladiatorsha. We think that's what they're calling the female Russian hitter."

"I'm on it. Give me sixty seconds."

Gwynn didn't wait. She wasn't going to miss anything Anya did inside that bedroom. When she stepped through the door, the already horrific scene had turned even more gruesome. Anya had Tornovich on his back with his hands and feet still bound and her blade poised just below his nose.

Anya spoke just above a whisper. "You will now tell to me who sent you."

Tornovich's eyes crossed as he struggled to focus on the fighting knife pressed to his upper lip. "They will kill me."

Anya smiled. "This is very good news. This means I will have both joy of depriving your boss of the privilege of killing you, and I will also have pleasure of draining your life from your body one incision at a time. Of course, I will keep you awake so you can also enjoy it."

"You're Russian. You know what they'll do to me. Please let me live."

Blood trickled from beneath his nose as Anya's blade pierced the skin. "I will be happy to let you live if you will tell to me name of men who sent you."

Tornovich hesitated, and the weapon sank deeper into his flesh. As he groaned in pain, Anya directed her attention to the two remaining Russians still sitting in silence on the edge of the bed. "I will give same offer to first person who gives me name of person who sent you."

The two Russians—who weren't bleeding yet—jerked their heads to stare at each other.

Finally, one of them said, "If we tell you, we will be dead very soon."

"Is okay," Anya said. "I have plenty of time to do terrible things to all of you. I am fair like this. I do not want any of you to have more attention from me than anyone else. Is only fair, yes?"

With every additional ounce of pressure Anya applied, Tornovich bucked as if convulsing from deep inside his soul. The two Russians on the bed turned away from the sight of Anya carving Tornovich's nose from his face, but Gwynn stepped in.

She slapped each of the men across their faces and ordered, "You will not look away. You will watch everything we do to him. With any luck, it'll remind you of the names we need."

Each of them grimaced, and one said, "Please, this is not necessary."

Gwynn chuckled. "Oh, we know it's not necessary, but it's fun for us. You get dispatched to find and kill us, and this is the result. Surely you can understand why we're enjoying ourselves."

The man swallowed hard. "I will tell you who sent us, but you must vow to take us somewhere we cannot be found."

Tornovich cut his eyes toward the man and growled in furious Russian. "You will be silent, or I will track you to the end of the world."

Anya giggled. "This is funny thing to say, Mikhail. You are in no position to make threats to anyone."

She turned her attention to the man offering to speak. "Do not worry about Mikhail. He is not a threat to you and will never again see sunshine. I have very special day planned for him."

The man on the bed glanced between Anya and Gwynn until his eyes fell on Tornovich. "We are afraid of him."

Anya leaned forward, applying the full weight of her upper body on her knife, and the steel disappeared to the hilt inside Mikhail Tornovich's skull. "Now, you have no reason to fear him. Give to me names."

Both men flushed pale, and the first said, "Please. You have to take us someplace safe."

Anya frowned. "I do not have to take you any place, safe or dangerous. You will now tell me names immediately."

The man said, "I have only two names. There are others, I am certain, but I only know of Ilya Gorshkov and Oleg Lepin."

Anya stood. "How do you know there are more?"

"I heard them talking, but I did not see them."

"How many did you hear?"

"I think maybe two more, but I cannot be certain."

She slid the knife back into its sheath. "Where can I find Gorshkov and Lepin?"

A look of panic overtook the man's face. "I do not know. I only talked with them on telephone, never face-to-face."

Anya scowled and turned to Gwynn. "This one is no use. He made up two names and told us nothing of value. Take him outside and shoot him."

Gwynn grabbed the man's arm, but he resisted, so she backed away and opened the door. "Mongo, would you please come give me a hand?"

An instant later, the big man filled the opening of the doorway. "Gladly."

She said, "The man on the right wants to stay here, but I need to take him outside and kill him. Can you help me with that?"

Suddenly, the man's resistance was meaningless, and Mongo dragged him from the room by a foot. Gwynn followed them through the door, and seconds later, two 9mm gunshots echoed through the house.

Anya nodded sharply. "Okay, is your turn. Tell to me where I can find Gorshkov and Lepin."

Tears fell from the remaining man's eyes, and his body quivered in terror. "I swear to you, I do not know, but I think maybe they are in Chicago."

"You think?" Anya asked.

"Yes, I am well-trained in . . . uh, *nablyudeniye*. I am sorry, but I do not know English word."

"Is okay. Word is *surveillance*. Who trained you?"

"SVR and FSB."

She shrugged. "Perhaps you were well trained in surveillance, but I think you should have paid more attention inside class when FSB taught resistance to interrogation. You are terrible at this."

Gwynn stepped back through the door. "All done. Did you make any headway with this guy?"

"He thinks they are maybe in city of Chicago."

"Chicago is a pretty big place. Can't he give us anything a little more precise?"

The man said, "I am sorry. I do not know anything more."

Anya motioned toward the door. "Take this one to join his friend."

The man recoiled and scampered backward. "No! You promised!"

Gwynn called out, "Mongo! We need you again."

The giant reappeared and plucked the one remaining Russian from the bed. The man fought hard, but Mongo made short work of rolling him up.

When Mongo left the room with the screaming man tucked beneath an arm, Anya said to Gwynn, "You did not really shoot him, did you?"

"No, of course not, but it sounds like it worked."

The women found Chase in the living room with the rest of his team.

"How'd it go?" he asked.

"We have names and also rough location of Chicago."

"Give me the names, and I'll have Skipper run them."

Anya said, "Is not necessary. I know who and what they are, and I am very pleased."

"Pleased?"

"Yes, Ilya Gorshkov and Oleg Lepin are very powerful men who have the ear of Putin. This means the Russians are very serious about this mission."

Chase nodded. "So, what's next?"

"Next, we must keep the two men alive while we search for Gorshkov and Lepin. You will help with this, yes?"

"Of course we will," Chase said. "We've got nothing else to do. Do you want to keep them here?"

"This is up to you. Wherever is convenient for you is fine for me."

"What about the lady gladiator?" he asked.

"She is first small roadblock for us. She is probably very dangerous, so we must eliminate or control her so we can get to people who are at top of all of this."

"How do you plan to do that?"

She said, "I do not know yet, but she will continue mission to kill us. I am certain of this."

"So, should we stick around to provide security?" he asked.

"No. We will leave island today. If men are in Chicago, Gwynn and I must also be there. I have strange request for you, though. Do you have friend inside government who can send diplomatic pouch to Kremlin?"

Chase tried not to laugh. "What are you going to put in the pouch?"

"Mikhail Tornovich's fingers."

Chase sighed. "Oh, boy. I'm afraid I can't get it directly to the Kremlin, but I'm pretty sure I could get a package on the desk of the Russian ambassador at the embassy in DC."

"This is wonderful idea. Wait here."

Anya disappeared and then returned in minutes with four of Mikhail's fingers.

Chase said, "Let's put those in a bag or something, if you don't mind. I really don't want to shove them in my pocket like that."

Gwynn's phone chirped, and she thumbed the answer button. "Hello."

"Is this Special Agent Davis?" a man's voice asked.

"Who's calling, please?"

"This is Sergeant Grimes from the hospital."

Gwynn said, "Please don't tell me you let my prisoner escape again."

He said, "I told you before that I can't be responsible for runaway patients."

"Stop stalling, Grimes. Is he there or not?"

"No, I'm afraid he's missing again."

Gwynn shook her head. "I can't believe you screwed up the one simple thing I asked you to do."

Grimes stammered. "Do you . . . Should I . . . Is there anything I can—"

Gwynn huffed. "No. There's nothing else you can do." She hesitated. "Wait a minute. There is something you can do. Are the handcuffs still attached to the bed?"

"No, the cuffs are gone."

"Do you know if he received an antivenin treatment yet?"

"I'm not allowed to give out medical information about patients. It's a HIPAA violation."

Gwynn said, "It's a violation of federal law to allow a prisoner to escape twice, so maybe you want to rethink that HIPAA thing. Did he get the treatment or not?"

"Yeah, they gave it to him."

"Then there's a possibility he's still alive, and you better hope he stays that way. If he doesn't, you may be the next person I put in cuffs."

Before Grimes could mumble through another sample of his incompetence, Gwynn ended the call. She said, "Johnny Mac's on the loose again."

Chase's phone was next to chirp, and he answered on speaker. "Tell me you've got good news."

Skipper said, "It depends on how you look at it. I found some background on our gladiator, and she's a serious player. Her résumé mirrors Anya's almost line for line."

Anya bit her lip. "This is good news. If she and I have same training, I will always know what she will do next."

Skipper said, "Her résumé *almost* mirrors yours, but there's one significant difference. She's a shooter."

"A sniper?" Chase asked.

"She's been to all the schools, so yeah, she qualifies as a sniper. She's also good with explosives and poisons."

Gwynn said, "This girl sounds like a real party animal. We should have her over for game night."

Anya ignored the comment. "You will send to us her dossier, yes?"

"It's already in your email boxes. There's one more thing. I don't think she left the island. Unless she turned into a ghost, she's still on Bonaire."

Anya said, "Yes, this is exactly what I would do. Do you have anything else for us?"

"I do. I ran down the phone numbers you gave me, and they come back to satellite phones on Lake Michigan. I even found two calls from Bonaire to one of the sat-phones. That's part of the reason I think this woman is still on the island."

"Please tell to me you have the number she called from."

"Of course I do, and it's in your briefing packet in the email. Let me know if you need anything else."

Anya said, "Wait. Do not hang up yet. I have two names for you. Oleg Lepin and Ilya Gorshkov."

Skipper said, "I'm on it. I'll get back with you when I dig up anything on those names."

Anya opened her email and read Gladiatorsha's dossier. When she finished reading it for the second time, she leaned back onto the couch. "I did not expect them to send a person with her level of skill so quickly. Mission is now much more dangerous than I originally thought."

"What can we do to help?" Chase asked.

"Take fingers to Russian embassy."

"Yeah, that's easy," he said, "but what can we do to help with the gladiator situation?"

"There is nothing you can do. Is now game of life-and-death chess between this person and me. I am older and wiser, but she is young and strong. I am not certain I will win, but game will not end with impasse. One Russian queen will fall, but I do not yet know which one."

Gwynn spoke up. "What do you mean, this person and you? I'm in the game, too."

Anya cast her eyes to the floor. "I cannot ask you to do this anymore. Is now far too dangerous."

Gwynn said, "Who's asking? We're partners, and that doesn't change just because the Russians launched a carbon copy of twenty-five-year-old you. We're in this together."

"You do not understand, Gwynn. This is very dangerous now. This woman will not stop until either she is dead or I am. If I take you into this fight, same will be true for you."

Gwynn didn't flinch. "You're wasting your breath. I told you before—we started this together, and now we're going to end it together."

"We can maybe continue this conversation later. I am going to make telephone call."

Gwynn said, "If you're calling Ray White or the attorney general, you're wasting your time. Neither one of them can stop me from coming with you."

"This is not who I am calling," Anya said. "I am dialing number of Gladiatorsha."

21

Siniy Dlya Svobody
(Blue for Freedom)

The line rang twice, and a young female Russian voice answered softly. "What took you so long?"

Anya said, "I am learning about you. Calling before I was prepared would have been foolish. And I am sure you studied me long enough to know that I do not do foolish things."

Gladiatorsha laughed. "You have already done many foolish things, beginning with falling in love with your target and deserting your countrymen and Kremlin."

"You were baby girl when I did these things you think you understand. You are still child, and I will use that to my great advantage. If you are wise, you will walk away before I am forced to kill you."

Gladiatorsha chuckled. "This pleases me greatly. If you believe I am only little girl, you will underestimate me."

Anya said, "I never underestimate my enemy."

"I hope that tastes like acid inside mouth when you call your former comrades 'enemies.'"

"It tastes only sweet to me," Anya said. "If you are warrior you claim to be, tell to me where you are. I will come to you, and we will fight until you are dead."

"What makes you believe I am not where you are?"

"You have no idea where I am," Anya said.

"Red or blue?"

Anya frowned. "I do not understand question. What are you asking me?"

Gladiatorsha said, "You must choose red or blue."

Anya studied the room in case her foe was watching in that moment, but nothing blue or red caught her eye. "I choose blue for freedom."

Almost before the words left her lips, the blue saltshaker on the table exploded into shards of glass and grains of salt.

As everyone in the room dived for the floor, Chase's phone chirped. Once in relative safety, he answered on speaker. "What is it? We're taking sniper fire."

Skipper's typical calm tone had become frantic. "Chase, she's there! I'm tracking the call, and she's a thousand yards south of your position."

The team dispersed in seconds, and boots thundered up the slope to the south.

Anya pressed the phone back to her ear. "Nice shot, but you should have killed me instead of showing off."

"I could have killed you a dozen times, traitor, but there would be no fun in killing you from so far away. I want to watch life fall from your eyes when I slice your throat."

"Tell to me your name," Anya said.

"You may call me Gladiatorsha."

"This is not your name. I am Anastasia Robertovna Burinkova. Now, tell to me your name."

"I will tell you as you are dying . . . not before."

Remaining low and hidden, Anya slowly made her way toward the back of the house before slipping through the rear door. As she moved, she scrolled through the dossier Skipper provided on Gladiatorsha. "I will make guesses, and you will tell to me when I have guessed correctly."

The sniper laughed. "You will never guess my name, but I will enjoy hearing you try."

Anya zoomed in on the first page of the dossier. "I think you are Mila Zakharina Vinogradova, but of course, this assumes that Zakhar was your real father."

The line was silent for several seconds. "So what if you know my name? This means only that you have connections maybe inside Kremlin. You will tell to me who these connections are, and I will also kill them."

Anya said, "You don't sound quite as confident as you did earlier. Did I spook you by knowing your name?"

"Nothing about you frightens me."

Anya said, "Then come to me, and we will see which of us will remain alive."

"I think I will not do this right now. You have too many friends around you, but I will find you alone, and that is how you will die."

Anya peered around the house, scanning every inch of the hillside. "Or perhaps I will find you."

The sniper laughed, said "TTFN," and the line went dead.

Anya dialed Skipper in the Bonaventure op center. "Where is she now?"

Skipper said, "I'm on the line with Chase and the team, so I'll patch you into that feed. Stand by."

Several clicks sounded on the line, and Singer, the Southern Baptist sniper and one of the world's deadliest marksmen said, "I've got her. Do you want her down?"

Chase said, "Put her down!"

But Anya yelled into the phone. "No! Do not kill her. She is too valuable."

Chase didn't question the Russian's order and instead said, "Belay my last. Take her down if you can, but keep her alive."

"She'll be over the peak in seconds," Singer said. "I've got the kill shot, but that's all. She's too fast to catch."

"Hold your fire," Chase ordered.

Skipper asked, "Did you say she was running?"

Singer answered, "Affirmative. She's cresting the ridge now."

Skipper said, "Her phone hasn't moved."

"She must've ditched it at her sniper hide," Singer said. "Talk me to it."

Skipper gave direction and distance calls until she said, "You're right on top of it. How can you not see it?"

Chase joined Singer at the GPS location of Gladiatorsha's phone. He kicked several large rocks until one of them moved a fraction of an inch. "Help me roll this one."

Singer bent over the stone and added his fingertips to Chase's efforts. Soon, the stone moved enough to provide an entrance to a small cave.

Singer pointed toward the hole. "I'll never fit through there. Hey, Anya. Are you on the comms?"

"I am here."

"We found your girl's hide, but the entrance is pretty tight. Do you want to give it a try?"

The sound of a helicopter filled the air, and Anya said, "I cannot do this now. I will be inside helicopter looking for her."

Singer stared up at Chase. "Where'd she get a helicopter on ten seconds' notice?"

"Her company owns four Robinsons they use for tours. I'm sure it's one of those."

A few seconds later, the bright yellow helicopter raced up the slope toward the crest, with Anya lying facedown and surveying the vegetation-covered hillside.

Mongo stepped beside Chase, planting his hands on his knees and gasping for breath. "I'm getting too old for chasing Russian girls."

Chase said, "If you think chasing them is tough, just wait until they start chasing you."

Mongo took a knee and shone his light into the small opening in the cave. "You want me to open that up a little?"

Singer said, "That's exactly what we want."

Mongo grabbed a pair of stones in his massive hands and pulled as if trying to move a freight train. With a mighty groan, the stones moved an inch, then two, then the opening tripled in size as the giant forced the stones over a small ledge.

Singer was first inside with his light leading the way, but before he was halfway inside, he froze. "Uh, we've got a little problem here."

"What is it?" Chase asked.

"It's a pressure plate trigger rigged to a MON-fifty."

Chase glanced at Mongo and shrugged. "I don't know what that means."

Mongo placed a hand on the back of Singer's leg. "Don't move."

Singer huffed. "Don't worry about that. I landed on the pressure plate. It's obviously rigged to fire when I move off the plate, so I'm staying right here until somebody disarms this thing."

Mongo said, "Tell me which rocks I can move."

Singer twisted awkwardly and groaned. "The big round one to my left is safe as long as nothing falls from overhead."

Mongo pulled the stone, but Mother Nature had concreted that particular rock into the earth, so even his massive strength couldn't budge it. "Find another one."

Singer said, "I'm in a fix here. I can't turn any more, so I can't see the rocks. Everything to my left is safe to move, but I'm blind to the right."

Mongo said, "Let me see what I can do."

He moved several smaller stones, creating a second entrance to the cave, and Chase crawled inside.

Once his head and shoulders were inside the opening, he shined his light around until it fell on Singer's elbow pressed against a round metal plate. "Are you okay?"

Singer nodded and pointed to the mine propped against a stone two feet beyond his reach. "Yeah, I'm okay for now, but that thing has great potential to ruin my day."

"That looks like a Claymore," Chase said.

"Yeah, it's the Russian's version of the Claymore, but it's a lot more volatile. Can you reach it?"

Chase squirmed farther into the mouth of the cave and stretched for the

MON-fifty antipersonnel mine. "I think I can get it, but you said they're volatile. Can I disarm it by breaking the wiring circuit?"

Singer said, "No, unlike the Claymore, the Russian version isn't that simple. You'll need to pull it outside, lay it on its back, and let it cook off."

"Are you serious? Is it okay to move it?"

"You can move it, but be careful with the wiring. If it separates, all three of us will turn into pink mist."

Chase cautiously gripped the mine and lifted it from its perch against the rocks. "Okay, I've got it. I'm moving outside."

Sweat dripped from Singer's face as Chase moved in slow motion, backing out of the cave.

Singer watched as the wire pulled tight. "Hold it! That's as far as you can go."

"I'm not clear of the cave yet. We can't set it off this close to you. The shock wave from the blast alone would kill you even if you don't get the shrapnel."

Singer closed his eyes and offered a silent prayer. When he opened his eyes again, he said, "We don't have any choice. Block it off right there with the front facing away from me and the back against the boulder Mongo couldn't move."

"I've never seen one of these cook off. Is the charge enough to move that rock?"

Singer said, "If Mongo couldn't move it, that mine ain't gonna do it. Just push it in there and get back . . . way back."

"I don't like it," Chase said.

"We don't have to like it, but it's the pot we're in. We can either let it boil us to death, or we can jump out."

Chase did as Singer asked and placed the mine against the heavy stone. "All right. That's the best I can do. Do you want a flak vest to cover your head?"

Singer said, "No, but I'd love a good pair of earplugs."

"Sorry, buddy. I can't help you with that."

Singer sighed. "In that case, just get away and let me know when you're clear."

Chase and Mongo backed away and yelled, "We're clear!"

Singer closed his eyes, turned his face away from the blast, and lifted his elbow from the pressure switch.

The earthshattering crack of the mine exploding felt as if the entire hillside might land in the sea a mile away, but the explosion isn't what held Chase's attention. Anya's bright yellow helicopter crossed the top of the hill, trailing a long stream of black smoke.

Rocks and dust filled the air above the cave instantly following the explosion, and debris rained down on them like a hailstorm.

Chase was torn between running in to make sure Singer was still alive and watching the smoking chopper limp through the sky.

Mongo was the opposite of torn. He dived into the dust-filled mouth of the cave and grabbed Singer by the waist. "Are you hurt?"

Singer rolled his head to the side, shook off the blast, and yelled, "Get me out of here!"

Mongo pulled the sniper from the rubble and was surprised to see a solid black rifle in Singer's hand when he was clear of the debris.

Mongo leaned down and stared into Singer's eyes. "Are you hurt?"

The sniper cupped a hand around his ear and yelled, "What? I can't hear you."

"They're going down!" Chase yelled from a dozen feet away, and Mongo finally turned his attention to the chopper.

"That doesn't look good."

Chase asked, "Is he okay?"

Mongo nodded, and Chase bounded down the slope toward the soon-to-be scene of the crash.

The chopper disappeared behind the wall of smoke pouring from what used to be its jet engine. The stream of smoke led into the trees, and limbs were turned to sawdust by the disintegrating rotor blades.

Chase continued his sprint to the crash site, determined to pull Anya and the pilot from the burning wreckage. When he finally reached the remains of the helicopter, Anya and Gwynn were pulling the pilot from the cockpit. Chase joined them and cupped his hands beneath the pilot's arms. "I've got him. Are you two all right?"

Anya said, "She shot us and escaped."

Once clear of the burning fuselage, Chase laid the pilot on his back on the sandy ground and stuck a pair of fingers against his neck. Next, he held a hand beneath the man's nose and pressed an ear to his chest. After ten seconds of feeling and hearing nothing, he began chest compressions.

Ten minutes later, Chase rolled from his knees and onto the ground, sweat pouring from his face, and his chest heaving for air.

Anya laid a hand against the pilot's chest and motioned toward a growing puddle of blood. "We must stop. He cannot be saved."

22

TORGOVOYE REMESLO
(TRADECRAFT)

Gwynn and Anya sat with the pilot's family for twenty minutes and apologized profusely, but nothing could quell the grief in their hearts. "I cannot tell to you how sorry I am for what happened. Your husband was marvelous pilot. He made terrible sacrifice by taking all of impact of crash on his side. He could have saved himself and killed us, but he did not."

The pilot's widow sobbed into her hands. "He loved flying for you."

"He was very good man, and he talked about you and his children every day."

The woman continued sobbing. "I don't know what we're going to do. I don't work. I just take care of the kids, so he brought home our only paycheck."

Anya placed a gentle hand on the woman's trembling arm. "Do not worry about money. I will continue to pay salary, and I will take care of all expenses for funeral. You have already enough to worry about, so do not add money to that list. I will take care of you and the children. I promise this to you."

Back at the rented house, where the two Russian surveillance specialists remained bound to the bed, Anya asked, "What was explosion on side of hill before we crashed?"

Mongo said, "It was a Mina Oskolochnaya Napravlennogo."

Anya gasped. "And everyone is alive?"

Mongo nodded. "Singer's going to be deaf for a few hours, but that's a lot better than forever dead."

The temporarily deaf sniper held up the rifle he pulled from the cave. "She left me a nice little present. It's a Lobaev SVL chambered in four-oh-eight CheyTac. It's one of the best sniper rifles ever built."

"Why would she leave it behind?" Chase asked.

Anya said, "If you were running for your life from our team, would you want to carry ten extra kilos on your back?"

"I guess not," Chase said. "She must've known we were tracking her phone, which is why she left that behind, too."

Anya cocked her head. "She left rifle *and* telephone?"

Chase said, "That's how we found the cave. Skipper was tracking the number you called, and it led us straight to the cave."

"Is old trick used by SVR. I was trained to find and exploit every tracking device. Using these things to lure pursuers into trap is basic Russian tradecraft."

Chase sighed. "It worked."

Anya said, "It always does. How did you survive explosion from MON-fifty?"

Chase told her the story of Singer's elbow on the pressure plate and moving the mine before setting it off.

"This was terrible plan. Touching that mine after it is triggered is suicide."

Chase shrugged. "I'm glad I didn't know how dangerous it was. If I had known, we might've lost Singer."

The sniper looked up. "What?"

Chase waved him off, and Anya asked, "Did you save telephone?"

Mongo shook his head. "We were too busy saving Singer to worry about the phone."

"This is very good answer," Anya said. "If you had taken it, she would have been able to track us. This is more of Russian tradecraft."

Chase said, "That's international tradecraft, not just Russian."

Anya extended a hand toward Singer. "Give to me rifle."

He furrowed his brow and passed the Lobaev. She opened the bolt and slid a finger into the chamber before holding it up to the light and peering down the barrel from the muzzle end. Next, she dismantled the scope and examined every piece of the optic. Finally, she drew her knife and unscrewed the butt plate. She shook the rifle violently, and a tiny electronic device fell from inside the stock and onto the table.

Anya placed the rifle on the floor and held up the small device. "Tradecraft."

Singer lifted the bug from Anya's hand. "I've got an idea. I'm going to find one of those island donkeys and send this little thing on an adventure." As the sniper jogged from the house, Chase chuckled at the absurdity of the moment.

Anya's eyes suddenly widened, and her perfect smile brightened. "This is very good situation."

Chase and Mongo leaned in as if hanging on every word.

"Mila knows her telephone was destroyed, so she will know also that mine exploded and her trap worked. She probably believes I am now dead. This is wonderful advantage for us."

Chase grimaced. "I don't agree. I don't think the mine was meant for you. She's been watching us, so she knows you're not alone. And she's too arrogant to kill you remotely—she said it herself. She wants to fight you face-to-face."

Anya stared at the ceiling. "Maybe you are correct, or maybe I am. There is only one way to know, and I have plan."

"This oughta be good," Chase said. "Your plans are never boring."

Anya said, "We must do more things to make Mila believe I am dead. Did you bring with you body bags?"

Chase said, "We never leave home without them."

"Good, then you will put me inside body bag and take me onto airplane. This will force Mila to make decision. She will either follow us to make sure I am dead, or she will report to her handler that I was killed with mine inside cave."

"I don't love that plan," Chase said, "but this is your operation. We're just here to support it."

For the first time in the conversation, Anya turned to Gwynn. "What do you think is best thing to do next?"

Gwynn recoiled. "Me? You want my input on this?"

Anya nodded, and Gwynn said, "I've got an entirely different theory. I think Mila saw you hanging out of the helicopter, so she knows you didn't die in the mine explosion. That doesn't necessarily mean she thinks you're still alive. She could believe you died in the helicopter crash."

Anya considered Gwynn's theory for a moment. "I think it does not matter how she thinks I died. It only matters that she believes her job is finished. If this is what she believes, she will relax and make mistake."

Chase said, "Never interrupt your enemy when she's making a mistake. I think somebody famous said that once."

Anya pressed a hand against Chase's chest and tilted her head. "You are famous person to me."

Gwynn swatted Anya's hand away. "Hey! Stop that. You're supposed to be dead, remember?"

Chase laughed. "If you do that when Penny's around, we'll both wind up in body bags."

As if on cue, Chase's phone chirped. "Hello, this is Chase."

"It's Cotton. Your plane's ready to go, and your suspicion was right on the money. It was sabotage for sure. The nose gear is good to go, and I checked out the rest of the plane for any lingering surprises, and it's clean. I'll take care of all the paperwork, but I don't have the equipment to lift the plane and cycle the landing gear. I recommend circling overhead and working the gear a couple of times just to make sure everything's functioning the way it was designed."

Chase said, "Thank you. I'm sorry to drag you all the way down here, but I don't want anybody's hands other than yours turning wrenches on our flying machines."

"You don't have to thank me. Just pay the invoice when it comes, and let me know next time Maebelle's cooking."

"I'll do that, Cotton. Thanks again. We're packing up to head back to the States, but we're pulling a little ruse, so don't be concerned when we show up with a body bag."

Cotton laughed. "I stopped being surprised by the crazy stuff you do a long time ago. Compared to most stunts you pull, a body bag is pretty boring."

"You make a good point, my friend. We'll be there in less than an hour. If you need a shower, there's one inside the FBO."

Cotton said, "You just don't want to smell me all the way back to Florida. I know your game."

"You nailed me. Get cleaned up, and we'll be there soon."

Anya said, "I must make telephone call before we leave."

Chase listened as Anya spoke in a language he didn't recognize, and when she hung up, he said, "What was that?"

Anya motioned down the hall. "We have dead body and two hostages inside bedrooms. We cannot leave them there, so I made arrangements for someone to take care of it."

"What language were you speaking?"

"Bonaire is Dutch territory. Do you not speak Dutch?"

Chase rolled his eyes. "No, I'm afraid I never found that one to be a tactical necessity."

Anya said, "It was this time, so is very good you have me on team."

* * *

When the convoy arrived at the airport, Cotton met them beside the planes. He, Chase, and Disco, inspected the work on the nose gear.

"I'm no mechanic," Chase said, "but if you fixed it, I trust it."

The team made a show of carrying Anya aboard the Gulfstream inside a black body bag. If anyone was watching, the show should've sold the performance, but only time would tell.

Chase and Cotton manned the cockpit of the Gulfstream *Grey Ghost*, and Disco slid into the cockpit of Anya's Citation. The Gulfstream spiraled upward above the airport, and Cotton cycled the landing gear several times.

After five cycles of the gear, Chase said, "I'm satisfied. Let's get out of here."

The flight to St. Augustine was uneventful, and the landing gear performed exactly as the Gulfstream engineers designed it to work.

After the mechanic and his tools were offloaded, he said, "Do I need to store Anya's Citation here for a while?"

Chase said, "No, Disco's taking it to Bonaventure. We've got plenty of hangar space, but I appreciate the offer."

They shook hands, and Chase said, "I'll have Skipper pay your invoice as soon as you email it."

Cotton gave him a mock salute. "I never worry about you paying your bills, Hotshot. Whatever you're in the middle of, keep your head down and your powder dry."

"Will do. Thanks again."

Back at Bonaventure, Anya walked off the Gulfstream wearing a hoodie pulled low across her forehead just in case Mila found a way to get to St. Marys ahead of them. Don Maynard, the airport manager, fueled and tucked Anya's Citation away in a vacant hangar before doing the same with the Gulfstream.

Inside the op center, the team, including Anya and Gwynn, huddled around the conference table while Skipper gave the briefing.

She said, "Things are really getting interesting now. I called in a couple of favors, so I've got temporary use of a pair of satellites the NRO isn't using at the moment." Skipper pointed toward a monitor. "Here's Anya's house in Athens, and if you look closely, you'll notice something is missing."

Anya studied the screen. "Johnny Mac's car."

"Exactly. Good eyes. He picked up the car within an hour of turning up missing at the hospital. Oh, by the way, the rent-a-cop almost screwed everything up."

Anya said, "He is very good at that."

Skipper said, "He went to the local police."

"Oh, no. This is terrible. We must—"

Skipper held up a hand. "Calm down, Nikita. I took care of it."

"Nikita?" Anya asked.

Skipper shrugged. "It was the first badass Russian name I could think of."

Anya groaned. "Nikita is name for Russian boy. Only in Western world is it feminine, and is spelled with two Ts."

Skipper said, "Thank you for the cultural education, but we've got a lot to cover." The monitor beside the satellite footage of Athens showed an aerial shot of the Caribbean, and Skipper pointed toward one of the three southernmost islands. "This is Bonaire. Let me zoom in."

She enlarged the image of the island until several red diamonds appeared in various places. "These symbols are satellite phones that called other satellite phones in the hours following your big adventure with the antipersonnel mine and the chopper crash. I'm very sorry about the loss of your pilot, by the way."

"This is very kind of you," Anya said. "His family is also very sad."

Skipper continued. "I'm tracking these calls and hoping one of the numbers is Mila's new phone. It's a bit of a waiting game, but I think it'll pay off in the end."

Anya said, "What about Johnny? Can you track him?"

"Oh, yeah, baby. He wasn't smart enough to dump his cell, so I've got him within a hundred-meter radius as long as the phone's battery is charged."

"So, where is he now?"

Skipper checked a third monitor. "He's making his way back to DC, but I don't know why yet. He did make one call, but it was brief. The only other activity on the phone lasted forty-five seconds and was an incoming call from just outside Chicago."

Chase watched Anya close her eyes—a habit he noticed a decade before when she was finalizing a plan to end someone's life.

When she finally opened her eyes, she said, "This is three times we have heard Chicago. Two times is coincidence, but three is operational intelligence. I would like to have Skipper continue what she is doing with satellites and telephones, but Gwynn and I are going to Chicago."

23

Chto Nashe, to i Tvoye
(What's Ours Is Yours)

After a night of sleep they both needed and deserved, Gwynn and Anya stepped into the kitchen at Bonaventure a few minutes after six the following morning.

"Good morning, friend Gwynn. You slept well, yes?"

Gwynn yawned and stretched in the doorway. "That bed is amazing. I need one of those mattresses."

Anya smiled. "Chase has very good taste in things. He buys only best of everything."

"You're going to be enamored with him until the day you die, aren't you?"

"Perhaps even longer."

Gwynn checked over her shoulder. "Are we the first ones up?"

"I think so. We should go for breakfast so we do not wake anyone else."

Gwynn grabbed her head of unruly hair. "We're not going anywhere nice, are we? I'm a mess."

Anya plucked a University of Georgia baseball cap from a hook beside the door and tossed it to her. "Here. Wear this. You will look perfect."

They slipped through the kitchen door and onto the back gallery overlooking the sloping backyard at Bonaventure. The first rays of the morning sun were showing themselves and glistening in the treetops. "Is beautiful place, yes?"

Gwynn elbowed Anya. "Jealous much? Come on. I'm hungry."

They climbed into the brown VW Microbus and buzzed their way down the pecan-tree-lined driveway, with Anya behind the wheel.

"This is a groovy vehicle," Gwynn said, rubbing a hand across the metal dash.

"It was my father's van. He left it to Chase when he passed away many years ago."

"I wish I could've met him. I bet he was an interesting man."

Anya dabbed at a tear she was determined to keep from falling. "He was wonderful man—brave and strong and also very smart. He loved my mother the way I hope someday Chase will love me."

"He was a professor, right?"

"Yes, he was greatest psychology professor in all of world, but only after being fighter pilot in war and covert operative for United States. I have every letter my mother wrote to him inside box at home. They are beautiful and full of love."

"I think that's the first time I've ever heard you use the word 'home.' I've known you a long time, but I don't know where you live when we're not together."

"Home does not always mean house. Sometimes, home is only feeling, and it does not matter where that is. I feel at home with you when we are together."

"Yeah, I get that," Gwynn said. "But I meant, where do you live when you disappear?"

"Most of time, I am in Bonaire with business, but sometimes, I am at my father's house in Athens."

Gwynn eyed the Russian. "Something tells me you're not lying, but you're definitely not telling the whole truth."

Anya sighed. "Okay, I have also dacha in North of Europe."

"That's a little vague."

"Is in Switzerland inside city of Bern."

"Why there?"

Anya said, "There is person there who is important to me."

"A man? Does Chase know? What's his name?"

"Is not man. Is just someone I must care for."

Gwynn said, "Stop it. You're killing me. Who in Bern is so important to you if it's not a guy?"

Anya stiffened in the driver's seat of the Microbus. "I promise I will tell to you everything about Bern and who is there when we finish mission. I have been waiting long time to tell you, so a few more days will not be too long."

Gwynn huffed. "That's cruel, but I'm holding you to that promise. In fact, I don't want you to just tell me. I want to go to Switzerland with you and meet this mysterious person."

Anya grinned. "That is wonderful idea. We will do that as soon as this is over."

Breakfast at the roadside diner was anything but continental. The waitress brought stacks of pancakes, biscuits and gravy, bacon, country ham, and gallons of piping hot coffee. With their stomachs overfull, they climbed back into the Microbus for the short drive back to Bonaventure, where the rest of the team should've been awake and stirring.

Gwynn buckled her seat belt. "What are we going to do about Johnny Mac?"

"He is no longer problem for us," Anya said. "Skipper will keep tubs on him."

Gwynn chuckled. "Tubs? What does that mean?"

"Is American saying for time when someone is recording where someone goes. You should know this."

Gwynn's laughter bubbled over. "I love you to death, Anya, I do. But you've been here way too long to screw that one up. The phrase is keeping *tabs*, not tubs."

Anya furrowed her brow. "Are you certain of this?"

"Yes, American girl, I'm certain. It's tabs."

Anya nodded. "Tabs does make more sense. Anyway, Skipper will handle it and give to us any information she finds that might affect our mission."

As they turned onto the street leading to Bonaventure, Anya glanced at Gwynn. "I need to have talk with you about something."

Gwynn straightened in her seat. "Sure, what's up?"

"This is maybe final mission against Bratva, but we are perfect team. We are Avenging Angels, and there are many people who need angels in their lives. Maybe we will be able to help some of these people in future."

"You mean, like the A-Team kind of stuff?"

Anya cocked her head. "I do not know what this means."

"Surely you know who the A-Team is. Hanibal, Murdock, Face, and Mr. T."

"I do not know these people. Who are they?"

Gwynn chuckled. "We've got some major vegging out and old TV show watching to do when this is over. If you're going to be an American girl, you'll need to know this stuff."

Anya smiled. "I like this idea. Vegging with you is always wonderful."

Back at Bonaventure, Skipper buzzed them into the op center. "Hey, guys. Come on in. Where'd you go?"

Gwynn said, "We were up before everyone else, so we went to breakfast, and now we're stuffed."

Skipper eyed Anya. "You must've gone to the diner."

"Yes, and they brought for us too much food. Is ridiculous."

Skipper said, "Yeah, they do that. Take a look at this. I've got some news for you."

She spun in her chair and brought up a map on the overhead monitor. "The red triangle is Johnny's cell phone, and the green square is his car. Nice job bugging the car, by the way."

Anya said, "Is what I do. Is that hospital on map?"

"Yes, it's Georgetown University Medical Center. I can only assume he's there to get more antivenin treatment."

Anya turned to Gwynn. "See? I told you Skipper would keep *tabs* on him."

"Yes, you did . . .sort of."

Skipper said, "We all need a hobby, and tracking former DOJ special agents who are working with the Russian Mafia is mine."

"You need better hobby," Anya said.

"Don't I know it? Anyway, I don't have anything new on the Chicago angle, but I'm still on it. If your bad guys can be found, I'll find them. Hopefully, I'll have intel for you by the time you get there. I assume you'd like to do a little shopping while you're here. Am I right?"

"Yes," Anya said. "Chase told to us we could have anything we needed from armory."

"Of course he did, but even if he hadn't, I would've told you the same. So, help yourself. You have the access code, right?"

"I do," Anya said as she and Gwynn stood. Just as they reached the door, Anya turned and said, "Thank you for doing this for us."

Skipper smiled. "You're part of the family. You don't have to thank us. What's ours is yours. Except for Chase, of course. He's just ours."

She winked at the analyst. "For now."

After Anya scanned her thumbprint and typed the code into the panel, the door to the subterranean armory clicked and swung open.

The lights came on automatically, and Gwynn inhaled deeply. "I don't know why, but I love that smell."

"Is gun oil," Anya said.

"Yeah, I know what it is, and it's a bit of an aphrodisiac for me."

Anya held up both hands. "Do not look at me. You are not my type."

Gwynn giggled. "I could be."

"You are funny girl. Let's get what we need and go. We have much to do."

They spent ten minutes collecting the gear they would need in Chicago, including weapons, ammo, surveillance equipment, and enough C-4 to level the city.

* * *

The flight to Waukegan National Airport, just north of Chicago, only took two hours thanks to a pleasant tailwind in the flight levels.

When they touched down and taxied to the Signature Aviation transient ramp, Anya pulled out her phone and showed the screen to Gwynn. "We missed call from Skipper."

"Call her."

Anya handed the phone to Gwynn. "You call her. I have to shut down airplane."

While Anya ran the checklist and the engines whistled themselves to sleep, Gwynn dialed Skipper's number.

"Op center."

"Hey, Skipper, it's Gwynn. We made it to Chicago and saw you called. I hope you have some good news for us."

"It depends on how you look at it. Johnny Mac probably isn't an issue any longer."

"What do you mean?"

Skipper cleared her throat. "His car exploded when he left the hospital in Georgetown."

"Was he inside of it?"

Skipper said, "Somebody was inside, but the body is too badly burned to identify. I hacked into the network at the hospital, and you were right—Johnny was there for another round of antivenin treatment, which he received. According to the hospital records, he left six minutes before the explosion. My guess is that the Russians weren't happy with his performance, so they canceled their contract with him . . . quite literally."

"Wow. I wasn't expecting that," Gwynn said.

Anya turned with curiosity on her face. "What were you not expecting?"

Gwynn said, "Hang on a minute, Skipper. I'm putting you on speaker."

She touched the button and laid the phone on the panel. "Skipper said somebody blew up Johnny's car minutes after he left the hospital."

"Is he dead?"

Skipper said, "It looks that way. The timing is right, but it just happened a few minutes ago, so details are sketchy at best."

Anya lowered her gaze. "I did not want this to happen, but I was afraid it would."

Skipper said, "I get it, but when you play Russian roulette with an AK-forty-seven, this is what happens."

"You are correct. I am sad, but from operational standpoint, this is one fewer player we have to monitor. Thank you for letting us know. Do you have anything on Ilya Gorshkov and Oleg Lepin?"

"I don't, but you'll be the first to know as soon as I dig something up. I recommend getting some rest. You two have had quite a week."

Anya said, "We do not have luxury of resting. I am certain that Gorshkov and Lepin tracked our flight."

Skipper said, "Oh, ye of little faith. I took care of that. Your flight plan never existed. Not even the FAA can find your airplane. I booked you a nice hotel, and I just texted the reservation to you, so make the most of it and wake up ready to kick some oligarch ass."

24

Nizkiye Druz'ya v Vysokikh Krugakh
(Low Friends in High Places)

Anya and Gwynn slid onto the front seats of their ubiquitous black SUV, and Gwynn said, "Nice ride. Skipper did well."

"She always does. Do you have everything you need from inside the plane?"

"I do. How far is it to the hotel?"

Anya entered the address into the GPS. "Is only fifteen minutes."

"Not long enough for a nap."

Jacketed bellmen opened each front door of the SUV when they pulled into the hotel entrance. "Good evening, and welcome to the Fredrick, ladies. May we help you with your bags?"

Anya said, "We do not need help, but we would like to have a luggage cart."

The bellman said, "I'm sorry, ma'am. We don't lend luggage carts, but we'll be happy to manage your bags."

The Russian sighed. "All right, but our luggage must not leave our sight."

"Again, ma'am, I'm sorry, but we prefer to use the freight elevators for luggage so our guests don't have to deal with them on the passenger elevators."

Anya scowled. "This is becoming absurd. We will ride with you inside freight elevators."

"It would be a much more pleasant ride for you inside the passenger elevators. The freight elevators are a bit . . . uncomfortable."

"Give to us luggage cart, or allow us to travel inside freight elevator. These are only two options. You choose."

Ten minutes later, they were checked in and riding the less-than-elegant freight elevators alongside one of the two bellmen from the front door.

"This is you," the man said as he wedged a rubber stop beneath the door.

He motioned them inside, and Gwynn shrugged off her backpack and took in the two-bedroom suite. "This place is really nice. Maybe Skipper should be a travel agent."

"She has very good taste in hotels."

The bellman unloaded five cases from his cart and asked, "May I unpack for you?"

Anya shoved a folded bill into his hand. "This is not necessary, but thank you."

He pretended not to glance at the tip and slid it into his pocket. "Enjoy your stay, and if there's anything you need, feel free to ring the concierge."

Anya said. "We have not had dinner. Do you have recommendation?"

He said, "Angelina's, downstairs, is as good as any five-star restaurant anywhere in the country."

Anya stepped toward him and slipped another bill into his palm. "You will make for us reservations for one hour, yes?"

The man made no pretense of eyeing the bill. "Yes, of course. Thank you."

He vanished, and the two women made short work of unpacking what they needed for the night.

An hour later, they were walking into the hotel's famous restaurant, and Anya's phone chirped from inside her purse. She stopped in her tracks and slid the phone from the clutch. "Is Skipper."

Gwynn held up a finger as the maître d' approached. "Give us just one minute. We have to take a call."

The man bowed without a word and backed away as Anya and Gwynn rounded a corner into a relatively quiet spot in the lobby. "Hello, is Anya Burinkova."

"Hey, it's Skipper. And you don't have to tell me who you are when I call. I've got some news. Are you somewhere you can talk?"

Anya said, "No, but I can listen."

"I guess that'll have to do, so here's what I've got. The coroner's initial report out of Georgetown is that the badly burned body and the remains of the car both belonged to a former DOJ special agent, but they haven't officially released the victim's name yet."

Anya checked the area and found no one close enough to eavesdrop. "Thank you for update, but this does not sound like real news. Is only one more reason to agree with your first opinion about Johnny being the victim."

"You're right, but I told you I'd keep you posted on anything I found, and this qualifies."

Anya asked, "Do you have more information for us?"

Skipper let out the breath she'd been holding. "Have you ever heard of a man named Yakov Arsenyev?"

Anya played the name in her head several times until a bell rang. "Yes, I know this name. He was major player in big scam against several banks in Ukraine and Poland. If I am thinking of correct person, he went to prison for these crimes."

Skipper said, "Yep, that's part of his history. Our boy, Yakov, apparently had some low friends in high places. There's no official record of his arrest, trial, or imprisonment, but there's a block of three and a half years in which he seemed to drop off the face of the Earth."

Anya continued checking for listeners. "Is not surprising that person disappears from official records in Russia. Someone probably needed him, so he was conveniently removed from prison, and record was washed."

"Yeah, well, that seems to be the case here. After his forty-two-month exodus from society, he showed up with two well-known, high-level Bratva. Namely, Ilya Gorshkov and Oleg Lepin."

"So, there is one more head of beast we must chop off."

Skipper said, "Yeah . . . about that. Someone beat us to it. His body was found floating in Lake Michigan three hours ago."

"How do you know this?"

"It's what I do. Chicago PD is calling him an unknown John Doe, but intelligence sources say it's definitely Yakov. Rumor has it he was shot in the head before going for one last swim."

Anya paused and then said, "This does not make sense. If this person was important to Lepin and Gorshkov, no one inside Bratva would kill him. And even if they did, they would not be so sloppy as to leave his body inside lake."

"I'm just telling you what I learned," Skipper said.

Anya considered the news. "I need to know if Yakov and Johnny Mac ever met."

"Why would you need to know that? What could that connection have to do with any of this?"

"They are both dead on same day. This alone is enough to make me believe they are connected."

"Yeah, but Yakov wasn't killed today. He was just found today."

"How do you know this?" Anya asked. "When was Yakov shot?"

Skipper paused. "Well, the truth is, I don't know when he was shot."

"So, is maybe possible they were killed at same time, yes?"

"Okay," Skipper said. "I'll admit it's possible, but it's unlikely."

"I have spent all of my life living the unlikely. This is what intelligence operatives and Russian Mafia have in common. Nothing is typical."

"I get it," Skipper said. "So, if they are connected, what do you think it means?"

"I have only theory, but is maybe correct. Perhaps Yakov introduced Johnny to Ilya Gorshkov and Oleg Lepin, and when Johnny failed to deliver me—or us—they had both Johnny and also Yakov killed for their failure."

Skipper sighed. "Okay. I'll buy that as a possibility, but I'm going to keep digging. I still don't think they're connected."

"This is why it is important to have more than one smart person in operation like this. We are both smart, but we have very different life experiences. We can look at many things and see them very differently."

Skipper said, "That's part of what makes this team of ours work so well."

Anya softened her tone. "I love feeling inside heart when you say to me I am part of team."

"Come on, Anya. Everybody knows you're an irreplaceable part of this team."

"Yes, maybe this is true, but I still like to hear it."

Skipper said, "That's all I have for you right now . . ." She trailed off and mumbled, "Wait a minute."

"What is it?"

Skipper said, "I have a background process running to trace any connections to Johnny Mac over the past two weeks, and I just got a hit."

"What does this mean?" Anya asked.

"It would appear that we have a third body, and there's no doubt who this one belongs to."

Anya groaned. "Do not make me continue asking so many questions. Tell to me what is happening."

Skipper said, "Sorry. I was reading and talking at the same time. My software found six connections between a guy named Vincent Arailia. He's a—or I should say—he *was* an analyst at the NRO. You know, the National Reconnaissance Office."

"Yes, I know this place. Go on."

"Anyway, he and Johnny talked on six occasions in the past five days, and even more the week before this whole circus began."

Anya gritted her teeth. "Why is this important?"

Skipper sighed. "Good ol' Vincent was found hanging in his garage in Chantilly, Virginia, an hour ago."

"Suicide?"

Skipper said. "I doubt it, but it's probably supposed to look like suicide. I'll keep digging, but if I had to guess, I'd say Vincent Arailia was Johnny's mole who was feeding him intel on you."

"This is not good," Anya whispered.

Gwynn leaned in. "Is everything okay?"

Anya grimaced. "Is not okay, but is getting better. Keep digging, Skipper. We need to know history on Arailia."

"I'll see what I can dig up, but the fact that he's dead tells us most of what we need to know."

"This is true, I suppose. If you have nothing else, we are going to have dinner."

Skipper said, "That's all for now, but the restaurant inside the hotel is magnificent. I highly recommend the filet mignon."

"We are standing in front of restaurant now. Thank you for tip."

"Anytime. Call me if you need anything or if you learn anything new."

"We will," Anya said. "Thank you for everything."

"You're welcome. Enjoy your dinner."

Anya spent a few minutes bringing Gwynn up to speed, and the lawyer with a badge and gun said, "Oh, they're definitely related. I've only worked six cases against the Bratva, but Johnny and Yakov being found dead on the same day has Russian Mafia written all over it."

"This is also what I believe, but Skipper thinks maybe not."

"When was the last time Skipper stood toe-to-toe with a member of the Bratva?"

Anya shrugged. "I think this has never happened."

"That's what I thought," Gwynn said. "We have to go on the assumption that they're related, right?"

Anya nodded. "Yes, I believe so, but I am hungry. We must first eat, and then we will put together all pieces of jigsaw."

* * *

A skillet of sautéed baby mushrooms in a port wine reduction landed in the center of their table just after the wine was poured, and both women dived in before the appetizer stopped sizzling.

Gwynn covered her mouth. "Oh, my God. If the main course is anything like these mushrooms, I may never leave."

Anya wiped the corner of her mouth. "I cannot wait to see list of dessert."

"Slow down, girl. You're getting way ahead of yourself. We've got a lot of food to get through before we start thinking about dessert."

"You are wrong," Anya scolded. "I can think of dessert anytime I want, but this does not mean I will not enjoy entrée first."

The steaks arrived and set a new standard. Anya said, "Filet is so good I have almost forgotten about mushrooms."

Gwynn swallowed a sip of her cabernet. "This is the best meal I had in months."

They ate in near silence until the server appeared with a small leather-bound book in her hands. "I hope you enjoyed your steaks, but it's time for the best part of the meal." She slid the book onto the table. "Take your time and peruse the dessert menu. The cheesecake is to die for, but the chocolate offering is my absolute favorite. I'll be back in a few minutes."

Anya said, "Do not leave. We are very good at making decisions."

Gwynn beat Anya's hand to the menu, and she spread it open between them. "I think we'll have one of each."

The server studied Gwynn. "One of each of everything, or just the cheesecake and chocolate?"

All three women giggled, and Gwynn said, "Well, honestly, I'd like to have one of everything, but we'll stick with the cheesecake and chocolate for now."

The server lifted the menu and disappeared.

Anya said, "You did not wait for my order."

Gwynn crossed her arms. "Nope, I sure didn't. I'm calling the shots tonight."

"I will let you believe this," Anya said, "but we both know who is really in charge."

In perfect unison, both women said, "Skipper."

Dessert arrived, and both Gwynn and Anya melted into their seats after the first bite.

Gwynn closed her eyes and sighed. "Have you ever tasted anything this good?"

"Only once," Anya said, but Gwynn held up a hand.

"Do not say the first time you kissed Chase."

Anya chuckled. "I was thinking of chocolate cake made by Maebelle, but now that you mention it . . ."

A new server appeared tableside and leaned toward Anya. In flawless Russian, she said, "I hope you enjoyed the final meal of your life. Is now time for you to die."

25

DUMAY KAK LISA
(THINK LIKE A FOX)

Determining which woman reacted first was impossible. Both Gwynn and Anya leapt into action immediately. Anya pinned Mila Vinogradova's knife-wielding hand to the edge of the table at the same instant Gwynn swept the Russian assassin's feet from beneath her. Mila jerked against Anya's grasp as she collapsed to the floor, and then Anya bounded from her seat and landed with one knee on Mila's elbow and the other on her throat.

Taking full advantage of the quick break, Gwynn held her credential aloft with the badge clearly visible. "Everybody, stand back. We're federal law enforcement officers, and we have everything under control."

Gwynn's calm, authoritative tone did little to calm the swelling, morbid curiosity of the other diners in the restaurant, but for a few seconds, it did change the odds of Anya's fight. With Gwynn's attention on the gathering crowd, Mila seized the momentary advantage of being in a one-on-one fight with her former comrade. She accepted Anya's foot on her throat and fired the opposite end of her body as a powerful weapon. Her forcefully rising heels caught Anya beneath her right arm, sending her onto her side on the floor of the swanky restaurant.

The younger Russian clearly had the advantage of speed and strength, but Anya had something Mila did not, and that secret weapon was only an instant away from rejoining the fight.

When Gwynn dropped her cred-pack, her role as public information officer was over, and she was once again the warrior Anya trained her to be. Leaping to her feet, Mila reclaimed the steak knife she'd lost as Anya rolled away. Gwynn shoved her Glock against the back of Mila's neck, forcing her to bend at the waist, and Anya threw a powerful kick to their attacker's gut, doubling her over even more.

Gwynn swept her feet again, and this time, the assault left Mila falling face-first toward Anya with a serrated blade protruding from her hand. Anya let her momentum carry her into one more roll on the floor to avoid having the knife find its way into her throat.

As she collided with the floor, Mila bore the impact on her rounded shoulder, allowing her to roll back onto her feet only inches away from her foe. There was no fear in the young Russian's eyes. If any emotion was there, it was excitement and the same look Anya wore when she locked horns with an adversary.

Mila kicked an abandoned chair into the air toward Gwynn at the same instant she retrained her muzzle on the assassin. Gwynn swatted the chair away, but not before it hooked her pistol and tore it from her hand.

Diners screamed, and several ran for the street, but many were mesmerized by the battle raging only feet from the kitchen door.

As she studied her situation, Gwynn concluded that continuing the fight was more important than reclaiming her Glock, so she dived back into the fray and wrapped both arms around Mila's neck in precisely the headlock Anya had taught her in hour after arduous hour of hand-to-hand training.

Instantly recognizing the maneuver, Mila imparted the only real defense against the hold that would render her unconscious in seconds. She mule-kicked Gwynn's knee, sending the agent's left leg backward after the thundering blow.

Fortunately, Gwynn had lifted the weight from her leg a fraction of a second before Mila landed the kick. The attack still hurt, but she hadn't lost use of the leg. If she hadn't reacted, the kick would've bent the knee backward, effectively destroying Gwynn's will and ability to continue the fight. Unfortunately, though, the mule kick did exactly what Mila needed it to do, separating Gwynn's arms from Mila's neck and giving her the freedom to continue the fight.

Gwynn shook off the pain and dived for her pistol that now seemed to be far more important than it had been an instant before. She planted her healthy knee on the ground and raised the pistol until it fell perfectly in line with her right eye and the center of Mila's back. "Step off! I've got the shot!"

Anya defied the order immediately and spun Mila around with a kick to her hip. "Do not shoot her! We need her alive."

The fight continued as both Mila and Anya ignored the muzzle of the 9mm mere feet away. Mila was determined to end the fight with Anya's soul in her hands, but Anya had other plans.

In the blink of an eye, she took inventory of her surroundings and stepped backward toward the swinging kitchen door, where faces were pressed against the small glass windows.

Gwynn closed the distance but didn't lower her pistol. "I can't let her kill you."

Anya's breath came hard as she absorbed blow after blow, delivered by one of Russia's newest assassins. "I cannot let you kill her."

With every attack by the young killer, Anya took one more backward step. The dance accomplished two things: First, it slowly moved the fight toward the kitchen, where a massive assortment of weapons waited. Second, the retreat served to soften the coming blows.

When she felt the door brush her heel, Anya kicked the hinged barricade, clamped down on both of Mila's wrists, and yanked her through the five-star décor of the dining room and into the stainless-steel world of the back of the house. Chefs, cooks, and servers scattered like terrified children as the three women crashed through the door.

Anya seized the first weapon her probing hand discovered, and she delivered a staggering blow to the side of Mila's head with a honing steel. The shot staggered the would-be killer, but she didn't go down. Blood oozed from her neck just below her ear, and when she wiped at it with a swift hand, the sight of the blood on her fingertips only seemed to further stoke the fire inside of her. She licked her palm, let out an animal's groan, and snatched a skillet hanging from a hook.

Anya spun like a tornado as she devoted every detail of the kitchen to memory in an instant. She snatched a massive knife from the chef's palm and lashed out wildly as Mila swung the skillet through the air like a baseball bat.

Gwynn came through the door, still in pursuit of the pair, and as Mila drew back to swing the pan and deliver one final blow at Anya, Gwynn grabbed the skillet with both hands and yanked it from the assailant's grip. Finding herself disarmed, Mila turned, grabbed the handle of a pot on the eye of one of the stoves, and hefted it toward Gwynn. As the boiling sauce inside the pot soared through the air, Gwynn covered her face and ducked away. The liquid missed her face but splashed across her hands and neck, scalding her skin. Even though the pain was more than she wanted to deal with, it wasn't enough to force her from the fight.

Gwynn came across with a long, thin filet knife and a steel bowl that made an excellent shield.

As Mila spun back to Anya, who'd finished her game of retreat, she suddenly found herself in one of the deadliest situations of her life. In front of her was an older version of herself—someone capable of fighting as long as breath remained in her chest—and behind her stood a federal law enforcement officer who'd spent the previous two years training under the legendary Anastasia Burinkova. To her right was a line of stoves and ovens, and on her left was a row of immovable prep tables. Perhaps she could kill or severely wound one of the women, but definitely not both. It was time for the fearless Russian bear to think like a fox.

Having endured the identical training as Mila, Anya knew every trick in the Russian's playbook, and her mind was churning a thousand miles per hour as she tried to imagine what the younger SVR officer might do next.

A dozen possibilities floated through her head, but the move Mila made was not on the list.

Instead of wildly lashing out by throwing everything in sight and making her escape, Mila became a politician and recruiter in the same moment. "Please help me! These women are trying to kill me, and I don't know who they are!" Her accent was gone, and the words flew from her lips as if spoken by a terrified local.

Gwynn reached for her badge to end the confusion erupting inside the kitchen, but her hand came up empty. The credentials remained on the floor beside the table where the skirmish originated, but even without the badge, Gwynn prayed she could make believers out of the stunned collection of employees.

She yelled, "We're federal agents, and this woman is under arrest. Stay back!"

The ploy worked on some of the staff, but not everyone, and Mila preyed on the lingering doubt. In her best English, she yelled again, "They are not police!" She pointed at Anya. "This one is a Russian spy, and the other one is her American traitor."

The word *traitor* didn't roll from her tongue the way a Midwesterner would pronounce it, and the gathered crowd was suddenly even more divided.

Reacting to Mila's desperate attempt to appeal to the workers, Anya said, "I am not Russian spy. I am American," but her accent was impossible to hide. With eight little words from her Russian tongue, Anya made Mila's point for her, and the crowd descended on her.

"Stay back!" Gwynn yelled as she threw down the filet knife and raised her Glock again. "We are agents of the DOJ, and this woman is under arrest!"

Gwynn was more convincing than Anya, but without a cred-pack, it was impossible to drive her point home. She wasn't going to pull the trigger, but no one in the kitchen was certain of that fact.

Dressed in the uniform of one of the restaurant's servers, Mila was, at first glance, part of the family, and no one knew Gwynn or Anya. The decision was made, and the gathered crowd became a mob, rushing Anya and Gwynn and sending both of them to the slick ceramic tile. Anya dropped her knife, and Gwynn lowered her gun. Stabbing or shooting one of the staff would only make the situation worse.

As the pair surrendered to the mob, someone kicked in the door from the dining room and yelled, "Chicago PD! Nobody move!"

Four uniformed officers, complete with vests, helmets, and riot shields, poured into the kitchen at the same instant the rear door of the kitchen briefly opened and slammed back into place. Everyone's attention turned to the door except for Anya's. She didn't have to look to know that the fifteen-year-younger version of herself had hidden in plain sight during the chaos and escaped into the night.

* * *

"You've got to be kidding me!" The Chicago police detective ran his hands through what was once a full head of black hair but now resembled the surface of a cue ball ringed by grey hair clipped close to the scalp.

The interrogation room looked exactly like every other such room on Earth, but Gwynn and Anya weren't accustomed to being the ones answering questions from their side of the table.

"Your men picked up my cred-pack from the restaurant," Gwynn said. "Call DC, and let us out of here."

A knock came at the heavy steel door, and the detective growled. "What?"

A younger man with most of his hair still in place stuck his head into the room. "I've got the Attorney General's office on the phone, and their story checks out. We've got no choice but to cut them loose."

26

Kogo-to Lyubit'
(Someone to Love)

Back in their hotel suite, Anya slid onto the plush sofa with her steaming cup of tea. "Well, that was exciting, no?"

Gwynn blew across her mug. "I'm not sure *exciting* is the word I'd use, but I can't say it was entirely unexpected."

Anya furrowed her brow. "You expected Mila Vinogradova to pretend to be server at restaurant? You should have told me."

"No, that's not it. I just meant that expecting the craziest possible scenario to pop up with you should be my constant mindset when we're together."

As if ignoring her partner's jab, Anya said, "I must apologize to you, friend Gwynn, because I am embarrassed and I should have died for being so careless today."

Gwynn gasped. "Don't say that. You couldn't have known that was going to happen."

Anya looked away. "This is not true. I should have known she would do exactly what she did because that is precisely what I would have done . . . with one exception."

"What exception?"

"I would not have failed. Mila made unforgivable mistake by letting us escape."

"I'm not so sure she *let* us escape," Gwynn said. "It's more like we let *her* get away."

"We made also many mistakes, but she had stronger position. She had benefit of surprise, she was standing while we were sitting, and she had knowledge of restaurant we did not have."

"Yeah, but there are two of us."

Anya frowned. "Please do not be offended, but I do not believe Mila thinks you are threatening. This is, for us, wonderful advantage."

Gwynn laughed. "I'm not offended. I actually like that she underestimates me, but something tells me she learned a little about me during our skirmish."

"Was more than skirmish. It was attempt to kill me."

"A lot of people have attempted to kill you."

"Yes," Anya said, "but most of them are now dead. This does not matter now. We must leave hotel today."

"Hang on a minute. Isn't that exactly what she would expect us to do?"

"Yes, of course, but it does not make it bad plan just because she expects it."

"But a better plan might be doing what she would never expect."

Anya raised an eyebrow. "I like what you are thinking. Tell to me what you have in mind."

"That's the thing. I'm not really sure. I've never had the training you and she went through, so I'm an outsider. What would you expect her to do if the roles were reversed?"

Anya thought for a moment. "I would expect the police to keep her in custody for longer than we were held. She does not have same connections as us, so it would take her much longer to escape from police."

"Put yourself in her position, though. If she didn't already know that we were feds, she does now, so we have to proceed with that knowledge, even if it's new information for her."

"It is not new information. I am certain SVR knows everything about both of us, so this means Mila knows as well."

"Okay, let's go with that. What would you do if you were her?"

"I would watch for our departure from hotel and follow."

Gwynn said, "Exactly. So, either we do the opposite, or we use what she knows against her and make a noisy escape."

"Noisy escape?"

"Yeah, you know. We should leave and make sure she sees us. If we know she's following us, we get to control where she goes."

Anya smiled. "You are thinking like spy. I like this."

"Does that mean you want to do it?"

"You gave two options. Which one is better inside your mind?"

Gwynn tapped her chin with a fingernail. "If we weigh the pros and cons, leaving seems to make more sense. If we stay, we're essentially trapped inside the hotel, and knocking off a potential assassin inside the hotel doesn't sound like a great plan to me."

"I agree. I think we must leave hotel, as I said, but we should make certain she is watching."

"I'll call the bellman," Gwynn said.

Anya reached for her arm. "No, do not do this."

"But we've got a lot of gear to move, and you know how they feel about lending their luggage carts."

Anya produced a plastic card. "I have key to all of hotel. We can have luggage cart if we want, and also, this gives us access to freight elevator."

"You stole the bellman's ID?"

"Maybe better word is *borrowed*. I will give back if we see him, or maybe I will keep for next time."

Gwynn huffed. "Next time? Please tell me we're never going to be in this situation again."

"I cannot make this promise to you. People like Mila are part of our lives now, so we must always prepare for next time."

Gwynn rolled her eyes. "Like I said, life with you is never dull. Do you want to get the cart or gather our gear?"

204 · CAP DANIELS

"I will bring cart. This will give to me opportunity to look for Mila. I am certain she will be watching."

Gwynn stepped around her partner. "I'll have everything ready to go when you get back."

At the same instant Anya moved for the door, a knock sounded. Gwynn froze, and Anya pressed herself against the wall of the short corridor. She pulled out her phone and stuck the camera lens to the peephole.

"Who is it?" Gwynn mouthed.

Before Anya could answer, the hiss of a suppressed pistol broke the silence, and her phone exploded from her hand.

Gwynn leapt for cover and slid her Glock across the floor toward Anya. The Russian kicked the pistol back to her partner and drew the knife she'd reclaimed the instant they returned to their suite. She locked eyes with Gwynn and pressed a finger to her lips, offering the universal signal for silence.

Gwynn obeyed, and Anya lay on her back, just inside the door, with one arm crossed over her face as if Mila's pistol shot had pierced her eye. The actions of her partner sent Gwynn into action. There was nothing inside the suite strong enough to stop a second bullet, so in the absence of adequate cover, Gwynn settled for a little concealment behind the arm of the sofa. She lifted her pistol and positioned herself with a perfect view of the entry corridor.

An instant after Gwynn crouched, the door flew open, and the second SVR assassin she'd ever met stood over Anya with the muzzle of her Makarov slicing through the air in the epitome of efficiency.

Gwynn's heart beat like thunder as her finger left the slide and fell perfectly into position on the Glock's custom trigger. Three and a half pounds of pressure would end Mila's life and erase the threat she posed, but having her alive was far more valuable than gunning her down.

Anya sprang the trap into which Mila stepped. From her position on the floor, she rolled onto her side and delivered a crushing side kick to the Russian's knee. Mila bellowed in agony as her leg bent backward and she collapsed to the floor.

Anya sent another powerful kick to her would-be assassin's chin on her way to the ground, rendering her former compatriot solidly unconscious. Back on her feet, Anya relieved Mila of her pistol and closed the door.

Gwynn stepped from behind the couch. "Nice work. Is she dead?"

"I hope not," Anya said. "Help me move her onto sofa."

They lifted the unconscious Russian, and Gwynn said, "She's heavier than I expected."

They moved awkwardly to the sofa and dropped Mila on the cushions.

"She is in good shape, and muscle is heavy."

Gwynn patted down the Russian while Anya bound her hands and feet. When the process was over, a pair of fighting knives, a second pistol, and two spare magazines of ammunition lay on the coffee table.

Gwynn unloaded the pistol. "Muscle is heavy, but hardware is even heavier."

After double-checking the bindings she tied, Anya moved quickly toward the kitchen. She returned with a pitcher of water, and Gwynn said, "Are we going to waterboard her?"

Anya's eyes lit up. "Ooh, that would be fun."

Gwynn said, "I'm not sure this is the proper spot to use that particular technique."

Anya shrugged. "A girl can hope, no?"

Gwynn chuckled. "So, what's the water for?"

Instead of answering, Anya emptied the pitcher in one swift motion, drenching Mila's face and shocking her awake.

The bound Russian bucked herself from the couch and fought against the restraints like a wild animal. Gwynn drew her pistol again, but Anya stood relaxed and watched Mila waste her energy and endurance fighting against the inanimate cuffs and shackles.

Anya said, "Is okay. You will not need gun. She will soon be too tired to fight."

Holstering her pistol, Gwynn joined her partner in watching their prisoner's convulsive thrashing.

Two minutes into the Tasmanian devil routine, Anya stepped toward Mila. "This has gone on long enough." She planted a heel against Mila's injured knee, pinning her leg to the floor and flooding her brain with sheer agony.

Mila bellowed in rage and pain until Anya's blade landed flatly on her tongue, silencing her outburst.

Anya's tone was soft and low. "You are not so beautiful when you act like animal."

Mila bucked and growled in piercing Russian, and Anya rolled the blade from the flat side to the honed edge. "We will have conversation in English, or I will turn you into reptile with forked tongue."

Gwynn watched in wordless fascination as Mila's eyes filled with temporary resignation rather than the fear that most people would experience in such a moment.

Anya eased the pressure of the razor-sharp tool. "How old are you?"

Mila stared up in confusion. "How old?"

"Yes. How old are you?"

"I am twenty-four. Why do you care?"

Anya smiled down at the woman as if staring into a mirror. "I was prettier, stronger, and faster when I was twenty-four. And from this position, it appears all of these things are still true, even now."

Mila's breath came hard and fast as her body tried to recover from the energy she spent during her voluntary seizure. Between powerful inhalations, she hissed, "Little child could kill me when I am tied up. If you are truly this legendary Anastasia Burinkova, you will fight me like real warrior instead of coward."

Anya wiped the saliva and drops of blood from her knife. "You are not important enough for me to waste time fighting with you. You will take me to Ilya Gorshkov, or you will die."

Spitting and jerking against her restraints again, Mila said, "You are coward."

Anya wiped the spittle and blood from her face. "You taste like fear and inexperience."

"Cut me loose, and I will show you how fear tastes."

Anya said, "Perhaps I will cut you loose if you survive interrogation."

"What do you want to know? You obviously know who sent me, and you have figured out that I am advanced evolution of what you were before you grew old."

Anya let the sting of Mila's verbal assault wash off her back. "I want to know where I can find Ilya Gorshkov and Oleg Lepin."

Mila smiled. "You have built for me trap. I will die no matter which path I choose. If I give to you information on these powerful men, you might let me live, but they will not. If I do not give information, you will kill me. Is better to die while protecting powerful men, so is now up to you. You can kill me while I am bound, and this will make you coward and murderer, or you can free me and fight with honor."

Anya relieved the pressure she was holding against Mila's knee. "You know nothing of honor. Is foreign word for you, and you are making terrible decision."

"There is no decision for me. I will die to protect my comrades and my country. I am giving you opportunity to fight to death instead of committing cold, cowardly murder of bound prisoner."

Anya studied the angular features of her adversary's face. "Do you have someone to love?"

"What are you talking about, old coward?"

Anya smiled. "You cannot hurt me with your words, little girl."

A demon's smile traced its way across Mila's face. "Since you asked about loving someone, is now my turn. How does it feel to know Chase Fulton, man you love, chose another woman . . . *Amerikanka*?"

27

Shpiony i Operatory
(Spies and Operators)

Anya raised her knife high above her head as fury overcame her, but before she could send the blade through Mila Vinogradova's flesh, Gwynn leapt toward her elevated arm. "No, Anya! Don't!"

The only native-born American in the room hooked Anya's arm at the elbow and tackled her against the sofa. "We need her alive until we know where Gorshkov is."

"Of course you are correct," Anya said, "but I will make her pay for saying such things."

Gwynn squeezed her partner's arm. "Don't let her get under your skin."

Anya pulled away and grabbed Mila by her belt and hair. With a groan, she hefted the bound woman from the floor and deposited her back onto the couch. She grabbed Mila's face with one hand and glared directly into her eyes. "You will not speak of Chase. If it happens again, I will do to you things you are too naïve to comprehend."

Mila glared back. "I expected more. They warned me of the mythical Anastasia Burinkova, but I have been only disappointed."

Anya tugged on the shackles. "I am sorry to disappoint you. I will make it better for you." She rolled Mila onto her side and pulled a second set of cuffs from her pocket. The chains rattled as Anya cuffed the ankle chain to the wrist cuffs. The unnatural position drew out a groan from Mila as her spine arched backward and she jerked for a breath. "I am going to make things very uncomfortable for you for a very long time. You should tell to me now where I can find Ilya Gorshkov and Oleg Lepin. This way, you will not have to endure prolonged torture."

"Nothing you can do to me would be worse than what Gorshkov would do to me."

Stepping between Anya and Mila, Gwynn seized the opening that Anya likely missed. "There's only one possible outcome in this scenario that lets you live."

Mila said, "Yes, I know this. I will only survive if I escape and kill both of you."

Gwynn made a show of examining Mila's restraints. "Yeah, I don't think that's a possibility. I was thinking more about a deal."

"A deal?" Mila asked. "What are you talking about?"

"Look, you've obviously lost. We have you, and you have no realistic possibility of escaping. We did exactly the same thing with Anya."

Mila tilted her head as Gwynn continued.

"She was busted. We had her dead cold on multiple murders, and she was headed for death row until we intervened with an offer."

"What is this offer?"

Gwynn waggled a finger. "I think you mean, what *was* this offer? For Anya, the offer was a life sentence or come to work for my agency."

Mila huffed. "You are recruiting spy."

"No," Gwynn said. "I'm recruiting an operator."

The prisoner looked to Anya as if asking for help, but the icy Russian stare was all she got in return.

"What kind of operator?"

Gwynn pointed toward Anya. "That kind."

Anya anticipated Gwynn's direction and said, "You were our target all this time. Like you say, I am becoming old, so is time for replacement. This replacement is you."

Mila grimaced. "You are asking me to become traitor—to desert my country and my comrades."

Gwynn shook her head. "No, we're asking you to work with us to make this country safer."

Mila laughed. "Why would I care if your miserable country is safe or not?"

Anya rejoined the discussion. "Because America is one of last places on Earth where a person can be free."

Mila continued laughing. "Freedom. This is funny. You are not free. You are puppet for American police."

Anya smiled, stood, and said, "Watch this." She walked to the door, opened it, and stepped outside the room. A few seconds later, she returned. "That is freedom. Now, you try."

Mila huffed. "Just because I am not capable of walking to door while wearing chains does not mean I am not free."

Anya said, "You are correct. You are not free because I could remove chains, but you would still be shackled by Russian Mafia. You could not walk away and survive. I can go where I choose, whenever I want. This is freedom, and we can make sure you have it, too."

"Are you telling to me that you will not kill me if I work for you?"

Gwynn said, "Not only will we not kill you, but we'll even pay you, give you citizenship, and protect you."

The prisoner's laughter returned. "You will protect me? This is ridiculous. Who is protecting Anastasia from me?"

Gwynn swept her eyes over Mila's bound body. "From the looks of things, that would be me. She's alive and uninjured, and the assassin trying to kill her is wearing a beautiful assortment of Smith & Wesson bracelets and anklets. From my perspective, we're winning."

"You do not have authority to make deal such as this."

Gwynn pulled her phone from her pocket. "Did you notice how quickly the Chicago PD released us?"

Mila didn't respond, so Gwynn continued. "We were out of there in minutes. That's the kind of authority I have. That's not all, though. I've got the U.S. Attorney General on speed dial. I can get her on speaker if you'd like."

"And you will give to me citizenship and name?"

Gwynn waggled her phone. "I've got the undersecretary of state on here, too. You can be an American girl by tomorrow morning, and we'll call you Betsy Ross. It just takes one phone call."

"How do I know you are not bluffing?"

"You don't, but I encourage you to consider the alternatives." Gwynn crossed her arms. "Which option seems just a little better than the others?"

"And Anastasia can walk away anytime?"

"Now that she caught you, we don't need her anymore. She can move to Moscow if she wants. We don't care."

Mila swallowed hard. "What do you want from me?"

Gwynn leaned in close and whispered, "We want you to tell us where we can find Ilya Gorshkov and Oleg Lepin. When you do that, we'll turn you over to the U.S. Marshals, who will protect you while you're being processed."

Mila said, "You said they will protect me. Does this mean I will be inside prison?"

"No, not at all. The Marshals Service is a little more civilized than that. You'll be comfortable and safe."

"But I will not be free?"

Gwynn shook her head. "Not until we verify your information on Gorshkov and Lepin. If you told us the truth, we'll start the conversation about your role in service to your new country."

"Call the marshals."

Gwynn tried to hide her disbelief by turning away and dialing the number for the Northern District of Illinois field office. While the line rang, she walked away, putting as much distance between herself and Mila as possible. Having the Russian assassin overhear the conversation Gwynn was about to have wasn't in their best interest.

Anya recognized the ploy and sprang into action. As if extending a Russian olive branch, she spoke in their native language. "Tell me where we will find Gorshkov and Lepin."

Mila swallowed the stinging bile in her throat. "I do not know address, but house is at end of street named Westminster in Lake Forest. This is where you will find Gorshkov, Lepin, and the dwarf, Nikita Obrosov."

Anya suddenly wished she would've studied the geography of Chicago. "Where is Lake Forest?"

Mila said, "It is suburb of Chicago to north of city."

Anya glanced down the hall and spoke quietly. "You are making excellent decision. You will be safe, and you will be free if you are telling truth. On other hand, if you are lying, there is no one who can protect you from me."

Gwynn reappeared. "Marshals are on their way, so let's have it. Where can we find them?"

Mila pointed her chin toward Anya. "I already told her. You will find these men at home at end of Westminster. Is maybe Street or Avenue . . . I do not remember. But it is in Lake Forest suburb. Home is at west end of street with very good security."

"You better hope you're telling the truth," Gwynn said.

Mila sighed. "I do not have another choice."

"You're right about that. Now, relax. I'm going to disconnect the hogtie. If you do anything stupid, you'll never get to meet the nice deputy marshals who are coming to pick you up."

Mila remained motionless as Gwynn removed the final binding Anya had applied— a chain between the shackles and handcuffs—leaving the prisoner looking more like a scorpion than the Russian honeytrap she was trained to be.

Anya snapped her fingers to focus their still-bound guest. "Tell to me about security at house."

As if trying to stretch away a cramp, Mila twisted her hips. "There will be men with guns at doors and many cameras. There is also security fence and gate. They have dogs, but I do not know what kind. Maybe German shepherds or Malinois."

Anya leaned to within inches of Mila's face. "You have no idea how badly I hope you are lying. I am now peaceful American, but I was first a deadly Russian spear with lust for blood. Part of me is still spear."

Sooner than expected, a knock came at the door, and Anya stepped into the foyer and peered through the peephole that had grown to the diameter of a 9mm Russian Makarov bullet. "Show to me identification."

A cred-pack appeared outside the hole with FBI embossed on the exterior, and Anya paused. Instead of inviting them in immediately, she pulled open the door and stepped into the hallway. "You are not marshals."

One of the two men shook his head. "No, we're FBI. I'm Miller, and he's Jake Pierce. The marshals passed this one off to us. It happens a lot."

Anya extended a hand. "Give to me your credentials, and I will be right back."

They did as she asked, and she stepped back inside, where Mila was still bound and sitting on the couch with her back to Anya. The Russian held up the pair of FBI credentials, and Gwynn nodded her approval. Soon, the two agents were walking out with a prisoner they had no idea what to do with, but when the attorney general says take a Russian assassin into custody, the FBI jumps.

With the damaged door closed, Anya said, "I thought you called Marshals Service. Those men were FBI."

"I did, but a field agent on a leave of absence doesn't exactly make marshals leap from their seats to come to my rescue. I handed it off to the AG, and apparently, she dispatched the feebs."

"Is okay as long as you know what is happening. Where will they take her?"

Gwynn shrugged. "I suspect they'll stick her in an interrogation room and chain her to a table, but I don't know for sure. Do you think she's telling the truth about the house on Westminster?"

Anya thumbed her phone and stuck it to her ear. "We will know very soon. I am calling Skipper."

28

Koshach'i Vzlomshchiki
(Cat Burglars)

Skipper answered from inside her lair at Bonaventure Plantation. "Op center."

"Is Anya Burinkova, and we have exciting story to tell to you."

"You're never going to stop that, are you?"

"Stop what?" Anya asked.

"You don't have to tell me who you are when you call. I know it's you. If you can't stop it all together, at least cut it back to just your first name. You're the only Anya I've ever met."

Anya and Gwynn briefed the analyst on their exciting evening with Mila Vinogradova, the Chicago PD, the Marshals Service, and finally, the FBI.

When Anya finished the briefing, she said, "Now, we need to know everything about house on Westminster. You can do this for us, yes?"

"I don't know if I can tell you everything about the house, but I'm already working on it. It looks like the house is owned by a Delaware corporation and a couple of holding companies. It'll take a while to get down to the nitty gritty about who owns it, but whoever it is, they don't want it to be easy."

"You can do it, though, yes?"

"Of course I can do it. I'm in the building permits archives for Lake and Cook Counties now. Give me a minute." Skipper drummed her fingernails against the desk as her computer whirred its perpetual whine. Finally, she said, "Here we go. I've got a remodel two years ago, and wouldn't you know it? I have the floor plan."

Anya said, "Send it to—"

Skipper grunted. "You don't have to tell me to send you anything. Trust me. I'm really good at this."

With a ding, the floor plans for each level of the house arrived on their tablets.

Anya scrolled through several pages. "This is wonderful. On page E-nine, there is electrical schematic for security camera network."

"Oh, goody," Skipper said. "I'll have some fun with that and see what I can do to exploit a few of their weaknesses." Skipper's fingers flew across the keys, but her mind was still on the mysterious Russian assassin. "So, you just surrendered Mila to the FBI?"

"Yes, we had to give her to someone."

"I get that, but the FBI?"

Gwynn spoke up. "I called the Marshals, and they routed it through the AG's office in DC. Somehow, the babysitting fell to the feebs. I don't love it, either, but beggars can't be choosers."

"We could've had a team there in a couple of hours. Don't forget . . . we're family."

"Thank you for this," Anya said. "But Gwynn played federal agent card, so we needed to keep up our story by using other federal agency."

"I get it," Skipper said. "Just don't forget that our assets are yours."

"Are you inside camera network yet?"

Skipper said, "Almost. It's a pretty good system. I can get into most networks in a few seconds, but this one's a little stubborn."

A few seconds later, she said, "I'm in, and it's a sexy setup. They've got a hundred and four cameras, twenty-six motion detectors, and it looks like everything is infrared. Don't worry about the motion sensors. I'll take care of those, but I don't think I can kill all the cameras. With triple and quadruple redundancy on most of the system, they're serious about their security. When do you plan to hit the house, and how many shooters do you need?"

Anya didn't hesitate. "We plan to hit house as soon as you know everything we can know about it. Sooner is much better than later."

"Oh, you're talking about right now."

"Yes, now."

"In that case, I can't get any shooters there in time to help, but if you'll hold off a few hours, I can put a couple tons of hunky men with guns and knives at your disposal."

"We cannot wait. We must go tonight. We have to claim Mila back from FBI before morning. If we leave her with them longer than that, they will do something to scour the pooch."

"Scour the pooch?" Skipper asked. "Is that what you said?"

"Yes, this is American saying."

Skipper chuckled. "It's *screw* the pooch. You know, as in . . . never mind. Give me five more minutes on the house, and I'll call you back."

The line went dead, and Gwynn said, "We're hitting them tonight, huh?"

Anya nodded. "We cannot wait. Mila was required to check in with someone on regular intervals. She can no longer do this, so they will soon know she is missing if they do not know already."

Gwynn grimaced. "That's makes sense. How do you plan to do it?"

"We will wait until Skipper has more information in two or three minutes, but hitting from west looks best. There is large open field with some trees."

Gwynn studied the aerial photos. "The front is definitely out. There's only one way in and out of the front of that place, and there's a ton of neighbors."

The phone vibrated, and Skipper's voice resounded through the speaker. "You're striking from the west, right?"

"We were just discussing this," Anya said. "And yes, this is only reasonable direction."

Skipper said, "I agree. I'm sending you recent aerials from about a week ago. There's good access and plenty of secluded parking on the west side. I'd stage a car out front, just in case, but that's up to you."

Anya asked, "How about cameras?"

"I can manage the motion detectors and one sector of cameras at a time. You'll need to move on my direction as you approach. If you make one step into a sector I don't control, you're busted."

"We have sat-coms, so we can do that. Who is notified if intruder is detected at house?"

Skipper said, "Funny you should ask. I was just digging up that information. C-One is an internal line at the house. C-Two is to a monitoring service in Montreal."

"Neither of calls goes to police?"

"No, apparently not."

Anya smiled. "This is very good for us. This means they believe they have manpower and skill to handle intruder without calling police, but we are going to prove to them they are wrong."

Gwynn said, "Yeah, we're not exactly cat burglars."

"Don't get overconfident yet. We've got a long way to go. How long will it take you to get into position?"

Anya checked her watch and consulted the map. "We can be ready to enter property from west side in less than sixty minutes."

"Good," Skipper said. "Hit your mark and tell me when you're in position. In the meantime, I'll keep digging and meddling, and I'll have a better briefing for you then."

Anya pocketed the phone. "We must eat. We will need calories."

Gwynn motioned toward the kitchen counter. "I put out a bunch of protein bars."

They ate and hydrated as they drove toward Lake Forest. It took forty minutes to arrive at the western expanse of the Westminster property and another ten to make two recon passes before pulling beneath a low growth of maple trees.

"This should be good place for hiding car, yes?"

Gwynn checked the perimeter. "It's as good as any. Let's check in with the op center."

Skipper answered without preamble. "They've got dogs."

Anya said, "Yes, we know, but is okay. Dogs love me."

"I've got some more not-so-great news. It appears they've got a satellite feed."

"What kind of satellite?" Gwynn asked.

Skipper said, "The Russian kind. I couldn't verify every feed, but they've definitely got some eyes in the sky. The current U.S. satellites show some cloud cover over Chicago. How does it look from there?"

Gwynn looked up. "We've got about eighty percent sky coverage, so that helps."

"Yes, it does," Skipper said. "Let's keep our fingers crossed for even more clouds as the night progresses."

Anya eyed Gwynn and offered a thumbs-up. Her partner returned the gesture, so she said, "We are ready to hit it. Are you ready?"

Skipper said, "Stand fast. There's movement at the front of the house."

"What is it?" Anya asked. "You have control of cameras, yes?"

"Yeah, I've got the camera. Hang on. It's somebody in a black sedan. They pulled through the main gate and beneath the portico."

"Who is it?" Gwynn asked.

Skipper groaned. "I can't tell. I'm on a perimeter camera and can't get the portico camera to come up. I saw at least two sets of feet get out of the car, but I've got nothing more than that."

Anya asked, "When they came through gate, did it look routine?"

"Oh, yeah. They drove right through. They're a definite known entity."

Anya considered the information. "It was probably late dinner run, but it does not matter who it is. Our mission has not changed. We are moving."

As they stepped from the vehicle, both women activated their satellite communication devices and linked them to the bone conduction audio transceivers glued to their mandibles.

"Op center, Alpha One," Anya said softly.

"Ops has you loud and clear. How me?"

Gwynn answered, "Alpha Two has all stations loud and clear."

"Alpha One has same. Moving to east and centered directly behind house."

Skipper said, "I've got both of you on the GPS. Move ahead at will, but don't stray more than ten feet left or right of a direct line to the back center of the house."

Anya conducted a tactile, silent inventory of her gear. With the tips of her fingers, she touched the handles of both knives strapped inside her thighs, then she let her fingers trace the butt of the Glock as her left hand danced across the four spare magazines of 9mm. A Taser rested just behind her pistol, and four pairs of flex-cuffs waited at the center of her back. Gwynn conducted the same inventory with the addition of a few tools, and she gave Anya a nod.

They moved with Gwynn one step behind and beside the Russian. The pace was moderate and deliberate, and they paused every thirty seconds to listen and look for dogs.

"You're coming up to a fence that appears to be chain-link or some variant. It's electric."

Anya said, "I see fence. Is not problem as long as there is no seismograph."

Skipper said, "I didn't see anything like that on any of the schematics."

Anya laid a hand on Gwynn's shoulder and whispered, "There is fence. We will cross using tree. You are okay with this, yes?"

Gwynn nodded and watched Anya start her slow, cautious ascent.

After inching her way across a long, thick limb, Anya sprang from the tree and landed silently on the other side of the fence like a graceful cat.

She froze in place until Skipper said, "No reaction from inside."

A few seconds later, Gwynn traced her partner's steps and landed beside her.

Skipper repeated, "No reaction."

They continued their measured progress toward the house until Skipper yelled, "Go to ground!"

Both Gwynn and Anya landed facedown an instant later and lay motionless, awaiting further direction.

Skipper finally said, "Sorry about that. They have the cameras on a frequency-hopping protocol that makes me lose control of the sector for a few seconds every twenty minutes or so."

"Are we okay to move now?" Anya asked.

"Proceed at will. I've got the cams."

They spent fifteen minutes crossing the expanse of property behind the target house until figures came into full focus at the rear of the home.

Anya whispered, "I have three men on left and one on right. Three are smoking."

"I've got 'em," Gwynn said.

Anya examined the layout of chairs and statuary. "We need to move to south side and approach man who is single."

Skipper said, "Give me a few seconds to work out the transition between sectors, but start moving south."

They moved in silence, alternating between watching the ground at their feet and the guards at the rear of the house.

"Hold position," Skipper said, and they halted. "When I give the word, take four fast strides forward and freeze. Got it?"

"Got it."

"Here we go. In three . . . two . . . one . . . move."

They took the four prescribed steps and turned to pillars.

"And . . . we're good to the south," Skipper said.

Every step was quieter than the previous stride, every breath was measured, and every sound was magnified a thousand times. The mumbled conversation from the smokers drifted on the night air—their Russian vulgarity and raucous laughter serving as a perfect shield for the advance.

They finally reached the corner of the house, and Anya spoke in Russian. "You have lighter, yes?"

The man answered in Russian. "Who is there?" Then he made the terrible and predictable decision to step toward the voice of the woman. He never saw her, but he felt her arms lace around his head and neck until the lights went out.

When Anya laid her unconscious victim on his side in hopes of preventing him from snoring, the heavy, deep barks of at least two dogs echoed from the front of the house.

Anya grabbed Gwynn's wrist. "Stay on me. We are going in."

The thunder of the dogs' paws striking the ground sounded like racehorses rounding the final turn and stretching toward the finish line.

Anya's hand hit the first available doorknob. She cranked it until it spun half a turn, and the door opened inward. Inside the house, they pressed themselves against the back wall and locked the door behind them. The dogs' toenails on the stone patio clicked, but the barking ceased.

Skipper said, "I see that you're inside. I've still got your GPS locations, and there are no interior cameras currently recording."

Anya clicked her tongue against her teeth to acknowledge the information. Their eyes slowly adjusted to the dim light inside the house, and they slowly moved away from the wall and toward the interior of the home.

Anya led the way around a cased opening into what could only be described as a banquet hall. A massive dining table spread the length of the room with no less than thirty chairs. Other than the furnishings, the room was empty except for one small detail . . .

SVR assassin, Mila Zakharina Vinogradova, stood near the head of the table with her palms resting on the pommels of a pair of gleaming swords. She glared across the room at Anya. "Why did it take you so long to arrive?"

29

Krik Vsego Dikogo—Nevesta
(The Cry of Everything Wild)

Gwynn froze, and Anya took inventory of everything inside the room that could be used as a defense against Mila's swords. Chairbacks and a polished silver coffee tray were the only items that remotely resembled shields, but without a weapon of her own that could outdistance the swords, the coming fight would be a massacre.

Exactly as she'd been trained to do at the Federal Law Enforcement Training Center, Gwynn drew her Glock and trained the sights on the center of Mila's chest. "Drop the weapons, and step to your left. Do it now!"

Mila ignored Gwynn and smirked at Anya. "Put your little guard dog away and fight me like the legendary warrior you are supposed to be."

Mila raised both swords and extended them in front of her body with their gleaming tips resting on the conference table. She raised the blade in her right hand. "This one was my grandfather's. He was great colonel in Soviet Army." She rested the tip back on the table and raised the sword in her left hand. "This one belonged to one of the many men he killed. It is impossible to know which one, but I like to believe this person was American like you . . . traitor!"

She slid the sword the length of the table, and the steel rang out like a bell as it came to rest in front of Anya.

Without taking her eyes from Mila, Anya laid a hand over the slide of her partner's pistol and lowered the weapon. "Do not kill her unless she kills me first. If this happens, do not hesitate, or she will do same to you."

"This is crazy, Anya. You can't fight her with a sword. Let's take her into custody and finish this by the book."

Mila laughed. "There is no book for what you are doing, Amerikanka. I have FBI in palm of hand, and I have also diplomatic immunity from your foolish American laws. Now, put gun away while real fighters end this."

Gwynn turned to Anya, but the two pairs of Russian eyes in the room were solidly locked on each other. "You can't do this, Anya. You can't. It's ridiculous."

As if Gwynn were a million miles away, Anya lifted the sword in her left hand, felt the weight, and leapt onto the conference table.

A ghoulish grin overcame Mila, and she mirrored Anya's jump with the grace of a dancer.

The two advanced on each other with their swords slicing through the distance between them until the blades met for the first time, and a mighty clash of steel on steel echoed through the room.

Mila was faster than her opponent, but Anya was more powerful, meeting every flight of Mila's blade with a crushing defensive counterstrike. The SVR officer lunged forward with her sword outstretched like the lance of a mounted knight, but Anya sidestepped the attack and sent a crushing blow to the back of Mila's neck with the pommel of her sword.

Mila fell to her knees, and Anya pressed the tip of the sword to the center of her back. "You have made terrible decision. You cannot defeat me. Drop your sword, and I will allow you to live. Continue to fight, and I will spill your blood."

From her knees, Mila spun, sending the razor's edge of her sword racing through a massive arc toward Anya's knees. The assault would've ended the fight with Anya bleeding to death on the table had she not reacted with blinding speed. She struck Mila's blade, stopping it in midair before it could meet the flesh of her legs. She followed the strike with a powerful front kick to Mila's shoulder, sending her facedown on the table, but she didn't stay down. In an instant, Mila was back on her feet and swinging wildly while advancing ever closer to her foe.

Anya smacked the attacking blade several times until the two women came to rest hilt to hilt and face-to-face. "Tell me, comrade. Have you seen American movie called *Princess Bride*?"

Mila narrowed her eyes. "What are you talking about? What is this movie?"

Anya said, "I know something you do not know." She leapt backward, tossing her sword from one hand to the other. "I am not left-handed."

"It does not matter, traitor. You will still die, and I will play in your blood."

Gwynn watched in awe as the two Russians fought like enraged beasts. Blood from each of them found its way onto both swords, but neither fighter wilted.

The lawyer with a badge raised her pistol again as she circled the room, desperately trying to get the angle for a shot, but it wouldn't come. Anya and Mila were too fast and the battle too volatile for Mila to maintain any position long enough to become Gwynn's victim.

Blood and sweat poured from each warrior, leaving a liquid diagram of their battle on the surface of the table. The sounds of Mila and Anya drawing air into their lungs as quickly as their bodies could demand it overshadowed the crash of sword against sword, and fatigue clawed at the women like a vulturous demon from the boundless pits of Hell.

As the speed of the battle diminished, Mila delivered a long, slashing blow to Anya's left bicep. An agonizing roar split the air, and Mila's blade was drenched in blood. Anya fell to her knees with exhaustion, and Gwynn bounded forward, raising her pistol as she closed the distance between herself and the table.

Throwing her head back, Mila howled the cry of a Siberian wolf as she hoisted her sword, preparing to deliver the final, killing blow that would split Anya's torso in half.

As if she could hear the springs tightening inside of Gwynn's pistol, Mila turned to see the white knuckle of her enemy's trigger finger drawing reward and promising certain death. In mortal desperation, Mila raised her sword again, but this time, instead of falling on Anya's flesh and finishing her, she opened her hand and launched the sword directly toward the muzzle of Gwynn's Glock that would soon belch orange fire and release its missile into her skull, where it would mushroom and demolish her brain.

The booming report of the 9mm round shook the room, and the light above Mila's head exploded. Anya dropped her sword, clutched the gaping wound on her arm, and instantly looked up, expecting to see Gwynn's bullet tear through Mila's chest. Instead, what she saw unchained the Angel of Wrath—an entity that could not be contained.

The overhead light crashed onto the table. Mila remained on her feet, her arm outstretched toward Gwynn, and converted her sword into an airborne missile streaking toward its doomed target.

Anya locked her eyes on the shimmering sword, its honed steel streaked with her own blood. The nose of the blade tapered elegantly to a point, designed to puncture flesh and refuse the bind of steel against bone. Flying like an arrow from an archer's bow, the razor tip found its mark two inches below Special Agent Guinevere Davis's chin.

Anya watched in horror as the blade buried itself through Gwynn's throat.

Gwynn dropped her pistol, and both hands flew instinctively toward the weapon piercing her neck. Her grasp of the blade opened the flesh on her hands, and she staggered backward, unable to cry out in pain.

Before her partner and dearest friend could collapse to the floor, Anya was on her feet again with both hands gripping the only remaining sword in the fight. The cry of everything wild echoed inside of her head as she stepped forward and delivered a shallow, descending slash from Mila's shoulder, across her torso, and to her hip.

As the wounded Russian pawed at her chest with terror-filled eyes, Anya delivered a powerful side kick, launching Mila across the room, where she finally came to rest against the wall.

Vaulting from the table, Anya took a knee beside the woman who'd become more than a partner, more than merely a friend and coworker. She held Gwynn's face in her hands. "Friend Gwynn! No!"

The Russian girl, who longed for nothing more than to become the American woman who lay dying before her, stared through death's falling shroud and poured out her heart in a wordless flood of emotion.

Tears streamed down Gwynn's cheeks, and she silently mouthed, "I love you."

Anya withdrew the sword from Gwynn's throat and then turned to see a wounded beast holding a fighting knife in each hand. Anya's first swing severed Mila's right hand, just above her wrist. Her second blow opened a laceration on the Russian's bicep, mirroring the wound she wore. But the next assault wasn't delivered at the edge of any blade.

She twisted Mila's one remaining hand backward until the bones split and separated. "You killed best person in all of world, you communist bitch! Hell is calling for your soul, and Hell shall have it."

Driven by a demon's rage, she thrust the sword through Mila's throat, delivering the same fatal wound that stole the light from Gwynn's eyes.

Anya stepped backward and collapsed beside Gwynn. She took her partner's cold hands in hers and whispered, "I would die a million times to undo this . . . to bring you back. I swear to you across great divide between life and death that I will tear souls from men who did this and send them to Hell."

30

SLED SMERTI
(A WAKE OF DEATH)

As the rage inside her erupted and flowed like scorching lava down the slopes of a trembling volcano, Anya forced herself to slow her mind and focus on survival. The wound across her left arm was serious but not fatal if she cared for it quickly.

A tourniquet between the incision and her shoulder would slow the bleeding, but it would also render her left arm practically useless. She tore open every drawer and cabinet inside the conference room until she found a first aid kit. Two pouches of expired QuikClot lay tucked beneath the box's white plastic lid, and she emptied the contents into her wound. The powder absorbed the blood and immediately began the clotting process. Six four-by-four gauze pads came next, with every inch of tape she could wind around her bicep.

Anya's brain refused to acknowledge the physical pain in the shadow of the agony of losing Gwynn. As her heart broke, and tears driven by emptiness and fury trailed down her face, she continued the self-assessment for injuries that required treatment before continuing her pilgrimage to the mountaintop of the Bratva that lay waiting for her somewhere deep inside the house.

With treatment complete, Anya knelt beside Gwynn and gently brushed the hair back from her fallen friend's face. "I will be back for you. I will not leave you here. My heart has never known pain like this, my friend . . . my sister. I will love you forever."

After downing two bottles of water she pulled from a small refrigerator, she press-checked her pistol, felt for the pair of knives she was never without, and stepped through the door at the far end of the room.

A pair of men with rifles at the low-ready position stood only feet beyond the door, but their mission to investigate the gunfire would never happen. The Russian raised her pistol and put a pair of rounds through each of their faces. Almost before their bodies hit the floor, she relieved one man of his rifle and a pair of magazines. The second man was smaller than the first, so she stripped his body armor from his torso and slid it over her head. It wouldn't stop a rifle round, but the protection would at least diminish the effects of pistol fire and a hand-to-hand assault.

Commotion rose down a corridor to her left, and she cycled the bolt on her borrowed AK-47 to ensure a round inside the chamber was waiting to take flight and deliver its lethal strike to anyone foolish enough to step in front of her.

Several feet in front of her, a door opened, and Anya stood in disbelief at the scene. A dwarf stepped around the door and stared, his mouth agape, stunned by the angel clad for battle.

She raised the rifle to her shoulder and centered the man's head above the front sight. "What is your name?"

He stood motionless as if he hadn't heard the question, so she repeated it in angry Russian. "*Kak vas zovut?*"

"Nikita Obrosov," the man said as he desperately scanned the environment for an escape route. Finding none, he snapped his fingers incessantly and pleaded in Russian. "Please do not kill me. I can give you whatever you want. I can make you wealthy. Anything . . . I will give you anything. Just name it."

Anya took four determined steps toward the tiny, trembling man and pressed the muzzle of Mikhail Timofeyevich Kalashnikov's greatest creation to his forehead. She hissed barely above a soul-stirring whisper. "Then give to me Gwynn's life."

His eyes locked on hers as something beyond terror took him. "*Pozhaluysta.*"

"You may plead all you wish, *karlik*, but you will never leave this house alive. Where are Ilya Gorshkov and Oleg Lepin?"

Nikita's lips quivered as Anya pressed the muzzle deeper into his flesh. "Tell me where they are, and you will live a little longer."

In quaking Russian, the dwarf said, "I do not know."

"Are they inside this house?"

"They were, but I do not know now. I do not know. Please—"

Anya shoved him away with the muzzle, and as he staggered backward, she said, "Run, little man."

Nikita swallowed hard, spun on a heel, and took the final step of his life. Before his first stride could strike the ground, Anya let the rifle fall against her body. She drew the smaller of her two knives and pulled the honed edge across Nikita Obrosov's throat. Without a sound, he fell where he stood, and she stepped across his corpse.

Another man appeared in Anya's vision down the corridor, and he raised his pistol. Without time to reshoulder her rifle, Anya used the only tool immediately at hand and launched her knife with unmatched speed. The blade pierced the gunman's right eye, and his pistol dropped to the floor at his feet.

As he bellowed and grabbed his face, Anya closed the distance, withdrew the knife from his eye, and buried it to the hilt in the man's abdomen. The injury to his brain through his eye would ultimately drain the life from his body, but her ravenous blade in his gut would punish him for choosing the wrong side.

Unable to distinguish the blood of her enemies from Gwynn's and her own, Anya wore the crimson as a badge of vengeance as she stepped over the second body she felled in the previous seconds.

Continuing deeper into the house, she didn't have to wait long for another target of opportunity. Two men rounded a corner only inches in front of her, and they leapt backward, surprised by her presence. They raised their rifles as they retreated, but Anya grabbed the barrel of the weapon directly in front of her and shoved the barrel toward the second man. With a punishing knee strike to the man's groin, she pressed his trigger simultaneously, and three full-auto rounds left his rifle and disintegrated his partner's skull.

Anya sliced the nylon sling of the man's rifle and yanked the weapon from his grip. She raised the AK above her head and sent the butt crashing down against the man's collarbone. The sounds of his breaking bone and cry of blinding pain were like carnival music to the Avenging Angel. A second butt stroke to the man's chin sent him crashing to the floor with Anya kneeling on his chest.

Kneeling on his chest, Anya said in calm, measured Russian, "Tell me where I can find Ilya Gorshkov and Oleg Lepin, and I will let you live."

Instead of an answer, the man spat at her, his defiance paving the road to his death. Never giving him time to inhale after the spittle left his lips, she sliced his throat and left him to die in an ever-expanding pool of his blood.

A voice sounded inside Anya's head, and she shook it off as if it were nothing more than a hallucination.

"Anya, what's going on? What's happening? Talk to me."

Skipper's voice grew more insistent with each word until the Russian realized who was speaking to her.

"Gwynn is dead. I killed Mila, Nikita the dwarf, and more men, but I do not remember how many."

"Are you hurt?"

"If I am, it does not matter. I will pay any price to cut off the heads of the men who started this."

"Listen to me, Anya. You have to slow down. You can't survive if you continue like this."

"I will stay alive long enough to make Gorshkov and Lepin pay."

"Get out of there, Anya. I'm calling the FBI. I can have the Hostage Rescue Team there in minutes."

"This is stupid waste of time. FBI is compromised. Mila escaped them and came here to kill us."

"You can't be serious. You think the FBI is working with the Russian Mafia?"

"I do not think this. I know this. If you call them, they will kill me first. I need to know where Gorshkov and Lepin are. This house is enormous, and armed guards are everywhere."

Skipper set aside her disbelief. "Okay. I've finally got control of the interior cameras. If Lepin and Gorshkov are in the house, I can find them, but it's going to take some time."

Anya sidestepped across the corridor and peered around the corner toward a staircase leading to the second floor. "I am at bottom of stairs. Tell to me where to go."

"They're not on the ground floor," Skipper said. "If they're in the house, they're upstairs. I'm still hunting."

Anya raised the rifle in front of her and raced up the staircase. One man appeared at the top of the stairs, and she ordered, "Freeze!"

The man did the opposite, dropping whatever he had in his hands and turning to run, but Anya put a 7.62mm round through the back of his knee. He crumpled to the floor and bellowed in pain.

She silenced the roaring man by driving the muzzle of her rifle into his mouth. "You will tell to me where I can find Gorshkov and Lepin, or you will die."

The man tried to back away from the rifle barrel in his throat, but he couldn't move.

Releasing just enough pressure, Anya allowed the man to speak.

He said, "They are in the library, but—"

With two presses of the trigger, she left the man's body without a soul.

"Skipper, where is library?"

"Okay, I've got most of the upstairs cameras. The library is at the end of the long hallway on the left. It has double doors. Do you see it?"

The Russian moved silently down the hall until she stood in front of the ornately carved wooden doors. "Yes, I am at doors now. How many are inside?"

"Three. Lepin is against the left wall, Gorshkov will be straight ahead, and the third man is near the left-hand door."

"Are they armed?"

Skipper said, "I can't tell if Gorshkov and Lepin have weapons, but the man by the door has a rifle."

Anya gripped the doorknob, but it wouldn't turn, so she squeezed and pressed against the weight of the heavy door. Nothing budged.

"Anya, get down!"

She dived left just as two dozen full-auto Kalashnikov rounds turned the library doors into kindling. Bounding back to her feet, she grabbed the rifle barrel as it protruded through the opening where the doors had been seconds before. The barrel's steel scalded her hands as she yanked the weapon and its owner through the doorway.

With a pair of butt strokes where he gripped his weapon, she broke both of the man's hands, and the rifle fell to the ground. Anya then delivered an uppercut with precisely measured force, leaving him practically unconscious but still on his feet. Spinning him around, she laced her wounded arm beneath his chin and used him as a human shield.

Anya forced the man back into the library, where Ilya Gorshkov and Oleg Lepin stood with fury of their own scorching the distance between them. Seeing neither man holding a weapon, Anya released her barely conscious shield and delivered two rifle rounds through the back of his head.

With a wake of death behind her, Anya Burinkova finally stood face-to-face with the two men she'd dreamed of tearing into unrecognizable remains from the moment she first heard their names.

Skipper's voice filled Anya's head again. "Uh, we've got a problem."

"There is no problem," Anya said, leaving Gorshkov and Lepin questioning who she was talking to.

Lepin spoke in gravely Russian. "We definitely have a problem, and that problem is you."

Skipper kept talking, but Anya wasn't listening. She slipped the rifle's sling over her head and let the killing machine drop to the ground, then she let her pistol join the pile of discarded weaponry. Finally, she pulled the Velcro from the body armor she'd taken earlier and let it slip from her shoulders. Slowly . . . deliberately . . . she moved across the room toward Lepin. "You are next to die, and it will be quick."

He swallowed hard and took a step backward. "I don't think you understand. You have taken this too far."

"No," Anya growled. "You are the ones who have taken this too far. You murdered Gwynn, and for this, you will pay with your very souls."

Gorshkov laughed. "Oh, how quickly you turned your back on your country and embraced the cowardly West."

His accent wasn't as harsh as she expected, and his English was good, but she would make him beg in the first language his mother taught him before erasing him from this world.

Anya growled, "My country is United States of America. I did not turn back on Russia. Russia turned its back on me."

Ilya checked his watch and smiled. "It is almost finished, and if you survive, you will spend the rest of your life in a prison of the country you chose."

"No one is coming to save you," Anya said. "You will die here in this room today, and I will gut both of you like miserable pigs."

"Anya, listen to me," Skipper yelled. "There's a SWAT team headed up the stairs. I didn't call them, and I don't know who they are."

She glanced back in an involuntary reaction to Skipper's announcement, but she didn't waste time waiting for the men with guns and shields who were apparently only steps away.

As she drew a fighting knife in each hand, the wound in her left arm screamed in protest. In an instant, her boot landed in the center of Oleg Lepin's chest, launching him backward against a bookcase.

She turned the longer of the two blades toward Ilya Gorshkov. "If you move, I swear to you, it will be the final step of your life."

Without waiting for a response from Gorshkov, she sank the blade into Leptin's gut. Groaning and gasping, he stayed on his feet, but with a mighty cosmic roar, Anya leaned into him and drew the blade upward, lodging it against the bone and cartilage where his ribs met his sternum.

The blade she chose for the task was designed and forged precisely to operate in that exact location, and its length and shape made it the perfect killing instrument from that position and angle. When the tip met the bottom of Lepin's heart, he fell against her with his life's blood gushing from his demolished body.

Gorshkov threw up both hands. "Wait! Don't do this!"

She spun like a tightly wound ballerina inside a jewelry box, but instead of the tinkling song that should've accompanied the dance, the only music in the room was the thunderous, fear-filled pounding of Ilya Gorshkov's heart beating against his chest.

Out of the spin, she threw a punishing kick to the front of Gorshkov's knee, reducing him to a terrified lump of flesh at her feet.

"Please do not do this. Just wait. Please!"

She took a knee in front of the man and pressed the bloody tip of her knife to his throat. "Russian. You will speak only in Russian. You have lost privilege of speaking language of free men."

In his native language, Gorshkov continued pleading. "If you let me live, I will call off the men who are coming for you."

Anya shook her head. "I do not fear these men. They mean nothing to me. I am alive for only one purpose . . . to kill you."

He continued begging in a desperate attempt to delay the inevitable—just long enough for the SWAT team to pour through the door of the library before Anya could stop his heart.

"Freeze! Drop the weapon and show me your hands. Do it now!"

Anya ignored the command, applying pressure against the blade poised at Gorshkov's Adam's apple until the steel pierced his skin and sank through the soft tissue of his neck, coming to rest between two vertebrae. His mouth opened, and he gurgled as Anya delivered the righteous reward for the life he had lived.

"Get your hands up, now!"

Still ignoring the barked orders, Anya raised her arm and threw a crushing elbow strike to the pommel of her knife, forcing the blade through Gorshkov's spine and severing his brain's only connection to what remained of his mortal body.

He collapsed beneath her, and she raised both hands as she slowly spun on a knee to face the wrath of the uniformed men at the door.

As her vision cleared, she saw six men in tactical gear, rifles shouldered and helmets strapped tightly to their heads. "It is done, and I am no longer threat."

Retired Supervisory Special Agent Ray White stepped through the phalanx of men making up the DOJ's Tactical Operations Team and knelt beside her. "You'll always be a threat, Anya."

He stared at the unimaginable pain in two of the most beautiful blue eyes he—or anyone—had ever seen. "I know about Davis, and I'm sorry. It never should've come to this. Somebody in the AG's office figured out what was going on in the FBI field office here in Chicago, and the boss dispatched us. Well, not us exactly. Just them. But I couldn't resist tagging along."

Anya looked up into his heavy eyes and wilted in exhaustion and agony too great to express in mere words. And the Avenging Angel wept.

Author's Note

I sincerely hope you enjoyed the Avenging Angel – Seven Deadly Sins series. I had a magnificent time creating these stories for you. This is the first series I've ever ended, so I don't know exactly how I'm supposed to feel about it. Every time I finish a manuscript, it's a bittersweet moment for me, and I believe most authors feel the same. I become so caught up in each story that it almost feels as if I'm living it with the characters, and when the story ends, I miss my imaginary friends. Secretly and selfishly, I hope you miss them too when you close a book after the last page.

These characters are quite real to me, and most of them are based on someone I've known or worked alongside in my life. It's an honor for me to bring these characters to life on the pages of my stories, and I'll always put them—the unsung heroes—first. Giving thanks for the brave men and women who do the jobs the rest of us cannot, or will not do, is part of my daily routine, and I hope you'll make it part of yours. We get to sleep in peace every night, warm and dry, while warriors lie in the scalding desert sand, or the frozen, muddy battlefields all over the Earth, paying the price for liberty, freedom, and the comforts of life here in the greatest nation on the planet. Pray for them. Think about them. And when opportunity presents itself, thank them for their sacrifice.

It's now time for confession. Forgive me, for I have lied, but it's kind of my job. I create fictional stories about fictional characters doing fictional things all over the world. This series was no exception, and I'll do my best to come clean about all the lies I told.

Let's start with the good ol' U.S. Department of Justice. The law enforcement agency I created for this series does not exist. The whole organization is completely fictional, and here's why: I don't know enough about any federal law enforcement agency to write stories set inside of the real ones, so I created my own. Likewise, the tactical operations team in the final scene is, just like the agency, completely made up.

Supervisory Special Agent Ray White is purely fictional, although I've known a great many bureaucrats in federal service with his attitude, level of frustration, and dedication to doing what's right, even when it's not exactly in line with laws and regulations. The world would be a better place if there were a few thousand more just like him. In the early days of creating this series, I thought a budding romance between Ray and Anya might come together, but now that we've reached the end, I'm glad it didn't happen. The stories are better without that element woven into them.

Just like Ray White, Special Agent Johnathon "Johnny Mac" McIntyre is also an amalgamation of overly ambitious, self-promoting egomaniacs in federal service. I've known too many of them to count. Here's a list of some of their real names . . .

Okay, that was just a teaser. I won't divulge their names because they would enjoy the attention too much, and I'm not willing to give them that pleasure.

Ah, the lovely Special Agent Guinevere Davis is next. The inspiration for her character came from a combination of some of the most capable and highly qualified women I was fortunate to work with through my years as a fed. Playing on her desire to be what Anya was, against Anya's desire to become the all-American girl, was one of my favorite parts of this series. I love people who are open-minded and willing to learn from people around them. Both Anya and Gwynn listened and learned well from each other, and I've always thought of them a bit like Xena and Gabrielle from the old television show. Perhaps the term Avenging Angel is interchangeable with Warrior Princess. At least that's how I imagine them.

I would now like to apologize for killing Gwynn. I'm writing this on a Thursday, after having spent most of the previous night tossing and turning, while trying to come up with a way to keep her alive and still incite Anya to maniacal rage. Ultimately, I chose to trust the story as it came to me. As you probably already know, I never write from an outline or plan of any kind. I simply sit down every day and write what falls out of my head. I thought Gwynn might not survive this final installment in the series, but I didn't know for sure. When it happened, it broke my heart, but it served a critical role in the story, pushing Anya over the edge and unleashing the wrath she's held inside herself most of her life.

I do have one request concerning Gwynn's death. If you leave a review or comment on Facebook, please don't mention Gwynn's death. That would be a pretty nasty spoiler, and I'd really like for future readers to experience the emotion of that scene without knowing that it's going to happen. Thank you in advance.

Let's touch on the attorney general for a moment. If you've read anything I've ever written, you know I'm a huge fan of extremely competent, powerful female characters. This also holds true for me in real life. It has become politically unacceptable to claim that men and women are different, but I'm not afraid to take that stand. I truly believe we were created differently to fulfill wildly different roles. Men are crybabies. I should know. I'm one of them. If I had to push a nine-pound baby through any orifice of my body, I couldn't survive it. I've been known to pull a muscle just by sneezing, so I'll never have the strength women possess. Again, I've never believed men and women are equal. That's a horrible insult to women. They will always be superior to us men, and they should never allow themselves to be reduced to equality with hairy, stinky men who scratch themselves and spit in public. I truly love writing powerful female characters. If you read my Chase Fulton Novels, you know how lost the team would be without Skipper.

And finally, we come to Anastasia "Anya" Robertovna Burinkova. One of the most common questions I receive from readers is, "Is Anya real?" Here's the truth about our favorite Russian. She is absolutely . . . undeniably . . . one hundred percent . . . I'll never tell.

If you like Anya, though, her story is far from over. She'll return to Chase's team in St. Marys and continue to play an enormous role in the ongoing saga of Team Anya versus Team Penny. I hope you'll stick around for the fireworks. They're coming. I promise.

Now that we've dealt with my lies, let's talk about the truth. Most of the criminal activity detailed in these seven books are based on reality. If you read the papers and pay attention, you'll find these unsavory characters with their hands in every pot imaginable. I like to pick on the Russians because they're an easy target, but immorality and criminal behavior isn't limited to any one group. It's rampant and out of control. I hope we have people like Anya and Gwynn kicking butt and taking names. God knows the world could use a little spring cleaning.

Another truth I told in these stories is the settings. Each of the seven books is set in a unique and complex location. Major cities are easy pickings for authors because they're so easy to research. Often, writers—including me—are lazy, and we try to write about things and places we don't understand. As I've mentioned on many occasions, I'm not very smart, so I like to see and experience the places I write about. It gives me intimate knowledge of a setting and allows me to turn the location into a character instead of just a backdrop. I hope you enjoyed my portrayal of the real places in these stories.

And finally, here it comes again. Words cannot express the emotion I feel when I think about the millions of you who open my books and spend hours of your lives lost in the same stories that live inside my head. You've changed both my life and my outlook on the world. At my core, I'm a storyteller, and you've given me a stage on which to perform. I love you for your acceptance and overwhelming support of my work. You've given me the greatest job anybody could ever ask for, and I'll never take that precious gift for granted.

This author's note feels a little different than the ones I typically write. It almost feels like I'm saying goodbye, but that's absolutely not the case here. This is meant to be a celebration of completing the series, and now I can focus more attention on my passion for Chase and his team of misfit toys.

There are plenty of surprises yet to come, and if I do my job well, a few tears might well up in your eyes in the coming years. I love making readers cry, but I also love making you gasp, laugh, shake your head, and experience emotions you never expected to feel. I truly love being your personal story-teller, and as long as you'll have me, I'll keep my fingers dancing across the keyboard so you can come out and play with my imaginary friends.

Cheers,
Cap

ABOUT THE AUTHOR

CAP DANIELS

Cap Daniels is a former sailing charter captain, scuba and sailing instructor, pilot, Air Force combat veteran, and civil servant of the U.S. Department of Defense. Raised far from the ocean in rural East Tennessee, his early infatuation with salt water was sparked by the fascinating, and sometimes true, sea stories told by his father, a retired Navy Chief Petty Officer. Those stories of adventure on the high seas sent Cap in search of adventure of his own, which eventually landed him on Florida's Gulf Coast where he spends as much time as possible on, in, and under the waters of the Emerald Coast.

With a headful of larger-than-life characters and their thrilling exploits, Cap pours his love of adventure and passion for the ocean onto the pages of his work.

Visit www.CapDaniels.com to join the mailing list to receive newsletter and release updates.

Connect with Cap Daniels

Facebook: www.Facebook.com/WriterCapDaniels
Instagram: https://www.instagram.com/authorcapdaniels/
BookBub: https://www.bookbub.com/profile/cap-daniels

ALSO BY CAP DANIELS

Stand-Alone Novels

We Were Brave
Singer – Memoir of a Christian Sniper

Novellas

The Chase is On
I Am Gypsy

Made in United States
Orlando, FL
13 September 2025

64946960R00146